Born in South Wales he began training as a mining surveyor before moving from working under the ground to above the ground by joining the R.A.F. to train as an aircrew navigator. After completing his service, he joined an international company and worked in sales, training and marketing before being appointed managing director of a subsidiary company. With a wide range of experience, he then became self-employed as a management consultant before retiring to build walls, play tennis and begin writing novels.

After convincing me that I should stop building walls and begin writing books for the plots scribbled over the years, my wife Margaret continues to encourage me, is meticulous in her proof reading and I owe her my thanks.

I am also grateful to my large family for their help and support and also to companion tennis players for their comments and contributions.

Tony Jenkins

SENIOR PLEASURES

AUSTIN MACAULEY PUBLISHERS™

LONDON • CAMBRIDGE • NEW YORK • SHARJAH

A CIP catalogue record for this title is available from the British Library.

ISBN 9781398411159 (Paperback)
ISBN 9781398411166 (Hardback)
ISBN 9781398416468 (ePub e-book)

www.austinmacauley.com

First Published 2022
Austin Macauley Publishers Ltd®
1 Canada Square
Canary Wharf
London
E14 5AA

Even when characters and plots have been created and the manuscript is written, progress to the printed book still requires months of work, but continuous guidance by Austin Macauley Publisers' staff made it possible. All communications were provided in a helpful and friendly manner which helped to create a team spirit.

Chapter 1
Newlyweds

Finally, the day of my best friend's wedding arrived and Dickie was overjoyed that Trudy was to become the new Mrs Chambers. Both had previously been living in miserable marriages and now hoped that they could at last spend their remaining years living and loving together. My name is Tom Hartley and Dickie and I have been best friends for many years, which is why today I will be standing alongside him as his best man. My fiancée Helen Marshall will be with me as one of the witnesses. I have a grown-up family of two daughters, Karen who is married with a new baby boy, Abby who works in sales promotion and is single and my son Michael, who is also single and presently working in Australia. Shortly after retiring my wife died and it took me two long years to adapt to my new life as a senior single. First, totally decorating and then selling the large family home and moving to a smaller more manageable three-bedroom townhouse. Not long after settling in at the new home and while digging up my overgrown front lawn, I met my neighbour Helen. We gradually became friends and often worked together on local community projects before suddenly appreciating that we were in love. Helen was reluctant to accept that she had strong feelings for me, especially since she was aware of my close, but brief encounters with friendly and unattached ladies. As a result, she insisted that before she would marry me, I had to agree to a one-year engagement to prove to her that I was ready to settle down and resist the attractions of friendly ladies.

After leaving my car in a multi storey car park, we stood together at the entrance looking out on the rain lashed street as gusts of wind drove papers and debris along the pavements in front of us. The registry office was only a ten-minute walk away, but in the appalling weather we knew we would all be soaked by the time we reached it. We had raincoats and umbrellas, but with the high winds we would probably sail up into the sky like Mary Poppins if we dared to open them. Unfortunately, Trudy had forgotten to bring a hat and Dickie generously gave her his cap to protect her hair from being soaked. He wanted nothing to spoil her very special day. Trudy kissed him as she accepted his offer and fitted the oversize cap over her curls. We stepped out of the shelter of the car park and immediately the wind and rain buffeted us as we hurried along the pavement, desperately holding on to our hats, or hoods with one hand. To make progress we had to physically force a way though the wind blowing directly into our faces. A wet newspaper flew through the air and wrapped itself tightly around Dickie's leg, but with one arm around Trudy, he ignored it and continued helping her along towards the steps to the registry office. Another gust of wind lifted Trudy's skirt around her waist and as she put both hands down to cover herself, we saw Dickie's hat go sailing up into the sky before vanishing over the roof tops. At last, we reached the protection of the registry office and were relieved to hurry inside to shelter before heading for the toilets to make ourselves presentable for the ceremony.

After taking off our wet outer clothes, we had to use toilet paper to dry our faces and Dickie also used it to dry his bald head. There was nothing we could do about our cold and wet trouser legs, but with hair combed, we managed to make ourselves as presentable as possible in the circumstances. I wrenched the wet newspaper from Dickie's leg and was amused to read that on a wet and windy day, his leg had been gripped by a copy of the Daily Sun. At twelve noon, we were seated in the wedding office waiting for the lady registrar to perform the ceremony which would make Trudy and Dickie a married couple. After the short ceremony and as we were signing the marriage documents, I was surprised to hear my name called and realised that the registrar was speaking to me.

"Thank you so much Mr Hartley for standing in for me at the Black Dyke concert. I let down my friend Magda at the last moment and it was really good of you to take her and save her evening. My name is Monica."

Seeing my surprised look, she smiled at me and explained a little more.

"Unfortunately, I suffer from arthritis and sometimes it gets so bad that I can barely walk. Magda told me you were kind enough to call at her home and take her to the concert, otherwise she would have had to cancel and forfeit the booking."

I nodded my head as I remembered meeting Magda at tennis and hearing that she would have to miss a Black Dyke concert because her friend was ill and unable to join her. I also remembered taking her home and joining her for coffee as she told me about losing her workaholic husband and selling their joint business. With a very interested listening audience, I wanted to be sure that my response made it clear that it was an innocent and generous gesture on my part.

"Oh yes, now I remember that evening. Magda is a very good tennis player and we have known each other for many years. I was glad to help her and really enjoyed the evening. I have always been a big fan of the Black Dyke brass band."

Glancing across at Dickie I could see him raise his eyebrows at me as one of my many evenings out with different ladies was revealed in front of Helen. I made sure that I continued smiling and deliberately did not look in Helen's direction. She was already aware of my meetings with other ladies before our engagement, but I was determined to convince her that I was now strictly a one-woman man. Of course, I mean one woman permanently, not one woman at a time and I still had nine months remaining on my probation period before Helen would marry me. I was sure that she would appreciate that taking Magda to the concert was an act of pure chivalry on my part.

After the wedding at the registry office, we had originally intended to have lunch at an exclusive Leeds restaurant, but as we stood on the steps and looked out at the rain sweeping along our route back to the car park, Trudy insisted that she was not bothered about the meal, but just wanted to get out of her wet clothes. Helen suggested that we should all go back to her house so that we could shower and change while she prepared a meal. Everyone agreed, but I said we were already wet enough and called a taxi to make the two-minute ride back to the car park so that we avoided facing heavy rain yet again. The ladies had wet shoes and stockings, but were not suffering as we were from cold, wet trousers plastered against our legs. I was pleased that Helen had offered a sensible solution to save the day, in spite of the terrible weather and told her.

"A great idea Helen, but if I drop off you and Trudy first, then Dickie and I can go to my house to shower and change before we meet up. It should give you ladies plenty of time to get changed yourselves and prepare the meal."

"Fine Tom, you two get changed and we should be ready to eat in about an hour."

As soon as we were alone Dickie had some questions for me about my evening with the registrar's friend Magda.

"Whenever I leave you on your own, I have visions of unattached ladies lining up outside your house, so when did you have it off with this Magda?"

11

"I did not have it off with Magda. We play tennis sometimes and she is a charming and attractive widowed lady. She lives on her own at Roundhay on the outskirts of Leeds where I picked her up and drove her to the concert. When it was over, we walked together to my car and I drove her home. She made coffee and we sat and talked as she explained how her workaholic husband died suddenly, which forced her to sell the business they had worked so hard to establish. We certainly enjoyed each other's company, but nothing improper happened and we just chatted until I finished my coffee and left to drive home."

Dickie was still not convinced and shook his head as he told me that I still had to convince Helen that nothing happened during yet another of my evenings at home with a widow. An hour later we were all sitting down together and enjoying the meal prepared by the ladies. Helen had taken a cordon bleu cookery course after retiring from nursing and complained to me that living on her own, she had no one to practise her skills on. I am a reluctant cook and immediately volunteered to be her official taster whenever she wanted to experiment. After we became engaged, she often cooked our evening meal and I was always happy to try out new recipes and enjoy her masterpieces.

The newly married couple would be living in York and we had all been drinking wine well into the evening as they spoke about their plans. The drive to York was therefore out of the question and Helen suggested that the newlyweds should spend their wedding night at her house. She would go with me to my house for the night, since it was only a two-minute walk away. In the morning I would drive them to York to collect their luggage before taking them on to the airport at Leeds Bradford for their honeymoon flight to Tenerife.

When we first became engaged, Helen suggested that since our houses were so close together, we should each continue living in them during my twelve-month probation period. We would follow a sequence by first sleeping together in my house, then alone in our own house, then together again in Helen's house. In this way Helen would have time to get used to sharing her bed, bathroom and breakfast with me after living on her own for so long. In addition, I would have time to adjust to living as one half of a couple again after my time as a single man. Once we were married, we would have to decide which house to keep and live in together. Helen had never been married and had no family, but she wanted to be sure that I was ready to settle down with her after my gregarious two years as a senior single.

After clearing away the dishes and washing up we left the newlyweds to enjoy their evening together with the help of a bottle of wine I provided. Arm in arm, Helen and I walked to my house and were soon cuddled up on my settee with coffee as we talked over our hectic day. I waited patiently for Helen to mention my evening with Magda at the Black Dyke concert, but nothing was said. Eventually, my impatience forced me to prompt a response from her.

"It was quite a surprise when the registrar spoke to me about taking her place at that Black Dyke concert."

Helen started to laugh before leaning over to give me a lingering kiss and letting me know what she thought about my evening with Magda.

"I wondered how long it would take you to ease your guilty conscience about yet another night out with one of your ladies. Now that we are engaged, I need to be sure that you have given up getting involved with friendly ladies, but it would be unfair for me to judge you for whatever you did before we became engaged. As usual, you went to the concert with Magda because you were trying to help and I want to help you to keep your over generous nature under control. Come on, it's time for bed."

Locked in the warmth of each other's arms I thought it had been a great day in spite of the awful weather. The following morning, I insisted that Helen should use the bathroom first because it takes me longer with having to shave. I had once tried growing a beard to avoid shaving and give me a nautical pose, but the beard irritated me and gave my wife a rash. Also, the beard and moustache both grew as bright ginger, which looked suspiciously like an add-on with my otherwise fair hair.

Each morning when we were together, I enjoyed watching Helen lean forward to slip into her brassiere before stepping into her panties. Probably because she is so used to living on her own, Helen always puts her underwear on after coming out of the bathroom, which gives me an early morning lift. While we were having breakfast, I told Helen about my discussions with Dickie on possible honeymoon venues. He was thinking of taking Trudy to Cyprus because it was where the two had first met. I persuaded him to choose Tenerife instead, since her best friend Jean had been with her in Cyprus and her subsequent death would still be a painful memory for her. Helen agreed with me.

"I'm glad you talked him out of it. Since it was intended to be a surprise for Trudy, she would have been upset when she found out where Dickie planned to take her for the honeymoon. Unfortunately, she would not want to say too much to avoid hurting his feelings and it might then have spoiled the honeymoon for both of them."

I asked Helen where she thought we should spend our own honeymoon, since I was sure that I would be able to prove my total reliability when meeting friendly ladies.

"Well, my love. Assuming that you can convince me that you will be a totally trustworthy husband, since you have travelled to so many places in the world, I am sure you will have somewhere in mind. Why not just surprise me."

We were not allowed to throw confetti when we were at the registry office and since we were using my car, I was not prepared to tie tin cans behind it. Nevertheless, I still wanted to follow tradition by somehow marking out the newlyweds and decided to use self-adhesive stickers. It seemed likely that the best opportunity would come at the airport. Next morning, I moved my car to park beside Helen's house and we called to see how our friends were getting on after their first night as a married couple. To our surprise, they were already dressed and waiting to be taken to York to change into their holiday clothes. After spending an hour making final checks on documents and their packing, as well as checking that their bungalow was secure, we arrived at Leeds Bradford airport in good time for their flight.

I gave Dickie a hand with the luggage and made sure there were bright red "Just Married" stickers added to every bag. As we said goodbye at the entrance to the departure lounge, I hugged them both and pressed stickers onto their backs before we waved them off. Established tradition had been followed and it was a case of duty done. Helen shook her head and glared at me as our friends made their way down the departure lane and said we would not be with them when they found the stickers. Even so, I told her that Dickie had been my best friend for many years and we both had a strong sense of humour.

We drove back to my house so that we could work together on our plan for an organised walk along the Leeds and Liverpool canal. We were both very involved in running the Fairfields Garden Club, which was now completely operated by willing local volunteers, who were also prepared to help elderly, or incapacitated residents of the estate.

After moving to a three-bedroom townhouse on the Fairfields estate, I was saddened to see a neglected and rubbish strewn patch of land at the entrance, which would give visitors a very poor impression of the area. It was also disappointing that there was no community activity, or support for residents on the estate. Having made friends with Rod, the landlord of The Yorkshireman pub, I approached him with my idea to form a garden club on the estate. Our first task would be to make a garden on the overgrown land at the estate entrance. Rod liked the idea and suggested that after he had explained his plan to form a neighbourhood watch at a residents meeting, he would introduce me so that I could speak about my idea. After first reminding everyone about the eyesore at the estate entrance, I received approval to form a garden club, which began by clearing the land at the entrance of our estate and turning it into an attractive garden site.

The Fairfields Garden Club members met regularly and initially gave their time to maintaining the garden site before later widening their activities to helping elderly, or handicapped residents with their gardens, or generally. I found a local sponsor to contribute funds and the area Rotary Club also raised funds to pay for materials, shrubs and equipment. The club mower, trolley and other garden equipment was stored rent free in an outbuilding at The Yorkshireman thanks to the generosity of the landlord. We had just added a walkers group and I had already tested an eight mile walk along the Leeds and Liverpool canal, starting in Leeds city centre. The canal is 127 miles long, has 91 locks and links the two cities. Residents had already been notified that the walk would take place on Sunday in two weeks' time, which was why Helen and I now needed to decide on likely numbers, transport, catering arrangements and costs.

Chapter 2
The Canal Walk

We were due to spend the night at Helen's house and after waving goodbye to our friends at the airport, it was nearly 5 o'clock when I parked the car and Helen began preparing our evening meal. Anxious to help, I joined her in the kitchen, but was soon driven out because Helen was accustomed to moving around on her own and I always seemed to be standing in the wrong place. Cast aside like a used teabag, I retreated to the lounge to watch television and patiently wait to be summoned to the table. Helen really was a superb cook and I appreciated just how lucky I was to have an attractive fiancée who played tennis and was learning to shoot, as well as being able to create delicious meals. When living on my own I often couldn't be bothered to cook and frequently skipped meals altogether, but with Helen making us regular and very appetising meals, I could well end up becoming overweight. Fortunately, Helen achieved flavour without bulk in her cooking.

After we finished eating, we settled down to finalise plans for the first organised walk for residents. We began by considering how best to get walkers to the starting point in Leeds, where parking was limited and fairly expensive. The Fairfields Garden Club (FGC) had money in its account and to avoid parking problems, we chose to hire a coach and offer seats at a price to match the cost of parking. If the number of seats sold was insufficient to cover the cost, we would suggest that club funds be used to make up the deficit. The coach would take walkers to the starting point and collect them at the finish before returning to Fairfields estate. The walk would end at Thornhill Bridge on the canal at midday and lunch could be arranged at the nearby Rising Sun pub, but the publican wanted diners to choose meals and pay in advance. This would allow him to stock up with food and protect himself against those who booked and failed to arrive. We decided to ask walkers to book coach seats with, or without the pub lunch and choose and pay from the lunch menu at the same time. We would print the tickets and our helpful landlord Rod at The Yorkshireman would sell the them. He would validate them by using The Yorkshireman pub stamp and enter names on a list. Meal orders would then be telephoned through to the publican at Thornhill Bridge to allow him to stock the necessary food. Money paid for meals would be given to the publican when we arrived and members who had not booked meals would pay at the pub. The small coach would carry twenty-five passengers, which was a reasonable number to take along the narrow canal path.

Helen would lead the walk and I would bring up the rear wearing a bright yellow tabard with "RING BELL" in red lettering written on the back. During my test walk I often had to jump aside to avoid near collisions with cyclists racing up from behind and failing to ring their bell to warn me of their approach. We suggested that walkers should take waterproof clothes and drinking water and they could bring dogs, but would have to keep them on a lead to avoid fights with other dogs. They might also want to bring their walking sticks. Wheelchairs were not practicable, due to the uneven and stone cobbled surfaces at the canal side. After finishing our planning, I put my arm around Helen and thanked her for her help in saving the wedding day after our experience in the rain and preparing the wedding dinner at her home. She responded by giving me a lingering kiss and just as I was thinking that it might be an invitation, my mobile phone rang. The call was from Peter, an old work colleague who retired some five years before me. He wanted to invite me to a reunion of retired executives of the international company which had employed us and said he wanted to talk to me afterwards. Helen only heard my side of the telephone call, but could tell from my voice tone that I was puzzled about something. After switching my phone off, I told her about my concern.

"Peter worked in a separate division of the company, but I often met him with his wife at various functions. Unfortunately, his wife died about ten years ago and I believe they had they had one daughter, but we have not been in contact since I retired. He is obviously troubled about something and wants to talk to me, although we were never close friends and he was unhappy when I was appointed to a position which he very badly wanted. He subsequently had an affair with Alice his secretary, who was the wife of a colleague who was our company's advertising manager. When her husband found that his wife had been unfaithful, he stormed into Peter's office and punched him in the face. He then took Alice away after they both resigned from the company. Peter was lucky to keep his job and had no prospect of promotion after such a public exposure. Fortunately for him the company took into account his good record, the loss of his wife and the fact that he was nearing retirement. Peter never mentioned it to me, but his office affair had killed off his promotion prospects and enhanced mine. Whatever his problem is, he sounded really desperate to talk to me."

Helen poked me in the ribs and warned me about getting involved.

"I know you will want to help, but just remember that the problem, whatever it is, is his alone so don't get too involved."

Now that we were engaged and almost living together, I accepted each day as how my life would be once Helen and I were married and enjoyed every minute. When we were in bed, Helen was determined to take my mind off Peter and wondering about his current problems and she succeeded really well.

I had bought her a 12-bore shotgun as a wedding present and promised to teach her to shoot. My newly married best friend Dickie would now be living in York and was now unlikely to find time to join me at the clay pigeon shooting ground. We were lucky in finding a second-hand gun for Helen, which was a perfect fit for her arm length. Next morning, we drove to a shooting ground not far from Skipton where Helen could actually experience firing her Browning over and under 12-bore shotgun. Beginners tend to hold the gun slightly away from their shoulder for protection and suffer bruising when the recoil drives the gun butt hard against them. It usually results in a bruised shoulder, but I made sure that Helen always mounted the gun with the butt pressed firmly against her shoulder to avoid this. I also spent time showing her how to hold the gun and practise aiming by pointing at a table tennis bat taped to one end of a broom. As I moved the "target" sideways, Helen practised swinging the gun barrel tip to follow it, aim slightly ahead and keep swinging the gun barrel as she fired.

At the shooting ground we chose a sporting layout since there were quite a few mixed pattern stands available, which were more suitable for beginners. I was pleased to find one where clays were launched from left to right and then the reverse, which would be ideal for Helen to use for practise. Initially I loaded the gun for her until she felt confident enough to take over. At the end of her sixth shot she hit her first clay and was surprised and thrilled. After hitting five more clays I suggested that she had done really well and it was time to pack up and look for somewhere to have lunch. She became very excited about her first shooting experience and was already asking when we could come back again.

At 9 am on Sunday morning we were waiting near the bus hired for the canal walkers. Since Helen was leading the walk, we thought it would be unwise to bring her small dog Billy, since he was still under training and had yet to learn how to behave on his lead. Rod had sold twenty-three tickets and I checked off the names on his list as the walkers boarded the bus, which with Helen and myself was filled to capacity. Three walkers with their dogs then arrived at the coach without tickets and I tried to persuade them to make their own way to the starting point since the bus was already filled with walkers and dogs. They were not happy to have to drive themselves and park at the starting point and walked away in disgust. The walk had been well advertised and we could not organise, or cope with casual attenders. On the day, the walking group was made up of four children, five dogs and the rest were adults.

After arriving by coach near Leeds Wharf in the centre of Leeds, the group of walkers set off with Helen leading the way and me on guard at the rear to fend off racing cyclists with no bells. Looking at the large group of walkers which completely filled the towpath, I soon realised that it would be impossible for a cyclist to find a way through without persistent bell ringing and my earlier worries were groundless. As we moved away from Leeds the size of the group and the noise sent Mallard ducks diving from the towpath and skidding to safety on the canal surface alongside, as well as disturbing birds which began flying out of the trees during our passage through a previously silent area.

All went well for just over an hour until we rounded a bend and suddenly found ourselves facing a mass of large Canada geese spread across the path in front of us. As soon as they saw us, the big birds reared up on their legs in alarm and stretched out their wings to their full extent before making defensive lines three geese deep. They then squatted motionless and showed no inclination to move aside for our group to pass. A golden retriever took the initiative by pulling the lead from his owner's hand and racing straight towards the birds. It was immediately followed by three other dogs who could not resist joining in the fun. The remaining handbag sized dog barked furiously for a few minutes before retreating between his owner's legs for safety.

Seeing the dogs racing towards them the geese immediately began honking and flapping their wings to warn off their attackers. Once the dogs were amongst them however, feathers began to fly and the large honking birds were forced to give ground, or take to the air. The noise of the honking, flapping wings and barking dogs was increased by owners frantically shouting at their dogs to try to get them to stop. Whether by accident, or design, as the big geese began to fly over us, they deposited copious amounts of excrement on their intruding visitors. A dog leapt in the air to try to catch a goose, missed and toppled into the canal. Once the angry geese had flown off calm was gradually restored, but the dog in the canal was trapped by the steep muddy sides and his lady owner was unable to help. The bottom of the canal has a deep layer of soft mud, which now covered the dog and changed it from a golden retriever into a brown retriever. Fortunately, the ground alongside the canal was dry and using my tabard to kneel on, I reached down to grip the dog's collar and help it back to solid ground. It immediately pushed forward into my chest and my shirt, trousers and tabard became smeared with soft wet mud from the canal.

It took twenty minutes to reorganise everyone as unlucky walkers cleaned bird droppings from their clothes and the large muddy dog rescued from the canal was wiped down with grass and tissues. The tabard came in useful to wipe most of the mud from my trousers and pale blue shirt, which now had a large brown stain across the front. I telephoned the publican to warn him that we would be roughly twenty minutes late and explained that we had been ambushed by a flock of Canada geese. He seemed quite surprised to hear about the attack, but thanked me for my call. At last, we reached the Rising Sun pub and waited patiently to take turns to enter the toilet where we could clean ourselves, or wash off bird droppings and in my case canal mud.

The group of hungry walkers enjoyed the pub food and ample servings were washed down with local Yorkshire beer. By the time we were back on the coach taking us home, we were all in happy mood and talking over our unexpected adventure on our first organised club walk. The owner of the golden retriever made a short speech, thanking me for rescuing her dog and praising Helen and me for organising a good day out. The other walkers joined in with praise for our efforts and were looking forward to telling their friends how they had survived a Canada geese attack. Helen went home to feed her dog Billy and take him out for a walk after being left in her kitchen during her absence. I went home to get changed and put my muddy clothes in the washing machine. Once this was done, I gave the car a thorough clean both inside and out and it was then 6 o'clock and time to eat. I knocked on Helen's door to see if she wanted to join me, but there was no answer.

After making a sandwich, I sat down to do some reading and finished off the last of an opened bottle of wine. This was one of the nights when we were due to be sleeping in our own houses and after the busy day and wine took effect, I fell asleep in the chair. Next morning there was a loud knock on my door and when I opened it I found Helen and her dog facing me. The previous night after returning from walking Billy she called and rang my bell, but there was no answer. She went down to The Yorkshireman where she was teased by Rod, the landlord, about the Canada geese battle. I checked my doorbell and was embarrassed to find that the battery had expired, which was why there were no chimes. I was building a reputation with Helen for falling asleep, but since it was another sunny day, we went off together to walk the dog and make up for my lapse.

The day for my reunion lunch with former colleagues finally came and we met up at the Wood Hall Hotel near Harrogate. Our gathering began with drinks in the lounge and introductions. In total there were twenty-eight diners and although I just managed to recognise most of them by sight, I had more difficulty when trying to remember their names. Since we all seemed to have the same memory problem, we finally resorted to telling each other our last position in the company before our retirement and then everything fell into place. Having finally remembered who we were we reminisced about our happy, or in some cases miserable days with the multinational company which had employed us. One guest was in a wheelchair, some used walking sticks and another, who was losing his memory had been brought by a kindly colleague. Time passes and takes a toll on both our appearance and physical and mental abilities, but it is irrevocable.

The lunch ended and we all shook hands and hoped that we would still be around to meet at the next reunion, while Peter and I settled down in the lounge for our chat. He began by explaining how he had become involved with Alice, his secretary, and the subsequent confrontation with her husband in his office.

"After my wife died and with my daughter living in France, I was very lonely and spent as much time as possible on my work and hoped to catch up with you in the promotion race. Alice came with me to a presentation to a major customer, followed by an overnight stay in a hotel. Naturally I kept off the drinks when with the customers and when we returned to our hotel, Alice suggested a drink in the bar. It was a relief to relax and unwisely we had a few too many drinks. Alice had a room next to mine and had difficulty trying to unlock her door, so I helped by using her key to open it for her and we were standing close to each other and then suddenly we were kissing. I slept with her and was surprised to learn that she was just as lonely as I was, since her husband showed her little or no affection. After that we met whenever we could and inevitably, we were seen together and our affair became common knowledge amongst staff. I ended up on the floor of my office with a bloody face. I felt guilty and was lucky to keep my job, but I wanted to spare Alice as much of the blame as possible. Now you know why and how I became involved and I hope you understand that an innocent drink led to me writing off my career prospects."

"Thank you for telling me that Peter. It came as a shock to me when I was asked to take over another department and lose even more of my free time with my family. So, what is troubling you just now?"

Peter frowned and began to explain.

"I still live in my family house, although it is now far too big for me, but looking after the garden and house helps to fill up my time. I went to a local concert and during the interval an attractive woman suddenly bumped into me and spilled her drink over the front of my trousers. She was very embarrassed and insisted on using tissues to wipe them dry before buying me a replacement drink. After that we began to meet regularly and eventually, she moved into my house and we became a couple and went on holiday together. She told me that she had been engaged to an army officer who was killed in Afghanistan. She had been forced to give up her job as a bilingual personal assistant and move back in with her mother when she unexpectedly found that she was pregnant. She is twenty years younger than me and very affectionate and attractive. Her mother had a fall recently and Jan asked if she could move her in with us until the cast on her wrist was removed. The cast was removed two months ago, but each time I raise the subject of her mother returning to her own home, Jan pleads for her to be allowed to stay for just another week. After that another week and then another.

The day I telephoned you, Jan and her mother had just given me an ultimatum. They want me to give Jan a half share in my house so that she has some security in the event of me dying, otherwise she will have to move back to live with her mother."

As he was speaking, I noticed a faint bruise on Peter's cheekbone and asked him if he was subject to domestic violence. He explained that at first, Jan moved in with him on her own, but he often found her crying because she missed her 15-year-old son Rodney. To please Jan, he agreed that Rodney could move in with them and then found that the boy was autistic and also had a tendency to lose his temper, smash furniture and hit his mother. Recently he tried to restrain him and the boy, who was big for his age, turned on him instead and the police had to be called. It took two constables to finally subdue him. When Jan moved in with him, he felt as if he had come alive again and his bedroom became a haven of love instead of just a room where he felt most lonely and forgotten. He had no idea how much time he had left to live and was frightened about ending his days living alone. He gradually realised that Jan was manipulating him and had no one he could turn to for advice. When we worked together, he saw that I put all my energy into my work and kept out of company politics. He was sure that I would listen and be willing to offer him honest advice. Since I had never attended the company reunion lunches, he decided to invite me and seek my advice at the same time.

When he finished telling me about his affairs, he sat watching me with a gloomy expression on his face as he waited for my reaction. I had a lot of sympathy for him and knew that I should respond to his request for advice, but he would have to make his own decision about the demand from his partner Jan. I explained my views.

"If you give Jan a half share in your house you will have to accept that both her mother and son would remain permanently in your home. Rodney is already becoming a threat to you when he is only fifteen. As he grows older and stronger, you will be growing older and weaker and will eventually be totally at his mercy. The mother will support her daughter on every issue and you will have no control over your life, or affairs. You may well come to feel trapped and be victimised in your own home with no way of escape. You would be unable to sell your half of the house and might well be forced to move out and find alternative accommodation, if you can afford it. Your decision must either be to reject the ultimatum by Jan and her mother and return to your old single life, or face the future with company you may well find very unpleasant. You must already be concerned, which is why we are having this conversation. Your instincts in seeking advice were good and it is up to you whether you accept it. Do you think the story about Rodney's father being an army officer and dying in Afghanistan is true and do you also think your meeting over the spilled drink was an accident, or did this woman choose you as her target?"

I watched as Peter's eyes filled with tears and he locked both his hands together as he struggled to accept that he had been duped. After a long pause, he responded to my question.

"Recently, I have begun to see a different side of Jan and it is very possible that the army officer story she told me is untrue and Jan almost certainly chose to spill her drink on me. Since she moved into my house, she has gradually taken over my life and I don't like to think where it will end. I realise I have to stop it now before it becomes even worse and I want to thank you for listening and helping me to make a very hard decision."

We shook hands and hoped to meet each other again at the next annual company reunion. I was glad I had finally learned the full background of his affair with his secretary Alice and had some sympathy with his reaction. I had heard stories before of ladies surprisingly being unable to unlock their hotel room doors, leading to them spending the night with a previously innocent male companion. I also remembered how lonely I felt after losing my wife, but fortunately by adding new activities and friends I was able to fill the void. If Peter had done the same, he would not have been as vulnerable to Jan's calculated approach.

As we walked outside to our cars, I wished him luck in sorting out his problems and hoped we would meet again at the next reunion. As I was driving home, I wondered how I would have reacted in the same set of circumstances.

Chapter 3
Horse Attack

Helen was very interested in hearing about my meeting with my ex-colleague Peter and she agreed with me about his live-in partner Jan scheming to move in her family and probably make him a prisoner in his own home. She told me.

"It was good of you to meet him and I hope the poor man takes your advice and gets them all out of his house before it is too late. It was really devious of that Jan woman to tip her drink over him to set a trap for him. You must go to the next reunion and let me know what happens."

We were at The Yorkshireman later in the day and our friendly landlord, Rod, told us that he had decided to stand for a seat on the council. He had always been a good friend and supporter of our community projects and should be able to give us even more support as a councillor. I could not resist teasing him.

"You should make a good councillor Rod. It's not as if you have a proper job and you can always give the voters free drinks."

"Thank you for that Tom. Did I tell you I was thinking of charging you a big rent for filling up my store with your club gardening equipment?"

I should have known he was the wrong man to tease, since he spent most of his life handling troublesome drinkers. I thought it wise to give him a little encouragement instead.

"You will definitely make a great councillor Rod, especially with the Fairfields, Garden Club supporting your election campaign to get you all the votes you need."

Rod told us that the councillor who currently looked after our area was retiring and had suggested to Rod that he should become a candidate. He was hoping that we would help him by delivering leaflets and canvassing local residents, since there were two other candidates from different political parties. I had a tennis match and Helen and I were going shooting during the coming week, but we agreed that we would spend at least one full day delivering leaflets to encourage residents to vote for Rod.

The location where we were to deliver leaflets covered the whole of our Fairfields estate as well as houses in the surrounding areas. We had more than a thousand leaflets to deliver in total and agreed to work together, with Helen delivering one side of each street, while I worked down the other. We began at the Fairfields estate, which was mainly on level ground with semi-detached, or blocks of town houses. There were gates to open and steps to climb, but our only problems came with killer letterboxes. Many of the springs were so strong that I was worried about losing fingers if I pushed my hand in too far with the leaflet. Instead I used one finger to press the flap open and slipped a folded leaflet through the gap with the other hand. This worked in most boxes, but not those with particularly strong springs. Rather than risk my fingers, I began to use a screwdriver which I pushed through the letterbox to keep the springs open and allow the leaflet to pass through. Some houses had "Beware of the Dog" notices, even when there was no dog. Working on the assumption that the postman would not deliver if there was a lethal four-legged guardian present, I bravely delivered to all these dog guard houses. Eventually I called at one house which did actually have a dog and it was big and black and very nasty. Fortunately for me, it was also on a chain as it bared it's teeth and snarled at me with the chain fully extended. Nervously keeping my distance, I dodged past to slip the leaflet through the letterbox and hurried away in case the chain snapped under the strain, wondering whether there was any insurance cover for injured leaflet deliverers.

Some of the elderly residents sat near their windows and having seen me approach with my hands full of leaflets, were waiting on the door to have a chat, or even invite me in for tea. I put this down to my grey hair and friendly approach, or perhaps they knew me as the FGC organiser. I warned them to be careful about being so trusting when there are unscrupulous people targeting the elderly. Perhaps they were lonely and glad to meet friendly visitors, but with so many leaflets to deliver I had to gently limit the length of these conversations. I always told them how much Rod supported the community and how much more he could do if they voted him in as their councillor. Most houses had letterboxes in the door at the front, but some had them at the side, or even in the back door. With these I had to walk down the side of the house to find the letterbox to deliver a leaflet and often met startled owners working on repairs, painting, or gardening. Having set up the FGC many of them knew me and wanted to chat, which often led to Helen coming to check if I had been attacked by dogs, or residents supporting the other candidates.

On rounding the corner of one house, I was startled to find a tanned young woman in a very brief bikini stretched out on a sunbed on her back lawn. As she raised herself on one elbow and smiled, I recognised Marigold, who was a regular and very popular customer at The Yorkshireman. She usually perched on a bar stool wearing a very short skirt and tight blouse with lots of cleavage. Rod had told me that when she was there his bar takings went up by 20% and I told him it would be worth providing her with free drinks to keep her there. Waving a small tube in her hand she gave me a big smile and welcomed me.

"Oh, hello love. Fancy meeting you here. I'm just topping up my tan in all this lovely sunshine and want to turn over, but I need some cream on my back first. since I don't want to get burned. With my fair skin, unless I put cream on I know I will. See, the tops of my legs are already going red. Do you think you could be a love and do it for me?"

As I looked down at her tanned and over exposed body, danger signals flashed in my mind as I thought about Helen finding me massaging cream on a young woman's back, even if it was to protect her from the sun.

"I'm really sorry Marigold, but I have all these leaflets to deliver and if I get cream on my hands, they would all be ruined. Why not try putting some cream on the back of that hairbrush and then use it to smooth it over your back?"

After watching her pick up her hairbrush and hold it as she thought about my suggestion, I gave her my best smile and hurried away to find my next letterbox, relieved that I had been able to resist temptation. It was only after reaching the road that I suddenly realised that I had forgotten to give her a leaflet. It would be unwise to go back to her now and I thought it might be possible to give her one in The Yorkshireman, but that might look suspicious to Helen. No matter, I was sure Marigold would be a Rod supporter. Once we completed delivering to all the houses in Fairfields estate we moved on to the surrounding older houses, which were a mixture of back-to-back, or top and bottom terrace houses with no rear gardens and very small front gardens. Their small gates often had to be lifted to open and since they were built on steep slopes, there were also lots of steps to be climbed up and down again. Because of their close proximity, it was faster to deliver leaflets to these houses, but constantly mounting and descending steps put a noticeable strain on my knees. Many of the small front gardens held toy bikes, prams, or plastic swimming pools, as well as the odd settee, or old bath. Probably the owners were forced to use any space available to them.

We met up with other Rod supporters delivering leaflets and heard about helpers for one of the other candidates removing and dumping Rod's leaflets, which they had pulled out of the letterboxes. There was a confrontation and the culprits agreed to stop their despicable behaviour, but our team were keeping watch to make sure it was not repeated. We agreed to push all our leaflets completely through the letterbox to be sure that they reached the householders. By the end of the week, leaflets had been delivered to all the houses in the area Rod would look after if he was elected. With two weeks remaining to election day Rod planned to hold a meeting of supporters in his pub. I suggested he should hold it immediately after our Sunday meeting for FGC members, which was usually well attended. It was now up to the voters to choose who should represent them on the local council, but I was convinced that Rod would win.

Helen and I were driving to the sports ground to play tennis and ended up at the end of a long line of cars waiting to overtake a slow-moving horsebox on a narrow country road. One by one the cars ahead of us pulled out to overtake and after checking that I had a clear road ahead, it was my turn. As I passed the horsebox, I was horrified to see a large horse rear up on its' hind legs with a rider in the saddle and it was on the road and immediately in front of the car pulling the horsebox. After staggering in front of my car, it suddenly began to topple and all I could see through my windscreen was the large rear end of a horse falling backwards towards me, I slammed on my brakes, but with a ditch on my right and the car on my left, there was no room to turn my car aside. The horse then fell down crushing my bonnet and windscreen. Under the massive impact I felt the car shake and watched as my windscreen completely disintegrated in front of me. Scores of small fragments of glass flew everywhere and Helen and I were peppered, but fortunately not injured. Jumping out of my car I ran to help and found the horse lying on the road and threshing its' legs dangerously near the rider, who was just out of reach of the flying hoofs. The engine of the car pulling the horsebox was still racing and the woman driver was frozen at the wheel. Worried that the car might surge forwards and run over the rider, I reached through the open window and switched off the car ignition. As I phoned for the ambulance and police, Helen attended to the motionless rider, who fortunately was wearing a helmet. With help from Helen, the rider was then gently moved to safety further away from the frantically kicking horse.

Finally, the woman driver got out of her car and ignoring the rider lying on the road, came hurrying over to me and began shouting.

"You were driving too fast. You should never drive at that speed with a horse on the road."

I could not believe what I was hearing, or understand how she could possibly ignore an unconscious rider lying on the road to come and shout accusations at me. I deliberately lowered my voice and kept calm.

"Do you realise madam that by putting that horse in front of your car and on the road, instead of in the horsebox where it belonged, motorists like me would have no idea that it was there, which just caused this accident."

Ignoring my remarks, the woman again began shouting accusations, but fortunately the ambulance and police arrived and she finally gave up. A policeman approached me and asked if I was the driver of the damaged car. The woman attempted to intervene, but a second policeman took her to one side to listen to her account. Helen had now joined me and I told the policeman I had no idea there was a horse on the road because I could only see the back of the horsebox. It was moving very slowly and as I overtook, the horse leapt in front of me. I added that I had slammed on my brakes but could not avoid hitting it with a ditch on my other side. My speed could barely have been 20 mph maximum in such a short distance and starting from 10 mph. Helen mentioned that the woman had stayed frozen in her car and I had to switch off the ignition to stop the engine. There was a risk of having the car surge forwards over the horse and injured rider. I later found out that the rider was the car driver's daughter, which made me even more disgusted by her appalling behaviour.

We were then joined by the second policeman, who told us that because the horse was acting up and refusing to enter the horsebox, the daughter decided to ride it with her mother following behind with the horsebox. Neither of them realised that this would hide the horse from the sight of following motorists. The horse was so badly injured that it would have to be put down before it could be removed. The rider was not seriously injured, but was taken to the local hospital for a check-up. Surprisingly, there was never a word of thanks from the woman driver for our help and she continued to hide her own negligent behaviour by complaining to everyone that I had been driving too fast. I later found that she was a local riding school owner who had a reputation for being a dominant and unpleasant lady and might want to put the blame on me to avoid having the cost of the accident added to her insurance policy.

I remembered how I had been badgered by my two teenage daughters to let them have riding lessons, because all the other girls in their school were having them. After talking it over with my wife, we booked them each twelve lessons with a local riding stable at a reasonable cost as their Xmas presents. When the lessons ended, Karen said that although she had enjoyed them, she thought that horses were mucky and smelly and she wanted no more to do with them. Abby however, loved horses and riding and arranged work mucking out and cleaning the stables in return for free rides.

Predictably, she then claimed that all her friends had their own horses and although we lived in a nice house, her friends had far more generous parents. We were not prepared to spend so much money buying a horse for one daughter, but Abby then found an owner with no time to ride who was willing to lend Abby his horse for up to six months. Under continued pressure, we caved in, but had to rent a stable to garage the horse overnight. On Saturday mornings, I then had to push a small trolley into the city centre with Abby to buy strawbales and feed. During school trips, exam periods, or when Abby felt unwell, it was left to me to persuade the horse out into the field in the early morning and then try even harder to persuade the animal back in again at night. I was not popular and the horse showed its' displeasure by regularly lashing out with its' hind legs and knocking chips off the brick stable side. I had to be pretty nimble to avoid having chips knocked off me instead. There were also expensive vet's bills when the horse ate what it should not have and when the six months loan ended, Abby was at university and raised no objections to having it return to the owner, while I was happy to pay the cost of hiring a horsebox to make the return journey.

After taking her degree Abby returned to riding and was appalled to be told that I was responsible for killing a horse and injuring a rider when driving too fast down a country road. Knowing my feelings about horses, she called to see me to learn all the facts. After hearing the true story, she was very angry and immediately returned to the riding stables to make sure that my accusers heard who the real culprit was in the accident. Helen and I finally decided that it was time to put a stop to the lies being circulated at our expense and visited a solicitor. A letter was sent to Mrs Horsebox warning her that if she continued to make false accusations, she would be sued for defamation of character and soon afterwards the lies stopped. My insurance company read our report and the police analysis of the accident and charged the full cost of my car repairs against Mrs Horsebox's insurance company. The police view was that I had neither the time, nor space to avoid hitting the horse in the circumstances. I hoped that in spite of the lies, the full cost of the accident would be paid by the culprit.

My car had to be towed to the main dealer garage for repairs, but fortunately a passing friend gave us a lift to our home in his car. Once we were back in my house, I got changed and was startled to find that my socks were soaked with blood from small fragments of glass which had somehow worked their way inside my shoes. When I walked around the accident scene, I assumed that I had grit in my shoes and ignored the irritation. Fortunately Helen did a super job of removing pieces of glass and bandaging up my feet as I lay helpless and uncomplaining on my settee. For the rest of the evening, I did my very best to be a brave and model patient and thoroughly enjoyed taking advantage of the sympathetic attention I was being given.

Chapter 4
The New Neighbour

With my car in the garage for lengthy repairs, hopefully charged to Mrs Horsebox's insurance policy, I was fortunate in having Helen to drive me around. Until my tender feet healed, she also had to ferry me to The Yorkshireman when we went along for the evening to celebrate our lucky escape from serious injury from the horse crash. As we went into the pub, we heard the sound of horses neighing as the comedians amongst the regular customers showed that they already knew about the accident. Although they were our friends, we made sure that they all learned the true facts.

Rod was grateful for all the help he received from his customers and was hoping that their efforts in supporting him would result in his election as our local councillor. Dogs were not allowed in his pub after a vote was taken with regular customers and Billy was left at home in his basket. This made me think about the problems we were likely to face when we made trips and took Helen's dog with us. Billy was a very bad passenger in my saloon car and regularly jumped on me to lick my face when I was driving. If we wanted to take him with us regularly in my car, or in Helen's small runabout, we would have problems. I thought about changing my saloon car to a model with a hatchback so that he could ride in the back in his basket. I started searching for a six-month-old demonstrator car offered by a main dealer. These were usually in very good condition with low mileage and offered a good saving against the new purchase price. I located a petrol hybrid, which would be economical on petrol and taxation costs since it used a combination of petrol driven and electric motors. When my saloon car was repaired, I drove it straight to a main dealer garage as a trade in against a used hybrid hatchback. We would now be able to start training Billy to accept a new dog travelling position.

I parked my new car on my drive and began fitting a dog guard, which would prevent Billy jumping over to join us in the front of the car. Having fitted the barrier, I was just starting to install a dashcam to record the circumstances if I was attacked by another horse, or anyone else. Helen was helping out at the local hospital while I was working on my car. I watched as a large furniture van pulled up outside the empty house next door and guessed that I was about to gain a new neighbour. After watching three men in overalls ferrying furniture from the van to the house, I thought it time to work in my back garden to avoid appearing too inquisitive. I did some weeding and gave my flagstones a good brushing down until the whole area looked clean and tidy. The area looked so inviting that I wondered if Helen would like to join me in setting up a barbecue on Saturday when we could invite my daughters. Better still, Helen might like to take over the cooking. I would suggest it to her over dinner.

After getting back to working on my drive again I began fitting the dashcam. I was upside down under the dashboard when I heard someone tapping on my car window. I peered out through my open door and was surprised to see a short skirt and brown legs standing alongside. Slowly unwinding myself, I eased my way outside the car as the woman moved away to make room for me. Standing on my drive I found myself facing a slim and attractive woman, who was probably middle aged, with short cut blond hair and good features. I guessed the unknown woman must be my new neighbour. Smiling to show very white teeth, she introduced herself.

"Hello. I hope I didn't drag you out from doing some essential work on your car. My name is Catherine Rawson and I'm your new neighbour, but please call me Kate."

As I shook her hand, I wondered if there was a Mr Kate somewhere, or was she a divorcee, a widow, or just a single retired lady. Whatever, an attractive and possibly unattached lady would now be living next door which could add temptation during my remaining probation period.

"Welcome to Fairfields estate Kate and I hope you will be very happy here. I'm Tom Hartley. A horse jumped on the bonnet of my old car last month, so I am busy fitting a dashcam on the new one to record any future collisions or horse attacks."

Kate patted my arm and laughed before saying that it sounded like a dangerous area for drivers and then asked me what happened to the horse. I gave her brief details in case she ever met up with Mrs Horsebox. Turning and pointing at her house she asked if I was ready for a break and would I like to join her for tea, or coffee. As my new neighbour I could hardly reject her friendly offer and followed her into the house and edged past the unopened boxes and scattered furniture.

Kate showed me to a chair in her crowded kitchen and explained that she had just taken early retirement from her work as a lecturer in Leeds University. She was very keen to settle in her new home as quickly as possible and become involved in the local community. She had been told by a friend who already lived on the estate that there were a number of organised activities available to residents. I told her how the FGC had been formed and the current range of activities, including the recent addition of the Walkers Group, which was very interesting for her and she explained why.

"At university, I was a member of the Moor & Fell walking group which organised walks once a month throughout the year. In winter, we even walked over the moors through sleet and snow and regularly covered twelve miles, or even more when we took a wrong turn."

"Very impressive Kate. We are not likely to attempt anything as demanding as that, but we have a meeting of our garden club on Sunday if you would like to join some of the residents involved. We have only just had our first walk along the canal and we now need someone to organise members to plan and test routes for future walks."

I expected retired university lecturers to be modestly dressed and quiet mannered, but instead, my new neighbour in her very short skirt was very glamorous and forceful and could well add temptation during my probation period. I explained about the fracas with the Canada geese and Kate could hardly stop laughing and reached out and squeezed my arm. I took her to be a tactile person who liked to touch those she was speaking with. She seemed knowledgeable about the hazards faced by country walkers.

"I have never heard about attacks by Canada geese, but I know that the birds are territorial. We were always careful on our walks to avoid areas where there was a bull on the loose and even cows can sometimes be aggressive, particularly if you have a dog beside you. I would love to join your Walkers Group."

Checking my watch, I said it was time to get the work on my car finished and after thanking her for the coffee, I left and was soon back working under the bonnet. I was struggling to push a wire through from the engine compartment to the dashboard to power my dashcam when someone pinched my bum. Thinking it was Kate, I turned quickly and was relieved to see that it was Helen, who laughed when she saw the expression on my face. She was on her way home from the hospital and saw my rear protruding from under the bonnet.

"Sorry if I startled you Tom. I just couldn't resist when I saw you and you would have done the same to me you devil, given the chance. No need to look so serious."

After finding that it had been Helen doing the pinching, I gave her a hug and was pleased to have her help with finishing off the connection before putting the car in the garage for the night.

In the evening, we were at our usual table in The Yorkshireman. We were talking to Graham, one of the FGC helpers who had just finished cutting the grass on the estate garden and had problems with our mower switch. I told him I would get it checked and then saw Kate holding a drink and walking towards us. She gave me a big smile before introducing herself to everyone.

"Hello Tom. I hope I didn't keep you too long this afternoon and you were able to finish the work on your new car."

Looking at my companions she then explained.

"I'm Kate Rawson and I just moved in next door to Tom."

Hearing these comments, Helen gave me an accusing look and I regretted not having described having coffee with my new neighbour. After the introductions, Graham left us and I explained to Helen about Kate's experience with a walking group at Leeds University and that she was keen to get involved with ours. I wanted to visit the toilet and told Helen I would get more drinks on my way back and left the two ladies to get to know each other. At the bar the only room was alongside Marigold, who was perched on a bar stool and showing a wide stretch of bare thigh to drinkers generously giving her ample space so that they could enjoy the view. As I ordered drinks, she nudged me with her bare knee to get my attention and then spoke to me.

"Hello again, love. Did you finish? You know you forgot to give me one before you rushed off, but your idea about using my hairbrush for the cream worked really well and I got plenty on before I turned over."

I could feel my cheeks reddening as the listening drinkers drew their own conclusions and I heard someone mention that I had "given her one" and that she had to turn over. I tried to explain and prove my innocence.

"Sorry about that Marigold. But if you are at home tomorrow morning I can drop in and give you a leaflet. We had lots of houses to visit and are all doing our best to get Rod elected."

Not stopping to listen to any more remarks from the very interested drinkers around me at the bar, I took the drinks to our table. As I was putting the glasses down, I noticed the silence and thought I detected a slight air of tension. Could Helen possibly be jealous of my glamorous new neighbour? My probation period was going really well, but I might have to take special care and avoid too much contact with Kate. We were joined by Rod, who was glad to meet a new customer and like us, was interested in her walking experience. As soon as she finished her drink, Helen rose and told me that it had been a busy day for her and she was now going to go home. Seeing me stand alongside Helen, Kate looked surprised and I told her Helen's house was quite near mine as we left together. After taking my arm there was no mention of Kate, but Helen wanted to know what caused titters at the bar when I was pressed up against Marigold.

"Darling, I was not pressed up against Marigold. That was the only free space at the bar and I just managed to edge myself in. She was perched on top of a barstool and prodded me with her knee to draw my attention, because I had forgotten to give her a leaflet when I found her sunbathing in her garden."

Helen grunted and shook her head as she spoke.

"With the way she was sitting Marigold already had everyone's attention and you must surely have had the best view."

I tried to explain my complete innocence by describing our meeting on her back lawn when delivering leaflets.

"Marigold wanted to protect her back from sunburn and asked me if I would put cream on for her, but I told her I had to keep my hands clean to avoid spoiling my leaflets."

Helen started to laugh as she told me that Marigold would certainly have had to remove her bra for me to spread cream on her back, which would have left her front fully exposed. My imagination flared as I thought of being caught in her back garden with a half-naked Marigold, but Helen was sympathetic.

"I am really proud of you my love for resisting temptation and protecting the leaflets. You know that is the first time you have called me darling and I rather like it, darling. So how did this Kate take up your time when you were supposed to be working on the car?"

Relieved by the change of subject, I described the tapping on my car window and being invited in for a coffee, which I hoped was enough to explain Kate's friendly approach to me in the pub. Helen nodded her head, but said nothing more and I was sent into the lounge while she made us coffee, since we were staying the night at her house. When she returned with coffees, she had changed into her dressing gown and wanted to know if it would now be possible to take Billy with us in the car. I told her that a dog guard was now in place and he could travel in his basket in the back. She put her cup down and snuggled up close to me. My spirit rose and I knew that not only had it been a good day for my probation prospects, but it looked like being a good night as well. Perhaps there would be real benefits from having a glamorous neighbour living next door to me after all.

My idea about a family barbecue had to be put on hold because Rod needed more leaflets delivered and Helen wanted to be taken shooting again after being thrilled by hitting her first clays. Between us we were able to deliver a further five hundred leaflets in a morning, without injuring our fingers, being chased by dogs, or embarrassed by topless, or bottomless sunbathers. Election Day arrived and I agreed to stand alongside one of the council workers checking the voting slips and placing them in groups for each of the candidates. As the slips were opened, I could see which candidate name was marked with an X and watched to make sure that it was placed in the correct candidate bundle. During two hours of watching the work, I spotted eight voting slips which were wrongly sorted and saved Rod losing five votes. The final count was announced and with whoops and clapping from his supporters in the counting hall, Rod was elected for the Fairfields area. A celebration was held at The Yorkshireman that night and as Helen and I were at our table enjoying free drinks with our new councillor, we were joined by an obviously tipsy Kate. She had been chatting with other residents celebrating at the bar and must have just noticed us with our new councillor. She gave me a big smile and pushed her way in to sit between me and Rod.

"Hi neighbour and congratulations to you Councillor."

Rod thanked her for her good wishes and I nodded, smiled and nudged Helen, to try and stop her from glaring at Kate. Kate had no drink in her hand and Rod generously offered to get her one and asked what she was drinking. Waving her arm around, she told him she was on Martini cocktails and I decided it would be a good way to avoid a strained situation and allow him to escape to his bar by volunteering instead.

"You have lots of people waiting to congratulate you Rod. Let me come with you and I can bring Kate's drink back."

When I returned with the drink, Helen was sitting alone at the table and she assured me that Kate had walked off just after I left and she thought she might have gone to the ladies.

"Did you say something to her."

"No and she said nothing to me either as she watched you two men walk away, which may be the reason for her leaving. Now, why don't we just leave her drink on the table for her? I would like to go home now and have a quiet night watching your television."

I knew I would not learn any more from Helen and was glad that for whatever reason, we had probably avoided an uncomfortable evening with the tense atmosphere prevailing between the two women.

Chapter 5
Broads Experience

With the dog guard in place, we could now take Billy with us for a drive in the country and hoped that he would behave when sitting in his basket in the back of my new car. We decided to drive to Bolton Abbey alongside the river Wharf where I knew there was a large car park as well as a number of walks to take, whether going up or down beside the river. I put the dog on a lead and walked him to the back of the car before lifting him into his basket and closing the hatch. We drove off and Billy immediately began barking his protest at being separated from us. Determined to make his point, he continued barking all the way to Bolton Abbey. When we arrived, we were relieved to get out of the car and welcome the silence and non-doggy fresh air as we drank coffee at a table outside the café.

Helen had never owned a dog and was obviously determined to face up to any problems which emerged as long as she could keep it. When my children were growing up, we had rabbits, hamsters, dogs and even a horse for a short period. Taking care of them added work for both my wife and me, particularly since little girls think all animals should be hugged and rabbits and hamsters can easily wriggle free and scamper away. One hamster escaped and somehow found its way into our roof space and we could hear it scampering around on the ceiling above us for some weeks. I never found it and assumed it had either died, or somehow made its way outdoors to bolster the local wild hamster population. Losing pets led to lots of tears and pleas for replacements and I thought my days with animals were over until Billy attached himself to Helen.

Our day out went very well and we enjoyed walking to Burnsall with Billy racing around and sniffing and raising a leg at many of the trees we passed. Although he sniffed most trees, he only raised his leg on some of them, possibly those previously selected by other passing dogs, or ignored by them. Billy was a small Border Terrier and with the number of trees he baptised, I thought he would soon run out of liquid, but he kept at it for tree after tree. From time to time, he plunged into the river and must have topped up his storage facilities by drinking more water because he was able to maintain his tree marking work throughout our walk. I carried a walking stick and the dog cowered whenever I raised it, which showed how his previous owner had controlled his exuberance. With the dog on his lead, I found a gentle tap on his rear was all that was needed to stop him from furiously trying to pull away from me.

At Burnsall, we chose a central pub for our lunch, but had to eat outside since dogs were barred. Luckily the weather was fine and I tied Billy to my chair to prevent him from racing around while we were eating outdoors. I wanted to take Helen on an overseas holiday, since the FGC was now running very smoothly and Dickie and Trudy were on their honeymoon. It would be wonderful to celebrate our engagement together under the hot sun on some tropical white sand beach. Unfortunately, we could not fly to overseas locations with a dog and since Helen was reluctant to put Billy in kennels, we could not go. If instead we chose to drive to The Lakes, Scotland, or North Wales we would have to book accommodation where dogs were allowed and accept whatever stringent rules were applied at the location. I was disappointed, but perhaps Helen would change her mind when Billy had fully settled in his new home. At some point she might have to choose between a tropical holiday with me after putting her dog in kennels, or me on a tropical beach while she remained at home with Billy. I really enjoy snorkelling in tropical waters and would be unhappy about being held back by a dog.

I got up and began walking towards the pub to use the toilet inside and the dog immediately tried to follow me and dragged my chair behind him. Helen just managed to grab hold of the chair and stop Billy from joining me in the forbidden area and bringing my chair with him. I shook my head and spoke to her.

"Thanks love. I will look after him when I get back if you want to pay a visit."

Helen nodded her head and told me she was sorry that the dog was not trained and she would have to teach him how to behave. Since he was now at least three years old, I wondered if she realised how difficult training the dog might be.

On our walk back to Bolton Abbey, Helen was quieter than usual and I assumed she was aware of my irritation and was possibly reconsidering her decision not to put Billy in kennels and prevent us holidaying abroad. The dog continued his ritual leg lifting and I wondered if he was now taking aim at the opposite side of the same trees he had visited previously. A human attempting the same procedure would need to make copious notes on which trees had been previously baptised, but Billy only needed his nose. For the return car journey, he barked furiously for the first twenty minutes and then stopped. Either he realised it would not get him back to the front of the car, or he had a sore throat. It was his first experience travelling in the back and he would just have to get used to it. We returned home and since it was our night to sleep in our own houses, I dropped Helen off with Billy and said I had some work to do and would not be visiting The Yorkshireman that night. Helen's face showed her surprise, but she said nothing.

I was wondering about trying a holiday on the Norfolk Broads. We should be able to take the dog on a boat and I had often thought about hiring a cruiser for a week. It should be possible to get all the information I needed on the computer and after our big pub lunch, I would be happy with a light evening snack before going on-line. By 8 o'clock I had printed off twenty sheets of information on hire boat sizes and costs, as well as possible routes along the Norfolk River systems and my table was filled with pages of information. Engrossed in the research, I had not heard the doorbell, but I did hear furious knocking and when I went to my door, I was surprised to see Helen. I later remembered the battery had expired and my doorbell was dead.

"Hello love. I was busy and didn't hear my bell."

"I thought you might welcome some company after your doggy day out."

I put my arms around her and gave her a kiss before taking her to the lounge so that I could make us some fresh coffee. She asked me if I was annoyed with her because of the dog preventing us taking the overseas holiday I was so keen on.

"No problem darling. I am sure we can find ways of having a holiday, even with the dog."

When I returned with the coffee, she was engrossed in reading my information on holidays on the Norfolk Broads. I got a hug as she praised me.

"You must have spent ages online to get all this information about a holiday where we could take Billy, you lovely man."

For the next hour, or so, we got our heads together over boats and prices before making our final choice. We decided to begin at Wroxham, where we would hire a two berth 27ft cruiser for a week. Surprisingly there would also be a weekly charge for Billy, plus of course, non-refundable damage waiver, fuel deposit and a security deposit per berth. We would have only days to prepare following the FGC meeting on Sunday. Having decided on all the essential details, I made all the reservations online and then lay back on my settee to rest after spending at least two hours on the computer. Helen draped herself over me and whispered in my ear.

"I know it's our turn to be in our own houses tonight, but why don't we just celebrate our first holiday together in advance in your house instead?"

I am a firm believer in sticking to established rules, but when an amorous woman makes a perfectly reasonable suggestion on my settee, I have to be prepared to make an exception.

At the FGC meeting, I introduced Kate as our newest member and with her previous walking experience she was voted in as leader for the Walkers Group. She would help to plan monthly walks with members taking turns to choose the routes. Winter walks would depend on the weather and turnout and might have to be arranged every two months. Kate was also willing to take her turn looking after the estate garden and helping elderly residents. She made it clear that she was anxious to get involved in any future new activities I had in mind. Her enthusiasm began infecting other members, who wanted to hear more about my future plans for the FGC. I insisted that they should wait until I had finished my research and would then give them full details. I could not help watching Helen's tense expression, which definitely did not reflect any enthusiasm for having Kate become so involved with me and club activities.

I moved my car out onto the drive to check tyres and engine oil as Helen was preparing our lunch in my house. Later in the afternoon, she would be going home to get her packing done for our holiday on The Norfolk Broads. After lunch I told Helen I would give the car a really good clean and check so that it was ready for our journey to Wroxham. Shaking her head, she insisted there was no point because it would get dirty anyway during such a long journey. I was quite surprised that she was so positive that the car did not need cleaning, until I glanced outside and saw Kate wearing some very short shorts and working in her front garden alongside my drive. I had already been rewarded for finding a suitable holiday with Billy and I resisted the temptation to exploit possible approaches by my glamorous new neighbour.

We packed the car with a selection of groceries, taking coffee-mate in place of fresh milk and olive oil in place of butter, since they would be unaffected by the heat inside the car and boat. Driving down the A1 motorway there were few locations with trees to tempt Billy to lift his leg, nevertheless he managed with pillars and walls and then refuelled from water in the car. We also carried a supply of plastic bags for collecting doggie deposits, which was essential, but not very pleasant. The dog was still not receptive to being tethered with his lead and had already raced off and dragged chairs and a table behind him. We now had to find solid objects to make sure that he was firmly anchored in place.

We arrived in Wroxham in time for a late lunch and chose to eat outdoors at The Kings Head since the weather was still warm and sunny. After leaving the car in the boatyard car park, we transferred our belonging to our floating temporary haven after we had been introduced to the Lady Jane, our home on the water for the next week. We were shown how to use the controls of our river cruiser, empty the storage container of discharge from our chemical toilet and navigate our way along the river system. As the sun was setting, we were sitting in our open cockpit in shorts and tea shirts while drinking our coffee as I steered along the river at a reckless four miles per hour. Billy was pacing around and around our boat deck, but fortunately had so far not slipped, or jumped into the water surrounding us. Thinking that the dog was searching for suitable trees, I steered to the bank and moored for the night before taking Billy for a short walk amongst the trees he had been watching so keenly. It had been a long drive and a hectic day and we were soon ready to try our cruiser two berth bed. Helen insisted that I close up the waterproof cover over the open cockpit to prevent intruders jumping into our boat during the night and with the dog settled in his basket, we were soon asleep. I always have wonderful dreams and in the middle of my exciting role as The Sheikh of Arabi, with at least four hundred wives and still counting, my dream was cruelly shattered by a diesel engine roaring immediately alongside my head. I switched on my bedside torch and saw Billy sleeping and snoring within feet of my pillow. Leaping out of bed, I picked him up and returned him to his basket in the cockpit. With nothing to form a barrier, I wedged our suitcases across the entrance to our cabin after tapping him on the bottom and threatening him with lots of grr's for effect. Valiantly resisting the temptation to wake Helen and complain about her dog's noisy incursion, I settled back in bed to catch up on my rest. I soon drifted off to sleep, but this time without my four hundred or so wives. Loud noise woke me up for the second time and I reached for my torch, but recognised that it was Billy barking in his basket with the background noise of heavy rain drumming on the waterproof cover of our boat. Helen was also awake, and I grumpily suggested she should investigate.

"Your flippin' dog has already woken me up once tonight and now he is at it again. He's your dog so you can sort him out."

I turned over and buried my head in the pillow to try to get some sleep and incredibly, I did go back to sleep and awoke as light was filtering through the curtains on the portholes. I looked up to see Helen's face and breasts hovering above me and immediately reached up for her nearest part to pull her down on top of me. She had brought me a cup of coffee as a peace offering, but I was quite happy to let it go cold. I dressed and squeezed my way into our mini toilet, which must have been carefully measured to allow only entry, or exit and with extreme difficulty. I wondered how very large people would manage to make use of it and assumed they would just have to reverse in. The shower and wash basin were in an adjoining cubicle and with barely enough room for towelling, I stepped out to dry myself in the cabin. As I was getting dressed, Helen pointed up at the cover over the cockpit.

"Lucky you agreed to my suggestion to put that up last night, or we would be bailing out rainwater now. The drumming you can hear is the noise of heavy rain bouncing off the plastic cover, so we now have water below us and water falling on us from above."

Actually, Helen had wanted the cover closed to deter intruders, but it had certainly saved us from the overnight showers and I was concerned that it might be the start of a watery holiday. I looked out at the splashes as rain churned up the water alongside our boat and settled down to read about the history of The Broads. The Romans were the first to dig peat out of the area to burn in their fires and in the Middle Ages, monks from the monasteries dug out peat and then sold it as fuel in Norwich City. When sea levels rose, the pits and ditches became flooded and the present landscape of reed beds, marshes, rivers and dykes slowly developed. We were moored in Salhouse Broad and planned to stop for lunch on our second day at Neatishead on the River Ant, before spending the night on the river Thurne. Billy began his pacing again and Helen took this as a sign that he was ready for a walk and since I had a good waterproof, I volunteered to face the rain and lead him into the trees.

"Let me take him. I found his favourite trees last night and while I am out there, you can get ready for our move down river."

I peeled back a corner of the cover and bravely stepped out into the pouring rain. Billy followed and I had to grab him to clip on his lead before he raced off. The rain swept over my waterproof top and poured down onto my shorts as though I was under a shower. Anxious to reach his trees, the dog suddenly leaped forward and taking me by surprise, I was swept off my feet to land flat on my back on the muddy grass. Having lost my grip on his lead, I watched as he vanished into the woods. Thinking it was a game, Billy dodged as I tried to catch him until his lead became tangled in a bush and I was able to grab it and lead him back to the boat. By this time, I was soaked and covered in mud, as also was the dog. Helen opened the cover and after tossing her dog into the cockpit and removing my waterproof, I jumped into the river to get clean. I thought the river water would wash the mud off me and my shorts and save soiling our towels. Helen put Billy on his lead and tethered him outside the boat so that she could pour water over him to get the mud off, while I was doing the same thing alongside. We wanted him clean, but without having him muddy the boat, or jump into the water with me and find he liked swimming around our boat.

The river water was quite cool and the morning swim was exhilarating and by the time I climbed back up into the boat, the rain had stopped and I was looking forward to our first full day cruising along the waterways. First rolling back the plastic cover, I stripped down to my underpants before dropping down into the cockpit. After edging my way into the shower again, I changed for our move along the river. Helen told me she had cooked bacon and egg for breakfast and in my clean shorts and top I sat down at the small table, which held only an empty plate. Helen came out of our bedroom and as she sat beside me, I asked her if she had made breakfast. She looked at the empty plate and her face froze.

"I left your breakfast on the table for you and went back to change. If you didn't eat it then it must have been Billy."

I sat back on the seat and shook my head in frustration.

"We only just began our holiday and so far your dog has wakened me up twice in the night, pulled me onto my back in soft mud and now eaten my breakfast. I don't know if I can survive seven days in a boat with him."

Helen put her arms around me and hugged me.

"We are all closed up together on this very small boat and I have to learn how to train the dog so that he can cause you no more upsets. I am really, really sorry because I know it is all my fault. Let me pour you some coffee while I make you some more breakfast."

"What do you mean about making me more breakfast. I have yet to eat any breakfast, but I expect Billy would love to have more breakfast."

Helen's face coloured, but she remained silent as she hurried off to the kitchen area and left me to glower at the culprit sitting up expectantly in his basket and no doubt hoping for more walkies and bacon. At least now that the overhead cover was opened, we were able to breath fresh air without the heady aroma of hot, wet and smelly dog. After breakfast, we moved off along the river Bure towards its junction with the river Ant and were surprised by the amount of activity on the river alongside us. Yachts, cabin cruisers, rowing boats and even canoes all passed by, as well as ducks, swans, Canada geese and surprisingly, a couple of otters. Our fellow travellers were all very friendly and most waved and shouted greetings to make us feel part of the river scene. We wanted to reach Neatishead on the river Ant for lunch and with no locks to negotiate, I hoped to continue at a breakneck speed of three miles per hour, or more. With the steering wheel gripped firmly in my hands, I was not intimidated by the walkers and cyclists racing past on the riverbanks alongside us.

I noticed that Billy was pacing around the deck again and told Helen to stand fast with the mooring cable as I prepared to make yet another professional landing alongside the riverbank. She should have given her captain a salute, but instead she gave me a quick kiss. I chose a spot near a small wood to tempt Billy to give a prompt performance, but he took his time sniffing and discarding trees before making his final choice. On our way back to the boat, we saw an angler with a long fishing rod trailing a line at the riverside. I stopped for a brief chat to ask him what he was catching. He showed me a small basket with pike and an eel, but told me that the day before he had caught roach and perch as well. He was a regular visitor and thought that there were definitely more eels in the rivers this year than he had seen for some time. I was surprised that he was doing so well in competition with all the other anglers, as well as the disruption from the busy boat traffic, swans, herons and otters.

He finished drinking his coffee and after putting down his empty cup, he reached over to pick up his packet of biscuits and was surprised to find the packet was empty. Looking at Billy sitting quietly nearby, I was not surprised and quickly wished the man good luck and led the suspected culprit back to our boat. Helen had the coffee ready and when I told her about her dog eating the angler's biscuits, she was really embarrassed and wanted to walk down to apologise and give the man some of our biscuits. I had to work hard to dissuade her by explaining that we had to leave on the surging tide to pass through the rapids at the junction of the Bure and Ant rivers. I also pointed out that Billy had stolen biscuits because she had not given him enough breakfast. Realising that I was teasing her, she thumped my shoulder and told me to shut up before making her own reply.

"If you had been doing your duty properly and escorting my dog back to me, instead of your usual habit of chatting with everyone you meet, that poor angler would still have his biscuits."

Ignoring her insubordination, I gave her a kiss and told her that the captain's decision was final and as a crew member, I wanted her on the bow to watch out for oncoming traffic, or icebergs as we moved out into the river. This time, instead of a salute I got a very loud raspberry as well as a rude finger gesture, but my order was carried out and we continued our voyage down river to Neatishead. I asked Helen if she wanted to try steering the boat, but after looking at the heavy traffic surrounding us, she was happy to carry on as a crew member with Billy. We finally reached Barton Broad and made our way down the narrow Lime Kiln Dyke to reach the pretty location of Neatishead. There were already dozens of moored craft alongside the riverbank with no spaces available for us since the area is very popular. I steered as close as possible to the designated mooring area and waited for a parking space to appear. Finally, a boat moved out and I steered Lady Jane into the narrow gap and closed up the cover before we made our way to the White Horse Inn. It was a rather plain red brick building, but fortunately there were plenty of tables outside and Helen kept hold of Billy's lead as I went to place our food order. Not wanting to have our table, or chairs dragged across the terrace, I wrapped the lead around my leg. Helen was watching and beginning to appreciate the measures needed to maintain control of an active and unpredictable dog. Putting her hand over mine, she spoke to me.

"I'm sorry love. You really have been very patient and I know how much you are doing for me and Billy."

Suddenly my leg was yanked forward as another dog walked past and Billy was determined to sniff it out, or drive it from his temporary territory. I pulled the dog back and gave him a couple of my grr's as I shouted "stay" and hoped that eventually the command might actually work with him. After lunch, we followed the path through the very attractive Alderfen Broad Nature reserve and then continued along the Barton Boardwalk, where we sat on the viewing platform which gave us a perfect view of Barton Broad. From here we were able to watch herons, kingfishers and some terns, as well as otters in the water hoping to find eels, which are their favourite food. After a very enjoyable afternoon in the lovely village we set off back down the river Ant and made our way up the river Thurne, to moor for the night at Hickling Broad. We both wore our shorts and after being in full sun for two days, our bare arms and legs were already beginning to acquire a healthy tan. After closing up the cover we took a short walk arm in arm, with the dog held firmly by his lead. It is not possible to adequately secure your cruiser against burglars, or vandals, but while we were in the area with many other tourists, we neither saw, nor heard about any incidents. I felt happy and relaxed to be enjoying the weather and scenery with the woman I hoped eventually to marry.

During our remaining days we explored the Thurne waterways, as well as those of the Yare and made sure that we were back at Wroxham in good time for our final night. Our boat had to be thoroughly cleaned, but we still found time to walk along the river bank and make the most of the lovely sunshine. Helen kept a close watch to stop me from chatting with anglers and Billy from approaching their food stocks and we ate our last dinner outdoors at The Kings Head pub.

Fellow mariners had told us that it was essential to visit Roy's department store at Wroxham and although she assured me that there was nothing she really needed, Helen skipped off for two hours, leaving me with the cleaning and her agitated dog. On her return I was startled to see her carrying two large bags, which she insisted contained only essential household items. With a flourish, she then produced a blue captain's hat for me to wear on my last night in authority. Naturally we had to have a photograph taken of the boat with its' captain, plus two crew members smiling into our camera set on time lapse.

We were all awake and very active next morning to make final checks and guarantee the return of our full deposit. After handing over a thoroughly cleaned and immaculate Lady Jane for use by other careful users, we gave Billy another walk before returning to our car. Having spent an entire week in the car park with exposure to large squadrons of birds patrolling over it, the roof and bonnet were covered in bird deposits and I was convinced that only the really large birds had targeted my car. Not wanting to have the acid deposits mark the paintwork, we called at a carwash before heading north for home. When we were together in bed on our last night on the boat, Helen confessed that she had been wrong to insist that Billy should not go into kennels for us to fly abroad for our first holiday together. She thought that I had been very tolerant and understanding and a wonderful fiancée. She was actually lying across my chest at the time and my spirit lifted as she whispered all this in my ear. Foolishly, I mentioned that I was usually right and was punished by having a hair pulled from my chest and was forced to grab both her arms and avoid more hair loss, before being kissed as an apology for my injury. I was beginning to feel confident that I was going to come through my probation period without a problem, even though I was now under threat from a glamorous neighbour living next door and enthusiastically joining in all our FGC activities.

Chapter 6
City of Light

It was a long drive home and due to an accident on the A1 Motorway we had to spend an extra hour in the car. I lost count of the number of times we had to pull into lay-byes, or refreshment stops because our dog was furiously barking his request for more leg up exercises. When we eventually pulled up alongside Helen's house, I was feeling hot, sticky and really tired until she put her hand on my leg and told me that when she had settled Billy in his basket, she would be ringing my bell. I perked up immediately and after unloading the car and opening a bottle of wine, I rushed to my door as soon as my doorbell rang to lead Helen into my lounge. After giving me a quick kiss on the cheek she made me an offer I could not refuse.

"What a journey that was? You must be exhausted after all that driving and you really were so patient with Billy. I wondered if your fancy shower would help to freshen us up before I make dinner."

Ignoring the wine, I immediately led Helen to my bathroom and as soon as we had stripped off, we were together in the centre of the shower with jets of water striking us from all sides. Fortunately, she was already fully trained in the ritual of being soaped all over, two or three times. By the time we stepped out to dry each other with my big bath towels, our aches and tiredness had been washed away and Helen put on a dressing gown to prepare dinner in the kitchen. Our meal was over we went straight to bed and were soon asleep after our very busy day and shower. We were both still sound asleep when the telephone rang at 8 am the next morning. Surprise, surprise, it was my new neighbour Kate, who wanted to know if I had enjoyed my holiday and could we meet later to discuss some ideas she had for our next organised walk. Holding the phone for an irate Helen to hear and struggling to maintain my composure as she massaged my chest and nibbled my ear, I replied.

"Good morning Kate. Yes, our holiday was good fun and the weather was hot and sunny, apart from one heavy shower. I have to open my mail and probably make some phone calls first, but I'm sure I can make it by eleven this morning."

Kate wanted to know if I would come to her house to look at her plans for a new club walk and was obviously an early riser, but I needed time to shave and get dressed first.

"Alright Tom, come around at eleven then and I will have the coffee ready. Bye."

Helen was not amused to be woken up, or to hear Kate offering me coffee at 11 o'clock in her house. She continued to lie across my chest and incredibly with her arms around me, I worried about her dog.

"What about looking after Billy. Your poor dog must be bursting to get out in the garden by now."

"Oh yes, you're right, but I was so comfortable until that awful woman woke me up that I forgot all about him. Can you let him out for me?"

My inclination was also to stay and enjoy the warmth and comfort of the bed after waking up feeling relaxed and rejuvenated after my night's sleep, but it was essential to look after Billy's needs. Later, it was a mad rush to get shaved, dressed and have breakfast after refusing coffee offered by Helen.

"Sorry love, my glamorous neighbour will be preparing a really special coffee for me and I must not be late for our 11 am assignation."

"You monster. It had better not be an assignation, or you will be showering on your own tonight."

"Aha. That means I can expect another close encounter of the loving kind, with lots of soaping and hot water jets, always assuming of course that I manage to escape from Kate unsullied."

Before Helen could throw the coffee cup she was holding, I bolted for the door and cut across my paved front garden in time to ring Kate's doorbell promptly at 11 am. She opened her door looking immaculate in a short leather skirt showing her tanned legs, crisp white blouse and perfectly groomed hair.

"Hello Tom. My, you must have really caught the sun to get so much colour. Come in. The coffee is just brewed and ready for you in the kitchen."

As I drank the coffee, we spoke about my holiday and Kate told me she had a friend with a place on the Broads and knew well every single place I mentioned to her that we had visited. Although we had known each other for not much more than a matter of weeks, I had already classified Kate as one of those irritating people who had already done everything, or seen every place you happened to mention. She produced a tray of cookies, but I said that I had just finished breakfast. Leaning across the table and smiling, she complimented me.

"I can see now how you keep so slim and are so active. How long have you been living on your own?"

I explained that I was widowed three years ago and had been at the Fairfields estate for just over two years. I asked how long she had been living on her own and was surprised by her response.

"My husband was a mummy's boy and it took me years to persuade him to move from his mother's big house to a home of our own. Living with his mother was a nightmare for me. We made love on our honeymoon, but after that he had hardly any sex drive and eventually we moved to separate bedrooms. We lived separate lives and I poured all my energy into my work at the university. After his mother died, he became an alcoholic and died five years ago. I took early retirement to enjoy all the things I missed during my loveless marriage."

As she was talking to me, Kate was studying me closely and crossing and recrossing her legs as she smoothed down her short skirt at the same time and waited for my reaction. I quickly moved my gaze away from her exposed tanned legs and knew that I must not give her any encouragement to avoid finding myself on a slippery downward path to a broken engagement.

"Did you ever think of divorcing him and perhaps getting married again?"

Kate took a moment to consider my question before replying.

"I have always had money of my own, from my work and from my family and I didn't need to divorce and marry again to enjoy a full life. They say once bitten, twice shy, so I made sure I hung on to my independence."

"Well, you have certainly wasted no time in getting involved in our local activities and you told me you have already prepared a walk for the club."

I stood up to move the situation away from personal conversation in the kitchen to learning the details of the walk instead. Kate also got up from the table and led me into her dining room where she had laid out a large ordinance survey map on a table. I looked at it and saw that it covered the West Yorkshire area. The walk she had planned centred around Oxenhope and passed the station for the Worth Valley Railway. If the walk started and finished at the Wagon & Horses pub on the outskirts, it would be a good location for lunch and parking. Perhaps some of the walkers might also want to take a ride on the Worth Valley

Railway afterwards. The route covered roughly five miles and was hilly and would probably take about two hours to cover, which should be ideal for club members. As she was pointing out the route on the map, she was standing close alongside me and each time I approved her plan, she hugged me and moved a little closer. She had also put on a rather heady perfume, which I had never known before. Kate would certainly want to use an exclusive brand and had obviously made herself as attractive as she possibly could for our meeting. I decided to say as little as possible and brought the discussion to an end by moving away from the map on her table.

"Well done Kate, you have chosen well and I am sure the group will enjoy themselves on your walk. Having just got back from holiday, I must now get my shopping done and respond to some of the queries in my mail. Thank you for the coffee and for all your work on this walk and perhaps I will see you later in The Yorkshireman."

I made my way quickly to the door to avoid getting another hug and for the rest of my morning I was busy cleaning and tidying to restore the house to its usual standard of high efficiency after the holiday. The doorbell rang and checking the time, I was surprised to see that it was 1 pm. Helen was at the door and she told me she had been expecting me to join her for lunch and wondered if I was eating with Kate instead.

"My invitation was for coffee only my love and Kate assured me that it was freshly ground and specially made for me when I arrived. After looking at her plan for a walk around Oxenhope, I escaped and have some interesting information about her marriage. If you invite me to lunch, I could be persuaded to tell you all about it."

"OK it's a deal. Come on before it all goes cold."

Obviously, Helen had not really expected me to have lunch with Kate, since the meal had been prepared for two. As we were eating in her kitchen, I told her about Kate's loveless marriage and her mother-in-law's influence. As I finished my account, Helen began sniffing me and I became concerned.

"I hope you haven't got Billy's disease and are not going to start checking out the trees when we go walkies."

"I can smell scent and I recognise it because I could never afford it. How close were you to this Kate woman?"

I described being alongside Kate as she showed me the route for the walk on the map and her occasional pats and touches.

"She would have put scent on her body, but not on her clothes, so if you only rubbed against her clothes and I am sure you would never rub against her body my love, you should not be smelling so strongly of scent. I suspect that devious woman deliberately put scent on you to make me jealous. She must be a calculating and manipulative woman beneath that smooth and charming manner she shows everyone. I suppose she must be desperate for love after years of living with a cold husband and she has obviously set her sights on you."

"Kate told me they had separate bedrooms, but she still lived a full life, which I think means she must have had affairs with other men. There must be lots of single men who would be very willing to have an affair with an attractive woman like her. She knows we are engaged, so why has she picked on me?"

"You live next door and have been your usual charming and helpful self since you met her, which makes you an easy and obvious target. Come on, let's get ready for our tennis this afternoon."

Helen had taken tennis lessons just before we became engaged and we now played together regularly. I had become a reserve player for the local league team, because I needed to spend more time with my new fiancée. Helen and I also hoped to play golf together and if she agreed to put Billy into kennels, we would soon be off on holiday overseas. On our way back from the sports ground Helen suggested a change from our usual evening visit to The Yorkshireman.

"You still have that opened bottle of wine you abandoned last night to rush me into your shower. Why don't I cook us a meal so that we can curl up on the settee and plan this holiday you are keen on? I just happened to buy some monkfish in the market this morning."

"How can I possibly resist such a magnificent double indulgence? My favourite fish dish and planning a holiday with my favourite fiancée."

"Not just your favourite fiancée Tom Hartley. I had better be your only fiancée, or no monkfish, holiday, or showers."

The meal she cooked was superb and we managed to finish the bottle of wine before settling down with brochures on kennels which Helen had, as well as details of a two-week holiday in Vietnam which I had selected. Helen was still concerned about putting her dog into kennels so soon after settling him in to her home. I wanted her to be relaxed on our holiday and thought a long weekend break beforehand would help Helen and the dog.

"Why not put Billy in kennels for four nights while I take you to the City of Light? It will give the dog experience of being in kennels and I would love to show you the sights of Paris."

"Oh yes, that sounds wonderful and should be ideal for getting Billy accustomed to kennels before we fly off for two weeks. You are not just a pretty face my love."

Just as I reached out to take advantage of the warmth and special message in her eyes, the phone rang and I left the comfort of the settee to answer it. Rod from The Yorkshireman was on the phone.

"Are you alright Tom? Kate was expecting to see you here tonight and keeps pestering me to check that you haven't tripped over your wallet and injured yourself, or something."

"My wallet is certainly not as big as yours Rod and I have just had a terrific meal with Helen. We were planning a trip to Paris when you abandoned your bar to drag me from the settee."

"Sorry if I have interrupted your love life pal, but that woman never gives up and I am all for a quiet life with my customers."

"Just tell her that I am busy planning a short break with Helen in Paris and we are still sorting ourselves out after returning from The Broads."

Rod agreed to pass on my message and also told me that he had two requests from elderly local residents who needed help with their home, or gardens. I said I would drop in next morning to see if I could help them and hoped he would have a good night with the bar takings. Helen was really annoyed about Kate interrupting our evening and wanted to know if I had arranged to meet her. I explained that I was trying to get away from her and my remark about seeing her at The Yorkshireman was just a throwaway comment during my hurried exit. She was my neighbour and I was glad that she was doing good work on the Walkers Group, which made me more tolerant of her over friendly manner, but did not entitle her to question my movements. Helen had her own views.

"That woman is trying to make trouble and split us up so that she can have you at her beck and call. I know how much time you have put into setting up the FGC, but you must put an end to her approaches even if it drives her away from her involvement with the club."

I wrapped my arms around her before assuring her that there was no possibility of us splitting up and I would continue with her request to honour my probation before our marriage. If she was worried about Kate, or had any doubts about me then we could marry sooner, but my view was that we should not allow the woman to change our plans. Helen edged herself onto my knee and we agreed that we would fly to Paris for a long weekend, with Billy having his first stay in kennels. Next morning, I met Rod and collected the requests from residents before deciding that I could deal with them myself. Rod told me that Kate had been sitting at his bar and competing with Marigold to show an expanse of bare thigh when perched on a barstool.

"Kate told everyone that you had been in her house for coffee and she was expecting to meet you for a drink. Knowing how you feel about Helen, I guessed that she was exaggerating for her own reasons, but she insisted that something must have happened to keep you away. It was a busy night and I rang you to shut her up. A number of your friends are already beginning to dislike her and avoid sitting near her."

After thanking Rod for his help, I called on the first resident needing help and managed to free the jammed lock that was preventing her from entering her dining room. At my second call I was taken inside a house by a heavily crippled man relying on two sticks. James explained that he was waiting for a knee replacement and hoped to be in hospital within the month. He introduced me to his wife, Sheilagh, who had MS and was sitting in her chair. Their lawn was overgrown and although he had a mower, he could not use it. It only took me an hour to cut the grass and bag the cuttings and when I called to say goodbye, they insisted I stay for coffee. James had retired from working in insurance and Sheilagh had worked at Leeds University. I could not resist telling her that my new neighbour Kate Rawson had also worked at the university. The two looked at each other and James nodded his head before his wife spoke to me.

"We all knew Kate and about her abusive husband, who finally went off with another woman before getting himself killed in a car crash on the continent. Kate was always so quiet and hardly ever spoke, but after her husband was killed, she totally changed. She began to take good care of her hair and spent a lot of money on clothes, although her skirts were always too short. She also began paying a lot of attention to the male staff and got herself a reputation and a nickname, 'Matey Katie'. Sadly, she then began having affairs with male students and although I have been retired for some years, I still have contacts at the university. Recently there was an incident with a male student in her study when a member of staff interrupted them in a passionate position when both had hardly any clothes on. Kate was invited to take early retirement and must have sold her large house in Leeds and moved here. I think that she was bullied and repressed for years and is now unable to control her urges."

James asked me if I was married and I explained that I was a widower, but had just become engaged. He warned me that from what he had heard from his wife, Kate now saw men as a challenge and would pursue them until they were tempted and then treat them with scorn. He thought that she was punishing men for the way her husband had mistreated her for years. I said goodbye and drove home to go online and book our Paris holiday. Helen had been working at the hospital during the day and we met up at my house about 5 pm. Since she would be cooking our evening meal, I wanted to avoid crashing pans and slamming pots by postponing telling her what I had learned about my neighbour. Once the meal was over and we had cleared up, I would make coffee and settle her on the settee before telling her about the information I had received on Kate Rawson.

With our meal over and as we were drinking our coffee, I began to tell Helen about Kate's reputation at the university. She was immediately horrified that I was living next door to a nymphomaniac and wanted me to move into her house away from Kate as quickly as possible. I had to calm her down and persuade her to let me deal with Kate in my own way.

"Obviously the tale she told me about a husband with no sex drive and dying as an alcoholic was pure fantasy, but I am not prepared to let Kate influence our lives in any way. I am pretty sure that she would not want to have her past misdemeanours made public, just when she is trying to make a new life here. I also think that the poor woman deserves a chance to enjoy her life after her treatment by her abusive husband. I know exactly how I can warn her off, without any unnecessary aggravation and control her future behaviour if she causes problems with any of our male friends."

"What hairbrained scheme are you cooking up in that devious brain of yours?"

"Tonight, my darling we will again be staying away from The Yorkshireman, partly because we need to choose a kennel for the dog and also because we have to discuss our holiday in Paris. At the same time, I will be on the settee with you giving me your best and most loving attention until we receive a phone call."

"If you can see off that awful woman, I guarantee that you will have my most loving attention ever."

We chose a local kennel and I showed Helen the hotel I had selected and the times of our flights from Leeds Bradford airport to Charles de Gaulle and back again. Just after 8 pm the phone rang and Kate asked why I was avoiding her, which gave me my opportunity to make my response.

"Oh hello, is that Matey, sorry Katie?"

The phone was slammed down and I turned to Helen and opened my arms for my promised reward.

"You are a devious and scheming devil and I love you to bits. How did you know she would ring you?"

I explained that since Kate had pushed Rod into ringing me the previous night, he would not be willing to ring again. When we again failed to arrive at The Yorkshireman, Kate would not be able to resist ringing me herself to find out what was keeping me away.

There is no substitute for making love when you love each other and want to transmit that love and with our trip to Paris booked and approved, it had been a good day all round. However, Matey Katie might not agree. The following morning, I knocked on Kate's door and as she stood facing me and not knowing how to react, I stepped inside after telling her.

"We need to talk now."

With a tense expression on her face, Kate led me into her kitchen and stood waiting apprehensively to hear what I had to say to her.

"What happened when you were at Leeds University is known to me, but to no one else on the Fairfields estate and it will stay that way, as far as I am concerned. All you have to do is respect me as your neighbour and give up trying to make it something more. I love Helen and we intend to get married and I will allow nothing to jeopardise that. You can make a new life for yourself here, provided that you are discreet and that you are able to control your obsession with men."

Kate began to relax and nodded her head as I was speaking, but said nothing and I left her standing in her kitchen and looking out through her window as I returned to my house. I then told Helen about speaking with Kate and reassured her that there should be no more advances from my neighbour. We took Billy to local kennels and I drove to Leeds Bradford airport for our flight to Paris.

It was late afternoon by the time we arrived at our hotel, which was only a twenty-minute walk away from the Arc de Triomphe. As soon as we had checked in, I hurried Helen from our room and we walked down to the bank of the river Seine to enjoy a dinner cruise on a large Bateaux Mouches pleasure boat. As we were eating our food, we glided slowly along the river past Notre Dame and the bright lights of the city and it was a lovely beginning to our stay in Paris. When we returned to the mooring, it was still a mild evening as we strolled arm in arm through the busy streets to our hotel. Next morning, we left the hotel to walk to the Etoile station on the Metro and travel to Anvers in Montmartre. Leaving the station, we had to climb the 270 steps to reach the Sacre'-Coeur basilica on the top of the hill of Montmartre. It is the highest point in Paris and we had to stand outside for a few minutes to get our breath back, whilst enjoying the view with most of the city spread out below. The inside of the building matches its' lovely pristine white exterior, but it was very crowded and difficult to stand and admire the exquisite workmanship of the columns and ceiling. Leaving the basilica, we strolled amongst the many artists and art shops nearby, which were a feature of the area. As we were standing and watching one artist completing a painting, he took out fresh sheets of paper and quickly made humorous, but remarkably accurate sketches of us, which I bought to take back as souvenirs. Our next attraction was the Eiffel Tower and as we ate lunch on the first level, we were able to look through the large glass windows to enjoy panoramic views of Paris spread out below us.

During our remaining days, we climbed the steps to the top of the Arc de Triomphe and looked down on the five converging roads and lanes of traffic battling to cross and reach their chosen exits. We also spent hours wandering around the Louvre with its superb art collection and travelled to Versailles to explore its magnificent rooms and walk through the exquisite gardens. Unfortunately, as we were leaving the gardens through the large wrought iron gates, we were caught in the open by a heavy shower and were soon soaked and very cold. We were fortunate in finding a local café to eat as we sat near a radiator to warm up and dry off.

I can spend all day admiring the beautiful stonework and magnificent arched interiors of cathedrals. I took Helen to Notre Dame and pointed out the flying buttresses which support the walls and allowed the builders to create the high roof and spectacular coloured glass windows. The theory was that the higher the building, the closer to heaven it was. I had paid many visits to Paris, but showing Helen the many wonders I was familiar with gave me a special kind of satisfaction. As we flew home Helen took my hand and told me that it was the best weekend she had ever had. Naturally I suggested that we would have to use my special shower to freshen up after all our travelling and she squeezed my hand, but shook her head. I was sure that what she really meant was that she was up for it.

As soon as he heard our voices at the kennels, Billy began leaping up in his cage and almost licked all the skin off my hand when I was struggling to clip on his lead. He seemed none the worse for his stay and after giving him a walk he quickly settled back in his basket in the back of my car. I persuaded Helen to go with me to The Yorkshireman for our evening meal and as we were sitting at our usual table, we watched Kate arrive and give us a wave before taking a seat at the bar, just two barstools away from Marigold. Helen dug me in the ribs and said with two women in short skirts sitting at the bar the evening takings should be good, then congratulated me on my success.

"Well, well. Apparently, we are not going to be honoured by her presence tonight and you seem to have got the message across, you crafty devil."

"Aw shucks. Any charming, presentable, unattached retiree could have done the same."

"You need to make sure that you stay an unattached retiree, if you want to be walking down the aisle with me."

With the problems with Kate now resolved and with Billy showing no difficulties about staying in kennels, hopefully I could now begin persuading Helen to fly with me to Vietnam, which I had always wanted to visit. First though, we would have to meet Dickie and Trudy when they arrived at Leeds Bradford airport on their return from their honeymoon in Tenerife.

Chapter 7
Vietnam

We were at Leeds Broadford airport in the afternoon and waiting in the Arrivals area as our two sunburned friends approached with their suitcases towed behind them. After greetings and hugs we walked with them to my car and they could hardly get the words out fast enough to describe their wonderful honeymoon in the Canaries. The weather had been hot and they both enjoyed the local cuisine and in particular the variety of fish available, which Dickie insisted on matching with local wines. They stayed at a hotel in Puerto de la Cruz, which was near the sea water swimming complex of Lago Martianez, with channels of seawater running through the gardens and picnic areas. Dickie preferred the complex to sitting on black sand beaches and actually went into the water with Trudy to swim along the channels. They were obviously very relaxed with each other and seemed more like a long-established married couple than newlyweds. It was wonderful to see them finally enjoying such happiness together after living miserable lives for so long.

Trudy sat in the back of the car with Helen and Dickie joined me in the front and was keen to hear how my probation was surviving. When I told him that a glamorous widow had just moved in as my next-door neighbour, he raised his hands in horror.

"Oh my god. How do you do it? These women just seem to home in on you. That is bound to put a strain on keeping away from ladies during your probation. You only have to nip across your garden to enjoy yourself in the night, or even for a quickie during the day."

"Actually, my neighbour is the first nymphomaniac I have ever met and she has already done her best to tempt me, but with a fiancée like Helen I am not interested. Her name is Kate and she knows I am engaged and definitely will never be on her available list."

Muttering about my luck in having to live next door to a nymphomaniac, Dickie obviously did not believe me and kept shaking his head to show he was not convinced. However, since he would now be living with Trudy in Haxby on the outskirts of York, he was unlikely ever to meet Kate who would probably frighten the life out of him. Parking the car outside their bungalow I could not avoid thinking of my previous visits when Jean was still alive. She had generously left her bungalow to her friend Trudy to give her the independence she needed after her divorce. I had met her with Trudy when Dickie and I were on holiday in Cyprus and we became soulmates. I was desolated by her unexpected and sudden death, but had been fortunate in eventually finding love with Helen. Dickie had lived a solitary life since his own toxic divorce and had no regrets on selling his home to move in with Trudy at Haxby. Helen had thoughtfully brought a selection of groceries for the couple and insisted on preparing a meal while Trudy and Dickie unpacked. I chose apple juice when the wine was opened, since I did not want to face driving on the busy M62 Motorway with alcohol in my system. I was concerned to watch Dickie drinking too much wine and had a quick word with Trudy about getting him to restrict himself to no more than two glasses a day. She told me that he enjoyed wine and had assured her that it had helped him to survive into old age. I told her that at his age he should keep his alcohol intake to the absolute minimum and since she did not want to lose him, she promised to do what she could to reduce his drinking.

Helen told them about the enticing approaches by my new neighbour and my use of the information about her affairs with colleagues and students at the university to rein in her activities. Trudy said she once worked with a woman who lived in a loveless marriage and after her husband died, she too had become man mad. I was watching Dickie's face and knew he was about to make a comment about how most men dream about having a glamorous man mad neighbour next door and quickly headed him off.

"Fortunately, she now has to behave, or risk having her background made public and I think she genuinely wants to settle and become involved in the Fairfields estate."

Helen decided that enough had been said about my new neighbour and changed the subject by telling our friends about our voyage across The Broads. They were very interested and wondered if we would be prepared to share a boat with them sometime on a return holiday. Helen was watching me closely as I thought about four people and a dog on a boat and I tried to be diplomatic with my response.

"It sounds fine, but we are presently taking short breaks to get the dog accustomed to being in kennels and then we hope to have two weeks touring Vietnam."

Hearing this Trudy offered to look after the dog while we were on holiday and Dickie immediately nodded his head to show his agreement as Trudy continued.

"Your dog will probably be easier to look after than my Dickie here, who has definitely put on some weight after we ate out every evening in Tenerife. I can take them both for walks, which will help all three of us to get more exercise."

It was a pleasant evening and as we made our way home in the car, I thought about my remaining months before we too would be off on honeymoon. We had left the dog on a long lead in the garden and provided him with a comfortable kennel for use during the mild weather. Only guide dogs and those with security agencies are allowed in airport terminals and we could not have left Billy locked up indoors, or in our car for so long. After parking my car in the garage, I noticed the "L" plate attached to the back. Dickie had retaliated in response to my "Just Married" stickers placed on their honeymoon luggage. Since we now had a temporary holiday home offer for the dog, we could finally begin planning our holiday in Vietnam. During the evening we worked through brochures and checked locations online before making our plans. We decided to fly to Dubai and then on to Singapore with a three-day stopover, before continuing on to Ho Chi Minh City in the south of Vietnam. We would then work our way north to end our tour at the capital, Hanoi.

We had nothing planned for the weekend and I suggested a barbecue on my back garden with my daughters invited with their family and some of our friends. Fortunately, I had kept the barbecue I used at my previous house, but I would need to buy a gas cylinder. Helen immediately told me that if I operated the barbecue to cook the burgers, sausages and chicken drumsticks, she would prepare the food mix, including Caesar salad and crème brulee' ice cream. With such activity next door, I thought it would be unkind not to invite my new neighbour. I was pleased when Helen agreed with me that otherwise Kate would feel ostracised, when we were trying to help her to modify her behaviour and blend in with the neighbourhood. She did however make some suggestions.

"Kate will be a guest with all the others. She does not need any special help, or courtesies from you, although I feel sure that the other men will probably look after her."

I assured her that I would be far too busy making sure the sausages didn't burn to give any special attention to any of my customers. I had also kept my blue striped apron and chef's hat to be suitably dressed for my performance on the barbecue.

Next morning, we drove around to daughter Karen's house and had coffee with her as young Martin giggled and bounced in his suspended baby harness. As I chatted with my grandson about the barbecue, he nodded his head and gave me a big smile and a couple of "glugs" to show that he was all in favour. At least, I thought he was until he threw his rattle at me. Now a year old and with his first three teeth, he was a happy baby and Karen and husband Graham were very proud parents. It would be the first time that both my daughters and their partners would be together at my townhouse and Helen was as anxious as I was to make it a pleasant get together for family and friends. Trudy and Dickie were at her granddaughter's birthday party and Rod and his wife had a function at The Yorkshireman, but two couples from our FGC accepted invitations. The local newspaper reporter David Kane, who always printed details of our functions, accepted and of course my neighbour Kate. Helen thought it was unlucky to have thirteen people including us, but turned down my offer to grab passers-by to make up a bigger total.

David Kane often dropped in at our FGC meetings and as a reporter had helped to promote our activities with his entries in the local paper. We first met when playing tennis and had gradually become good friends. After years in a relationship with his partner, the two had split up and he now enjoyed "playing the field", as he put it. I invited him as a friend and because I expected him to find Kate a challenge and keep her occupied. When I approached Kate as she was cutting her lawn, she looked apprehensive at first, but when I invited her to our barbecue, she could not stop herself from giving me a hug and accepting. Helen and I could now get on with our preparations. Good weather was expected and I bought extra garden benches and hoped that by opening up the double doors between the dining room and garden, there would be ample space for guests to mingle, sit and eat. I collected a gas cylinder and went shopping with Helen for the food before getting out my string of Xmas lights to give the garden a festive atmosphere. We were due to fly off to Ho Chi Minh City in five days, after delivering Billy to his new temporary owners in York for the duration of our holiday in Vietnam.

It was a lovely morning and after an early start, Helen and I were busy preparing for our guests to arrive for our 1 pm start. A selection of drinks was available for guests to help themselves as I wielded my spatula to flick over the cooking sausages with Billy licking his lips as he sat hopefully nearby. My daughters and partners with baby Martin arrived first. Our remaining guests followed and as anticipated, Kate soon noticed that David Kane was unaccompanied and made sure that she was always by his side. Having eventually given up his position alongside the barbecue, Billy began prowling around and I warned guests about putting food down within his reach. David Kane was too interested in Kate to heed my warning and when he reached for his hot dog, he found an empty plate already cleared by a hungry dog.

The food selection as well as the efforts of the chef and barbecue expert were praised and all went smoothly until baby Martin suddenly began wheezing as he played in his little pen. Seeing him struggling to breath and holding his throat, Helen raced across to him, took hold of him and crouched down so that he lay head down along her knee, with his head supported by one hand. She then used the edge of her other hand to slap his back between his shoulder blades. We all saw a small bead drop from his mouth and suddenly Martin began to gasp and take in big breaths.

Lifting the crying baby, she handed him to Karen, who had been desperately worried as she stood alongside watching Helen deal swiftly and professionally with the crisis. After Martin and Karen had finally calmed down and everyone had thanked Helen, she explained that in her work as a midwife she was trained to use the Heimlich procedure to clear blockages in the throat. Babies put everything in their mouths and the bead had come from a supposedly safe toy rattle he had been playing with.

My family guests left first and Abby and Karen both kissed me before elder daughter Karen summed up the day.

"A really lovely afternoon, Dad, and thank heavens that Helen was here when Michael swallowed that bead, or we could have lost him. Abby and I are both delighted you are going to marry her. We were worried about you living on your own, but now we know that you will be in good hands with Helen."

Next to leave were David and Kate, who left together and caused Helen to wag her finger at me for plotting to link them. Just before our last guests left and it was dusk, I was able to switch on my coloured lights to complete the party mood as the evening finished with coffees. Left on our own we put away the garden furniture and cleared up. We thought Billy deserved one of our remaining sausages for behaving for most of the time. It was a relief to flop down on the settee as I hugged Helen and told her what a wonderful woman she was for saving my grandson and preparing the food. It had been an enjoyable day and we were both looking forward to a good night's rest to recover. The day for the start of our holiday in Vietnam finally arrived and the taxi whisked us off in the early hours to get us to the airport in time for flight and security checks.

Flying from Manchester we had a two hour wait at Dubai before our next flight to Singapore and Helen was bedazzled by the incredible selection of shopping outlets and the opulence of the large terminal. The rows of tall palm trees inside the terminal helped to create an eastern and very original atmosphere. Exploring the two floors also helped in giving us a chance to stretch our legs after being doubled up in our aeroplane seats for so many hours. Singapore is off the southern coast of Malaysia and by the time we reached our hotel after the two long flights, we were too tired to eat and went straight to our bed. We were staying at a hotel in the middle of Orchard Road, which has twenty-two shopping malls and six department stores, making it Singapore's shopping mecca. In the morning Helen checked out the ladies' clothes selections and I was impressed by the range and low prices of watches and electronic items. For lunch we visited the famous Raffles Hotel and drank Singapore Sling cocktails at the bar, where bowls of peanuts are provided free to drinkers. To follow tradition after eating the peanuts, the shells have to be thrown down on the floor. When we finished our meal, we left our table and crunched our way out across the layer of shells, which made me wonder how often the floor had to be swept during the day.

In the afternoon we took a taxi to the Botanic Gardens on Sentosa Island and walked into the National Orchid Garden. We found ourselves surrounded on all sides by orchids planted in the trees and on the ground around us, as well as on shelves in the roofed over area. The range and intensity of the colours was so breath-taking that I had to take dozens of photographs. Helen had never before shown much interest in plants or gardens, but surprised me by wanting to stay as long as possible amongst the colourful plants. I decided that when we returned to the UK, I would have to introduce her to Albert, our Freshfields estate orchid grower. He was a widower almost crippled by arthritis and when I was helping to clear the weeds from his garden, he took me into a bedroom which was completely filled with orchids. I was sure he would be delighted to show her his prized blooms and give her advice on growing the exotic plants. In the evening we walked along Clarke Quay until we chose a restaurant amongst the dozens located alongside the pristine Singapore river. Sitting at our riverside table, we were able to look down at the river taxis going up and down below us and Helen was thrilled by her first visit to Singapore. The river, the streets and the buildings were all so clean and completely free of litter and graffiti, which was a very pleasant change from most UK streets.

As we were walking back to our hotel, an elderly man suddenly stopped and turned back towards us with a big smile on his face, before returning to stand alongside me and call out a greeting.

"Well, fancy meeting you here. It is Tom Hartley isn't it? I'm Patrick Mulcahy if you can remember me."

The name was familiar and then I recalled meetings with him when he was our company agent in Singapore and having dinner with him and his lovely wife Shena. Patrick and I shook hands and then he insisted that we have a drink with him so that he could catch up on news of all his UK friends. He rushed off to get the drinks as we sat waiting at an outside table and I told Helen about my overseas visits with Patrick, who was our foreign company representative for Singapore. When he returned and sat down, he turned to take Helen's hand and smiled at me.

"And this must be your lovely daughter Tom."

Looking at the mischievous smile on his face, I remembered his wicked sense of humour, conditioned by his natural charm, which always endeared him to the ladies.

"Ha ha. You old phoney. This is my fiancée Helen and we are on our way to a two-week holiday in Vietnam after a three-night stopover here."

Patrick told us that after his wife died and since he no longer had any living relatives left in the UK, he decided to stay on in Singapore because he loved the city and had lots of friends locally. His wife Shena was buried there and he would eventually join her. After catching up on news of people he still remembered in my old company, he told us about some of the restrictions which apply in Singapore.

"For a start, you can't buy chewing gum, or discard it here and littering can bring you a fine of $300 and jaywalking up to $1000 in Singapore currency. Feeding birds brings a fine of $500 and spitting in a public place can cost you up to $1000. Parents are allowed to cane their children and gay sex is punishable by a two-year jail sentence. Look around and you will see how immaculate the city is, with no graffiti, or litter, no blobs of chewing gum on the pavements and scarcely any crime. It shows what can be achieved when the population works together to maintain a clean neighbourhood, which everyone can enjoy and they certainly have no difficulty in following the restrictions."

For almost an hour we were kept busy answering his questions on current affairs and life in the UK and agreed to meet him for dinner on our last evening in Singapore. Next day we toured the city on a Hop-On-Hop-Off bus after stopping first at Chinatown, where we visited the exotic Buddah Tooth Relic temple, but either the tooth was missing, or it was too small for us to recognise. After a further stop at the Indian sector with its glittering facades in gold leaf, we ended up at Marina Bay and admired the giant four metre figure of the Merlion. The statue has the head of a lion and the body and tail of a fish, with a jet of water spouting from its mouth into the bay below.

We met Patrick at 6 pm and he led us to Big Lulu's restaurant for dinner where he introduced us to the owner, a very tall Chinese lady, on arrival. The food was delicious and included an incredible mix of oriental and western recipes. It was a fitting climax to our stay in the city and a pleasure to meet up again with an old friend. When we were bidding him goodnight and thanking him for his hospitality, he gave me his phone number and urged us to make another stopover on our return journey, because he still missed England and had really enjoyed spending time with us. He also told me how lucky I was to have such a charming and lovely fiancée as he took Helen's hand and kissed it. He always was popular with the ladies and had obviously lost none of his suave manners. Back in our hotel, Helen told me how much she liked Patrick and that we seemed to have helped an obviously lonely man. She did not mention making another visit on our return, but I guessed that she would be quite happy to meet Patrick again.

Our flight left early next morning and after roughly two hours flying time, we landed at Ho Chi Minh City, which was previously known as Saigon. We took a taxi to our hotel in the bustling city centre, which was thronged with motor scooters darting in and out of the traffic and often ridden by attractive young ladies wearing long coloured dresses and masks. We thought the face masks were worn as a precaution against the dense fog and smell of the exhaust fumes, but many were used as protection against sunburn from the fierce rays of the sun.

The hotel had been built by the French when the country was known as French Indochina and it had a large central atrium with surrounding guest rooms opening onto a gallery, which looked down into the atrium. The style of the building and fittings were so typically French, that it was just like staying in Paris. We had already done our research and chosen the attractions offered by the city, beginning next morning, but tonight we would dine in at our hotel after yet another flight.

I had read about the vast tunnel complex prepared over many years by the Viet Cong in campaigns first against the French and then the Americans and we spent the morning touring the Cu Chi tunnels. The underground network extends for 155 miles and contains living quarters, storage areas, hospitals, canteens and workshops. Unexploded American bombs were dismantled by the North Vietnamese and the explosives removed to make booby traps and anti-personnel devices for use against US troops. Access to the tunnels was through a network of cleverly disguised trapdoors which allowed the Viet Cong to hide and emerge in the jungle behind their enemies, or take refuge during bombing raids. We were allowed to go down into the tunnels and although they were now lit with a line of low voltage bulbs, we were both glad when the tour was over and we returned to daylight on the surface. Visitors were taken only to tunnels where they were able to stand upright, but many of the tunnels were so low that the Viet Cong had to crawl along them on their hands and knees.

During the wars first against France and then the USA, the Viet Cong lived underground for weeks, or even months amongst the ants, poisonous centipedes, spiders, scorpions and rats. The Vietnamese combatants usually came out at night to attack invading troops, or set anti-personnel traps with sharpened bamboo stakes coated with poison. Roughly half of those living in the tunnels contracted malaria and most died. Our guide was called Tang and he spoke good English, but asked us to help with pronouncing written words. He could not understand how stake and steak were pronounced in the same way, or sent and scent. We explained that the English language has no markings over letters to help with pronunciation, as with French, German and Spanish. He would be with us again in the morning for our tour of the Mekong delta, no doubt with more problem words for us to explain how they should be pronounced. Helen found it hard to accept that the Vietnamese had dug such an incredible network beneath the ground and was horrified to learn of the terrible injuries inflicted on soldiers trying to destroy them.

Tang was late the next morning when collecting us at our hotel and when he arrived we saw that his trouser bottoms were quite wet. He explained that during the night there had been heavy rain in the Mekong headwaters, which caused the river to flood its' banks and his home had a metre of water inside. He had to wade through the water to leave, but assured us that the surge had passed and levels were falling so that his wife and baby were safe. Many people lived alongside the river and simply accepted the frequent flooding because land there was cheaper. Tang was a graduate, who learned English listening to British television programmes and had a Manchester accent after regularly watching Coronation Street. As well as night work, during the day he carried out work as a courier to save enough money to move to a drier, but more expensive area away from the river.

We boarded a flimsy looking wooden boat with a pole at the stern holding a large engine in the water, which was used by the boatman to propel and steer it along the Mekong River. Much of the river surface was covered with giant clumps of floating water hyacinth with greenery on the surface and an extensive root network beneath, which fed on nutrients in the river water. As we surged through the muddy water, our boat carved a swathe through a mass of water hyacinths which then divided into smaller clumps and floated away to join other masses, or regrow in the fertile Mekong water. We passed a variety of smaller and larger craft, some having giant fishing nets suspended on long poles above their sterns, which could be lowered into the water to net the fish as the boat continued along the river. Others carried crates filled with live chickens, or building materials piled high to force the boat low in the water. We then turned into a narrow subsidiary channel almost completely overhung by dense trees on both sides, which cut out the light and sheltered us from the blazing sun. Having heard about the venomous snakes which often lurk in the trees, I kept a careful watch overhead, but said nothing to Helen.

We landed at a small island and were taken to a wooden hut and given tea before moving outside to be entertained by a group of local dancers. Looking around I was surprised to see a big glass cage behind my chair and inside was a very large, coiled black python which completely filled the cage. We were assured that the reptile was sleeping, but I could not see the head and kept thinking about their muscular strength. I hoped this one would not decide to stretch and crash out of its cage to land on the ground behind me. The dancers finished their performance with a clash of cymbals and I noticed the snake lift its' head and open its' round black eyes to look at me. Naturally I said nothing to Helen and did my best to look unconcerned as I nonchalantly moved my chair out of range. At least I hoped that I was out of range, or if not, that I would be able to grab Helen and that we could run faster than the python could slither before the performance was over. I was very relieved when the entertainment finished and we returned to our boat.

Our entire day was spent under the hot sun, which seemed to reflect the heat from the river surface. In spite of a generous application of protective cream our faces, arms and legs were already quite tanned, but fortunately not burned. We decided to have a relaxed evening by eating in the hotel dining room, which had only half its' tables filled and was cooled by a large rotating overhead fan. We had ordered our food and were talking about our experience during the day when an elderly couple asked if they could join us.

"You two look like tourists just like us and surely know more about Saigon, shucks, I mean Ho Chi Min City and could give us some advice. It's our first visit to Asia and we just arrived from Angkor Wat in Cambodia. I'm Betty and this is my husband Frank and we hail from Philadelphia."

I watched as a very large lady and her much slimmer male companion sat down and beamed at us across the table. Helen immediately extended her hand and told them that we were from Yorkshire and it was our first visit to Vietnam. After introductions I told the Americans that we were at the end of our two day stay in Ho Chi Minh City and were off to Da Lat in the morning. Betty wanted to know what we thought they should see and I told them about our visits to the tunnels and the Mekong delta. Frank nodded his head and spoke to us.

"I was in the Air Force, but we all heard about those damned tunnels, which killed or maimed a lot of my buddies. We should never have got ourselves involved, because those people were never going to let the US decide their future."

Putting her hand on his arm, Betty consoled her husband.

"Put it behind you hon, it was a long time ago and these folks won't want to hear about it."

Anxious to change the subject, I spoke to Betty about my visit to Philadelphia.

"I was at your home town myself a few years ago and thought it was very English and I remember looking at the Liberty Bell with the crack in its side. I had my first ever Maine lobster there and the waitress came and tied a napkin around my neck with an image of a lobster on the front."

Frank smiled and told me that he knew the place well and it was famous and popular with tourists who were willing to pay the fancy prices. During his military service he had been stationed in Germany and had also spent time at a base in Yorkshire. The Americans were good company and after our meal together we stayed drinking in the bar throughout the evening and swapped holiday stories. They owned a farm and bred buffaloes and also packed steaks and buffalo burgers for sale across the country. The lean meat was growing in popularity in the US and while they were away in Asia, the farm, packing and distribution business was being run by their eldest son. The activities of Helen's dog really amused them, but they were particularly impressed to hear about my experience dancing with a belly dancer on a Nile river cruise. We wished them well in their tour of Asia and went to our rooms. The next day we arrived at our next location, Da Lat.

Again, our hotel had been built by the French during the time when Indochina was one of their colonies. Even the menu in the restaurant was written in French and the waitresses were all dressed as French maids, which reminded me of some of the racier leaving parties I had attended with work colleagues. Helen was intrigued by the quaint atmosphere and when given the choice between a cycle ride around the lake, or a ride on a chair lift over the mountains, she chose the chair lift. We had magnificent views of the valley and lake below us as we soared high in the air before descending to reach an ancient pagoda in the next valley and spend time exploring the building. Two days later we ended our very enjoyable stay in Da Lat and flew to Da Nang, where we landed on a long runway built by the Americans. During the war it was used for their large bombers to drop chemical and cluster bombs on the jungles and villages where the Vietcong were seeking refuge. Whole areas of forest were chemically cleared and took years to grow again, although not at the same magnificent levels. The US bomber base had now become Da Nang International Airport, although we were amused to see on the Departures Board that there were only two flights a day. One in and then the same one out again to make a return flight. The French had provided beautiful buildings, road systems and bridges and the Americans had left the Vietnamese with modern runways and a massive stockpile of military equipment which later helped them in their brief conflict with their powerful neighbour China to the north. During the war between North and South Vietnam, Da Nang was used as a relaxation area for US troops fighting the Vietcong and with its sandy beaches surrounded by the Marble mountains it was an ideal location. Our hotel was located on a broad promenade alongside the sea and with yet another chair lift to cross the channel between the mainland and an offshore island. We hired a small boat to take us out where we could snorkel in the warm Andaman Sea and swim alongside the wide variety of brilliantly coloured fish swarming in the warm water. After our swim and return to our boat, we were landed on the island and visited a restaurant set high on the hillside above the beach. As we ate our food under the hot sun, we looked out across the shimmering waters of the bay and watched other tourists riding high in the chair lifts taking them back to the mainland. After our visit to Da Nang, we could understand why it had been chosen as a rest and rejuvenation centre for war weary American military.

Our next stop was at picturesque Hoi An, a typical Vietnamese town alongside the Mekong River and our arrival was just two days after the town had been flooded, leaving the streets still coated with a layer of river mud. We were taken for a ride in a wooden cart pulled by an enormous horned water buffalo. The animal was at least six feet high, with smooth brown furry skin, which felt like silk when I stroked it. It was very docile and obviously had no fear of humans, but turned its head to look at me with big brown eyes when I stood alongside. We stopped near a long grove of trees planted in straight lines which interested me and as I was about to walk along between them, the driver stopped me. He warned that there could be king cobras in the long grass between the trees and knowing what aggressive and venomous snakes these are I immediately turned around and pulled Helen back up into the cart. The rubber trees were planted by the French, but had since been left neglected for decades.

We spent a full day on a boat-ride taking us between the scores of towering limestone islands of Ha Long Bay and when our boat moored offshore, we were allowed to snorkel alongside in the warm seawater. Many of the islands had caves and beaches to explore and there was also a floating village with a restaurant and shops, all connected by wooden walkways for tourists to move around over the sea beneath. Entire communities once lived there with schools and houses as the locals made their living from fishing. Recently the government moved villagers to the mainland to enjoy a better life, but the wooden buildings were retained as a tourist attraction. We moved north to Hue, the ancient capital of Vietnam with its massive stone wall forming a defensive citadel. The gardens and local pagodas were simply spectacular and we visited as many as possible during our short stay before continuing our journey to our last stop, Hanoi, the current capital of Vietnam.

The city is built around a very large lake where residents walk and cycle alongside to take their daily exercise, which together with their moderate diet ensures that very few residents are overweight. It was unusual to find shops grouped together by commodity in the central streets. One street had only shops selling shoes and leather goods, whereas the next only had shops selling ladies clothing. It would certainly save time when shopping for specific items, since outlets selling similar products were all near each other. We visited the forbidding stone walled "Hanoi Hilton" prison, built by the French and used to contain US fliers who were shot down after bombing Hanoi and survived attacks by locals. Prisoners were kept in small cells with a stone slab to sleep on and the most famous inmate was US Senator John McCain, who was a prisoner for some years before his release.

Since our tour was nearly finished, we spoke about making another stopover at Singapore, but reluctantly decided it was time to return home in view of the cost and our many local commitments. I telephoned through to the number given to me by Patrick Mulcahy and a strange voice answered and told me that Mister Patrick had died, but they had been expecting my call. I was asked to provide my home address, because Patrick had written to me and wanted to send me a wedding present. We were both sad to hear that the lovely man we had met so recently in Singapore was dead, but we were glad that we had at least been able to spend some time with him. The next day we took our flight to Singapore to connect with our onward flights to Dubai and Manchester and settle back to our quiet and uneventful existence on the Fairfields estate.

Chapter 8
Oxenhope and the Barn

As our flight landed, I looked out on the snow-clad countryside during our early morning arrival at Manchester airport after our holiday in warm sunshine and blue skies and shivered. We then had to struggle to see our luggage on the heavily loaded carousel because our view was blocked. In spite of notices urging passengers to stand outside the white markers to avoid blocking the view, there were many who ignored the request and stood immediately against the moving carousel. When I was finally able to spot our cases moving along, I had to force my way through a group of selfish passengers to collect both before they were carried off by the moving belt. Many elderly passengers simply had to wait until all those crowding them out had collected their own luggage and left. The taxi dropped us off separately at our houses so that we could first switch on the central heating before settling down to work through our mail.

After unpacking and filling our washing machines we drove across to York to collect the dog and were invited to stay to lunch with Trudy and Dickie, who wanted to hear all about our holiday. On the way back I stayed in the car with Billy while Helen shopped for food in our local supermarket. We were at The Yorkshireman in the evening to tell our friends about our holiday and catch up on the local gossip and I was surprised to find that Kate was missing. Checking with Rod I was told that Kate and David Kane were now smitten with each other after meeting at our barbecue and I would be able to see for myself at the Oxendale walk taking place at the weekend. Helen wanted to take Billy, but there would be other dogs on the walk and I wanted to take a ride on the Worth Valley Railway and dogs were barred. Billy was still difficult to hold back on his lead, particularly with other dogs present, but Helen was unconvinced.

"A walk across Oxendale would be ideal for him, especially after being farmed out with our friends for over two weeks."

I could understand how Helen wanted to give the dog a run outdoors, but over a three-hour period across moors, where there could be rabbits, or livestock, only well-behaved dogs would be safe to let off their leads, or mix with other dogs.

"Sorry Helen, but on or off his lead Billy is not yet ready for a walk like this with other dogs and would not be allowed on the Worth Valley train."

Helen was still determined to take Billy and for a moment I considered not going, but decided to say no more and hope she would change her mind. She did not.

"Billy is my dog and I will be responsible for him on this walk and I know he will love it."

"Quite right. Billy is your dog and it is your decision, but when he vanishes over the moors after a rabbit I will not be chasing after him."

Helen said no more and maintained a stony silence for the rest of the evening. After our experience on The Broads I thought it best to let matters take their course and avoid further upsetting her.

On Saturday morning a group of walkers shared cars to drive to the Wagon & Horses pub in Oxenhope to begin the walk and circle back to the pub for lunch. Helen had brought Billy and was probably waiting for me to comment, but silence still seemed to be my best option. Kate was dressed in leather boots and tight-fitting black designer trousers as she took charge and led the group off, with escort David Kane walking beside her. There were eighteen walkers in total and three dogs besides Billy, who was already pulling hard on his lead as it was firmly gripped by Helen. It was a dry day, but a little cool as we chatted and made our way steadily along the planned route.

All went well and we were more than halfway on the walk, when we came to a gate in a hedge enclosing a herd of a dozen or more cows in a field. Our path crossing the field would take us alongside the herd and as we stood near the gate, we began to feel nervous when the big beasts slowly turned their heads. We were being watched by some two dozen or so big brown eyes and as we hesitated, the cows continued to stare at us. A walker with a dog decided to carry on and passed through the gate and began making his way across the field. Two of the larger cows immediately began trotting towards him. Concerned about seeing such large animals bearing down on him, he turned and quickly made his way back to safety on the other side of the gate. Some of the other walkers who were following him also retreated from the field to seek sanctuary beside him. The walking group stood around muttering about not wanting to be attacked by the animals and waiting for guidance. Suddenly deciding that it was up to her to take the initiative as our group leader, Kate urged walkers to go around the field and she and David began striding up a steep hill to get to the other side. After taking a quick look at the hill the walker and his dog chose instead to move further along the hedge to look for another route and then made their way into the field by climbing over a low fence. This entry was well away from the cows, who ignored them and just carried on eating grass. Seeing this easier and safer path, the rest of the walkers followed them as the group leader and her escort vanished over the hill-top.

After continuing our walk without our leader, we eventually saw our pub in sight and looked forward to lunch. As we were passing an old barn, Helen stumbled on some long grass and the dog lead slipped from her hand to allow Billy to race off. After circling around and barking furiously for a few minutes the dog then headed straight for the old barn and vanished inside. After a minute, or two he then raced back out again but now with some long dark cloth held in his mouth which he was dragging along behind him. Helen's face showed her embarrassment and annoyance with her dog and I knew that it was up to me to try to catch him. Walking towards the dog I called out to him and at the same time rustled the paper on his favourite dog biscuits to try to get his attention. Billy dropped the cloth and ran towards me for his reward, which allowed me to take a firm grip on his lead. When we had finished our walk, we returned to the Wagon & Horses pub, but there was no sign of our leader, or her escort. Drinks were ordered and as we all sat down for lunch, David Kane hurried into the bar and asked me for a private word outside. Once away from the other walkers, he explained the problem.

"Your damned dog stole Kate's trousers and now she can't leave the barn."

I had to turn my head aside, but was still unable to control my laughter as I realised what Billy had been trailing and what Kate and David had been doing. Fortunately, David also saw the funny side of the theft and a smile slowly spread across his face as I told him.

"If Billy had stolen her knickers instead you would not have a problem. Have you tried driving your car up to the barn?"

"If I could get my car over the style, I would have done. So can you help?"

"I know exactly where her trousers are, but you may find them a little muddy. You were both lucky it was Billy and not the farmer who found you in the barn."

"I know that, but by God it was worth it. It had been building up all morning and when we saw that barn, we just couldn't wait any longer. Kate makes me feel like a teenager again and is the most enthusiastic woman I have ever known and believe me, I have met some ravers. But please, mum's the word on this, or Kate will be mortified if anyone finds out what happened."

I jogged over the field and picked up the muddied, but fortunately intact designer trousers and took them back to David, who thanked me and hurried off to take them back to a desperate Kate hiding inside the barn. As I took my place back at the table, I received enquiring looks from the walkers and told them that unfortunately Kate had turned on her ankle and David was now collecting her in his car to take her home. Helen kicked me under the table and growled into my ear.

"That is a load of bullshit. I want to know the whole truth when we get back in the car."

Giving her my best smile, I whispered to her that I would be happy to give her a full explanation, but of course there would be a price to pay. I received another kick under the table and had to rub a sore ankle. I knew that I owed it to my friend David to protect Kate from local gossip and embarrassment if the full facts were revealed. When we finished our lunch some of the group headed for the Worth Valley Railway and the rest of us headed home. Helen asked if I wanted to try the railway, but I reminded her that dogs were not allowed. I suggested that perhaps we could return some other time without Billy and Helen did not press the issue after losing control of her dog as I had predicted. In spite of strong and persistent demands and slaps on my shoulder I refused to give full details of Kate's injury.

When Helen had made dinner and we were enjoying a glass of wine together on the settee, I explained how Kate had first lost and then recovered her trousers, with my help of course. When she finally learned what had happened, Helen's shoulders shook with laughter and she was impressed by Billy's role in running off with Kate's trousers.

"I thought it must be something like that. Trust my lovely Billy to sniff them out in the middle of their naughties."

On Monday morning I received a neat parcel in the post and found a letter inside from Patrick Mulcahy, as well as two gifts. I walked along to Helen's house so that we could read the letter together.

Dear Helen and Tom,

It was wonderful to meet up with you both here and I hope you come again soon, since my doctor tells me I am now living on borrowed time. If you are reading this then my time must have run out and I will be with my wife again. My neighbours are wonderful people and they will share my furniture and property, but the enclosed items are for you and Helen to remember me. The watch was my pride and joy and I hope it will help to keep you on time. The necklace was given to Shena by her mother and she regularly wore it to functions here. If she had met Helen, I know she would have wanted her to have it as our gift for your wedding. If your marriage is as happy as ours, then you will be a very lucky couple. After meeting you both I am sure that you are perfect for each other.

My best wishes to you both, Patrick Mulcahy.

The watch was a Rolex Oyster and must have cost thousands of pounds, which is why I had never owned one. Helen was dumfounded when she saw the sparkling sapphire necklace since she had never imagined she would ever own such a beautiful and valuable piece of jewellery. I told her she would now look even more stunning when we finally got married and as she kissed me, I could feel the tears running down her cheeks. Patrick could always charm the birds from the trees and even exert that charm after his death.

It was my turn to tend to the estate garden and I used my hatchback car to load the FGC mower at The Yorkshireman and get on with the weeding before tackling the lawn. As I was checking to make sure that I had pulled up and bagged all the heavy crop of weeds, which had an uncanny ability to thrive whatever the weather, I received an unexpected visitor.

"Good morning Tom. I saw you working earlier on as I drove past and thought you might enjoy a break and some hot coffee."

My neighbour Kate, immaculate as ever in a short-pleated skirt and thick woollen jumper was holding out a silver flask and smiling at me. I pointed to the bench and we sat down together and shared the hot coffee. It was a cool day, but gardening quickly builds up body temperature and although I had not really felt the chill, the coffee was still very welcome. My smiling neighbour sat beside me and poured out two cups of hot coffee.

"I wanted to thank you for saying nothing about my indiscretions and recovering my trousers during my walk at Oxenhope and David is also very grateful to you. I was so embarrassed when I saw your dog run off with my them, but David assured me that you would help us and say nothing to the others. He thinks you are a very special person you know. I really love it here and for the first time for years, I feel I have found my home and appreciate how much you have helped me in settling here."

Her eyes were shining with tears and I almost put my arm around her to comfort her, but wisely kept my distance and assured her of my support instead.

"Kate. You are now a Fairfields estate resident and I will do all I can to help you to be happy here."

Telling her this was a big mistake with a touchy-feely woman like Kate, who immediately swung sideways on the bench to kiss me on the cheek. In her enthusiasm hcr very short skirt rode up to give me a view of bare thigh and frilly pantie edges. With the thought of someone seeing us embracing on a bench in the estate garden in mid-morning, I panicked and shot to my feet, knocking the coffee cup out of Kate's hand. Seeing the surprised look on her face I apologised and explained that there is always someone somewhere watching and likely to misconstrue her perfectly normal actions to cause embarrassment. Kate understood immediately and stood to give me a hug, but I moved back and warned her again about possible watchers. After thanking her again for her generous thought in bringing the coffee, we parted and I got on with my gardening. When the mower and tools had been returned to the store, I called at Helen's to ask if she felt like a game of tennis and tell her about my meeting with Kate. She was very impressed by Kate's generous gesture in taking me coffee and her enthusiasm in thanking me for my help, but perhaps a little cynical about me seeing a flash of Kate's undies.

"Oh, come on Tom. Surely a quick flash of your over enthusiastic admirer's undies is not a big deal for a man of your wide experience."

"It wasn't the undies that got me concerned. I was more worried about someone describing Kate kissing me on the estate garden bench with her skirt up around her waist. Although there seemed to be no one in sight when I was with her, from experience I was sure someone would have seen us and broadcast the information."

"Which is why my love I guess you are telling me about it now. Don't worry, I know you better than you think and there is no way I would expect you to perform on a bench on the estate garden in broad daylight in spite of Kate's warm feelings for you."

I had told Helen about my coffee delivery and embrace from Kate to avoid any misunderstanding by a garrulous resident, but she had simply shrugged it off at my expense. No matter, at least my probation had not been threatened.

We went off for our tennis game and as we were knocking up on court, we were approached by two immaculately dressed players who asked if we were interested in playing doubles. I looked at Helen, who nodded her head and we played two sets with the couple. Marie was dark haired, slim and vivacious and obviously much younger than husband Arnold. He was probably a good ten years older than me, but looked quite fit, if just a little overweight and had a magnificent head of long wavy grey hair. They were not strong players, but while Marie was very quick on court, her husband was slow to chase after balls, but we had an enjoyable game. They insisted on having us join them for a drink at their home, which they assured us was only minutes away. We followed their Bentley coupe to their large detached house with its imposing driveway and were then seated in their large drawing room as we drank Singapore Slings. When Marie asked what I would like to drink, I hesitated and she persisted until I told her my favourite, which we all then enjoyed. Helen explained how I had met an old colleague in Singapore and his touching letter and gifts to us. The couple were impressed by the story and Marie squeezed my knee as she gave me a big smile. I groaned inwardly at meeting yet another touchy-feely lady who might yet threaten my probation record.

Arnold was sitting next to Helen and giving her his undivided attention as she told him about our holiday in Singapore and Vietnam. Marie explained how she had taken a degree in History, had no interest in teaching and was only able to find work with an international charity. Arnold was the MD and at an office party they began chatting and eventually married. He already had children by a previous marriage and made it clear that he would not want to become a father again at his age. Marie would have liked children and I got the impression that she felt that life was passing her by, in spite of the comfortable lifestyle she enjoyed. When I told her that Helen had taken both golf and tennis lessons after we met, she asked if I played and nodded her head when I told her that I had played both for years.

"You are not married Tom, but I assume Helen is your fiancée. Will it be a long engagement?"

I was surprised by the question and was not prepared to explain the one-year probation period we had agreed before our marriage.

"I was married for thirty years and have three grown up children. Helen has never married and I suppose we are both making sure that after our different life styles over such a long period, we are ready to become a couple for our remaining years."

Marie was watching my face closely as I was speaking and reached out and squeezed my knee again before responding.

"Helen must think a great deal of you to take lessons in both golf and tennis to keep you company."

"We live close to each other and when I moved in as a neighbour after losing my wife, Helen was very helpful in working with me to set up the community services on our estate."

Marie wanted to know all about the services and as I was speaking, she edged closer to me and looked intently into my face as I was speaking, which made me feel slightly uncomfortable. Having just escaped from a possible entanglement with neighbour Kate, I thought Marie was taking too much interest in my affairs and it was time to leave. Telling Marie that we were meeting friends in York, I rose and fortunately Helen had heard me and also stood and told Arnold that she had enjoyed our game and their company. Holding on to her hand, Arnold insisted that we come to them for dinner soon and he would not accept a refusal. We exchanged telephone numbers and they walked with us to their door, where Marie gave me a quick peck on my cheek. As we were driving home, I told Helen that Marie was definitely missing something in her life and I wanted to be sure it would be me. She laughed and told me she had a similar view about Arnold who obviously assumed that his money could buy him anything he wanted.

"The man already has everything anyone could want, but I suspect he is just bored and looking for new distractions, or possible conquests to fill his days, or nights. Now that we have agreed to go for dinner we will just have to wait to find out when and whether it is just with them, or with their friends as well."

I had exactly the same impression and since we had told them we were meeting friends from York I suggested ringing Trudy and Dickie to see if they would like to join us for dinner. Helen thought that would make our little white lie more respectable and when I spoke to Trudy, she suggested meeting at an Italian restaurant in Wetherby.

Since it was midway between us, we both had an easy drive and luckily were able to find parking spaces. After being given our table I told them about the dog running off with Kate's trousers on the organised walk. They both thought it was hilarious and agreed that it was very kind of me to protect Kate's reputation. Trudy told us about her new granddaughter and how she opened her arms to Grandad Dickie whenever she saw him. It was good to see the couple enjoying their life together and involving Dickie with Trudy's family. He told us that since his marriage, his ex-wife and son had taken every opportunity to be unpleasant to him. Although at his divorce he had given his wife the large family house and half his investments she was now demanding that he clear her debts. Instead of moving to a smaller property with lower running costs after he moved out, his wife and son remained in the large family home. They had now run through the settlement money and accumulated debts which they clearly expected Dickie should pay off. He had no intention of doing so and no legal requirement to provide the money she wanted. As a consequence, he had to tolerate persistent telephone and written demands and insults from both of them. His wife was now threatening to take him to court, but after meeting with his solicitor he was advised that she had no case to answer after his generous settlement at the time that the divorce was finalised. After we parted company and were driving away, Helen told me how sorry she was to hear about the long-term persecution of my best friend by a vindictive divorced wife. I had my own view on the matter.

"Dickie is too generous and should have sorted the pair of them out long ago."

Chapter 9
Unwelcome Encounters

My next development for the FGC was to propose an Investment Club for residents interested in meeting once a month to invest in the stock market. Just like betting on sport, or playing amusement machines, investing in the stock market is a form of gambling since money can be lost as well as made. Members would contribute £5 a month for a share in the club, or £20 for four shares. Each month three members would meet separately to investigate which shares to buy, or sell and their recommendations would be discussed and the shares bought at the next monthly meeting. The following month a different trio of members would research and recommend shares they considered worthy of investment. Any members wishing to leave the club, or withdraw funds would be paid from the fund holding. Helen was very interested and suggested we set up separate clubs for men and women to introduce competition between the sexes. The women to meet on a different night to accommodate family commitments and prevent men from stealing their ideas. It was clear that Helen was hoping to show that women who were accustomed to balancing the household budget would also be good at investing money on the stock market. The plan would be discussed at our next FGC meeting and after talking it through with our new Councillor Rod, he thought it would be very popular.

In the middle of another busy week after returning home following a day of clay pigeon shooting, we received an invitation to dinner with Arnold and Marie for Saturday evening. Helen took the call and Arnold used all his charm to persuade her to accept. On the day we parked on our hosts large drive alongside the expensive cars presumably owned by our fellow guests. We were introduced to Kevin and Laura who had settled in Wetherby and Mike and Stephanie who lived in Leeds. After drinks and casual conversation in the drawing room, Marie led us into the dining room where the table was set for eight. The immaculate white tablecloth and sparkling cutlery must have taken Marie some time to prepare, unless she had domestic help. I looked at Helen who raised an eyebrow to show that she too was impressed.

Once we were seated the food was served by a maid, which allowed Marie, who was sitting beside me to rub her leg against mine. I had to fight my instinct to get up and leave since all the signs pointed to an over intimate evening in which we were intended to be the new converts. Seeing that Helen appeared to be enjoying the gathering, I felt I should bide my time. Marie was charming and easy to talk to, but with an intensity and direct approach that was making me feel uneasy. The food and wine were superb, but I frequently had to place my hand over my glass to avoid having it topped up. After dinner we moved to the sitting room and Arnold suggested a game of cards with £1 stakes. By 9 pm, just as I was thinking about leaving, Kevin suggested we make it more interesting by playing for items of clothing. I looked at Helen who hesitated before nodding her head and we began to play. After an hour I was shirtless and had lost my shoes and socks, while Helen had lost her shoes and stockings, as well as her blouse. Our host Arnold was without his trousers and Laura was sitting opposite me with bare breasts, which I noticed were very small while Marie was down to a ridiculously small pair of knickers and her stockings and shoes. Stephanie was a buxom woman and her bare breasts were large and heavy, sitting beside her husband Mike in shorts and his socks. Helen then lost two points and was urged by Arnold to take off her bra and skirt. I shot to my feet and looked around at my fellow guests.

"I am sorry, but we have to go. I am not prepared to have Helen strip naked for any sort of game. Put your clothes on Helen."

As we dressed there was silence in the room as our startled hosts watched us and then Marie came up to me and held my arm.

"It is only a bit of fun Tom. When we are on holiday on the Continent we are often surrounded by naked people on the beaches."

I shook my head as I buttoned up my shirt.

"I don't think that is quite the same thing Marie. But thank you for an excellent dinner and for your company. Good night everyone."

We left and my last view of our fellow guests showed them huddled together and having an animated conversation. Once we were in the car and on our way home Helen leaned over and kissed me before giving her view of the evening.

"Well done my love for helping me to hang on to my underclothes, although you are normally scheming to get them off. I think the striptease was just the preamble to swapping partners and Marie told us they do have five bedrooms, even though there are only the two of them living in the house. I could tell by your face that you were not going to tolerate it much longer and then you exploded into action. When I was doing my nursing training I heard about parties where you tossed your car keys into a bowl and when you were ready to leave you picked up a bunch and were expected to sleep with the owner. I always kept away from them because it usually ended up with married partners divorcing and then marrying the person they had slept with. The problems came with the poor children, who were confused by having parents in different marriages."

"I'm sorry Helen, I almost left it too late, but I must have been distracted by Marie's breasts. Did you notice how perfectly formed they were. I was wondering if they were implants."

"Trust you to spend time studying her breasts when I was losing my clothes and yes they were implants, I know the signs."

It was late and we were glad to go to bed and put the whole affair behind us. I was sure we would not be invited to dinner again, but we might well meet the couple when we next visited the tennis club.

Our Sunday meeting of the FGC took place and I explained that with no money coming from our Rotary friends we had only £20 in our kitty. Our sponsor was paying us £50 a month for the large notice featuring his building services on our estate garden, but we had no other source of income. I proposed that we took a collection with Marigold and Helen gathering the money and suggested that members contribute at least a pound since we were now providing a range of services for local residents. Marigold's blouse was so low that I found myself wondering if the men would be distracted and put the money inside her blouse by mistake. Since I would be counting the takings, I would certainly be responsible for helping Marigold to find any misplaced coins. We collected a total of £74 and I thanked our members for their generosity, although surprisingly, none of it found its way inside Marigold's invitingly open blouse.

When the plans for an Investment Club on the estate were outlined and a show of hands was requested, there were at least thirty interested members. I suggested that we call our club "Yorkmisers" and handed over to Helen to promote her idea of a separate club for women. Although there were only twelve women in the audience, every single one was interested. We split into two meetings as I launched our all-male Investment Club and Helen set up the Tea Caddy club for women. Most of my members chose to buy one share at £5 a month, or up to four shares at £20, as also did Helen's ladies. She was assured that each of her ladies had a friend who would probably be interested in joining so that the number should roughly match the male total. Each club then chose three members to study the market and come prepared with investment suggestions at the next monthly meeting. Men decided to meet every fourth Wednesday and ladies on Mondays. Following an approach by our local Councillor I added Rod as a member. Within days the membership of Helen's Tea Caddy Club had grown to twenty-two.

In the evening as we were snuggled up together on my settee, Helen wanted to know if I had now ended new developments for FGC and I told her about another possibility. I was thinking about holding a Car Boot Sale every fourth Sunday in the car park of The Yorkshireman. We all had items we no longer used, but which might be wanted by others. We would need to hire folding tables, but could add £5 to the hire charge for those using one to sell items on the day. If we averaged only twenty tables each month, we would put £1200 per year into our FGC account. I would have a chat with Rod to get his reaction on having the sale in his car park as well as having his Sunday takings boosted with beer and food sales to visitors.

Thinking again about our visit to Singapore and our meeting with Patrick, I suddenly remembered how fascinated Helen had been with the orchid displays in the Botanical Gardens on Sempora Island. I asked her if she would like to meet Albert so that he could show her his incredible collection and explain his passion for growing the exotic plants. She was very interested and was looking forward to meeting Albert and his orchid collection. He was a pensioner on the Fairfields Estate and I was sure that Helen would be as impressed as I was when Albert showed me his back bedroom completely filled with orchids which he had grown himself.

Chapter 10
Orchids, Family and Friends

Albert was a widower with severe arthritis in both hands and I had dug and cleared the weeds from his back garden before covering it with black plastic sheeting to prevent their return. Afterwards he invited me indoors for coffee and showed me his orchid collection which he tended in a back bedroom. Helen was standing beside me as I rang his door bell and when he opened his door and saw me, his face lit up. I introduced Helen and he welcomed us inside and insisted on making us tea. Seeing him struggling to lift the kettle between both his twisted hands, Helen persuaded him to let her make the drinks and I explained the reason for our visit. Once again Albert's face lit up with joy as he told us.

"My wife was always the gardener bless her and they were her passion, so when she died, I knew I should look after them for her. She showed me how to water and feed them and I spend time with them every day, which makes me feel as if I am still close to her. Come and meet my orchids."

He took us to the bedroom where the orchids were displayed on racks against three walls and projected a mass of brilliant colours, which left Helen stunned by the spectacle. The name of each species was written on a plastic tag attached to its container. Albert explained how he put warm water on them once a week and fed them once a month. At first, he had used special orchid food, but then found that watered down tomato fertiliser worked just as well and was much cheaper. For the price paid for a good bunch of cut flowers, he told us we could buy an orchid instead which should last months, or even years, while the cut flowers would be dead in days. His enthusiasm was infectious and by the time we had finished our tea we both wanted to try growing the beautiful plants ourselves. He invited Helen to choose an orchid and she picked a cerise coloured plant with flowers clustered on each of its two stems. He gave it to her in its container and explained that it was a Phalaenopsis, or moth orchid and is an excellent house plant, but must be kept at a temperature above 58f. He had few visitors and would be delighted to see her whenever she needed advice, or a cup of tea. Helen hugged him and thanked him for the gift.

As we were walking back home, I had an idea and mentioned it to Helen.

"How do you think our local residents would react to a lecture on orchids by Albert at the Yorkshireman one evening?"

Thankfully Helen's response confirmed my own view, since I needed to find a speaker for The Yorkshireman.

"I think they would all get the same enthusiasm for orchids from listening to that lovely man that he gave us and I am sure he would really enjoy doing it."

That was my thought too and more new ideas began to form in my head for involving residents of all ages on our Fairfields Estate. There could be others with special hobbies, or talents which could be shared with residents and they might welcome the opportunity to pass on their expertise. If like Albert, they lived alone it could also encourage them and provide an opportunity to become more involved with other interested neighbours. Returning with Helen to her house we looked for a suitable location for the orchid and finally chose the kitchen window. It was light for most of the day, but not in direct sunshine which might burn the plant and should average 60F in temperature. Helen liked pots and quirky items, but would have trouble finding room for more orchids if her passion developed, but we could always consider buying a greenhouse. Since my year of probation was nearly up, I thought it was time to think about which house we would choose to live in when we married.

Three-bedroom townhouses are easy to look after, but the gardens are small and space is very limited. Perhaps with two of us to cook, clean and look after the garden we could surely manage a larger property. Combining our possessions in one small townhouse might also prove difficult after we married and I asked Helen about making a change in plan.

"When we get married, instead of selling one house and both living in the other, how would you feel about selling both and finding a bigger house instead with a larger garden and space for both cars on the drive?"

Helen kept her eyes fixed on mine as she was turning my suggestion over in her mind before giving me her answer.

"I think it makes sense Tom. We both have things we want to keep, including our cars and I know how much you miss the garden and greenhouse, which you often mention."

I was pleased that my suggestion received her approval and although she was due to sleep in my house that evening, she had an upset tummy and thought it best to be in her own bed instead. Next morning, I telephoned to ask how she was feeling and although she was much better, she wanted to spend a quiet day at home and encouraged me to carry on without her. We arranged to meet for dinner at her house and I went to see Albert to sound him out on speaking to residents about orchids. He was surprised to be asked, but after being reassured that his expertise would be very interesting for other residents, we agreed the date of an evening presentation at The Yorkshireman. Next, I called to see daughter Karen and grandson Martin, who was now racing around on his knees and would not be long before he was standing, walking and grabbing anything within reach. From my own experience I warned my daughter about moving away from edges anything which could be pulled down, smashed or knocked over.

Karen asked me to give her regards to Helen and told me they were driving to Aberdovey in Wales for a long weekend with Abby and her boyfriend and invited Helen and me to join them. They were booked in at a small seaside hotel for three nights from Friday. We had nothing planned over the weekend and it could be a pleasant break with my family at this small Welsh coastal resort. I told Karen I would check with Helen and get back to her. Over dinner that night I mentioned the invitation, but Helen was still suffering stomach pains and had already agreed to stand in for a colleague at the local hospital over the weekend. Instead, she suggested that I should go without her.

"I am sorry Tom, but I can't face a long journey in the car at the moment and would not be very good company. It will be very light work for me at the hospital and I think I can cope with that. Please give my apologies to your daughters and by the time you get back I hope I have shaken it off. I feel very embarrassed to miss our first invitation to spend time with your family and hope they will invite us some other time."

I was accustomed to seeing Helen a picture of health and full of energy, but with her medical training I had to accept her reassurance, in spite of my concerns.

"This is the second time in the last few months that you have had stomach upsets and I think you should have a check-up to find what could be causing them."

Helen assured me that it was more an inconvenience than a serious issue and was nothing to worry about in her professional opinion. She insisted that I stop worrying and go off and enjoy myself with my family. After dinner she preferred to stay indoors and I walked to The Yorkshireman to meet Councillor Rod. I wanted to discuss the timing and arrangements for Arthur to give his orchid presentation to residents. We settled on a 7 pm start the following Thursday in the pub function room. Albert would need a table as well as a screen to cover his plants before introducing each species to his audience.

I was just about to leave when David Kane suddenly appeared and asked me to follow him to a quiet corner which would be out of sight of the bar. He quietly explained to me that he wanted to avoid being seen by Kate, but needed my advice on how to curb their over passionate relationship. After seeing them so obviously infatuated with each other I could not understand how when she was so passionate, he now wanted to avoid her.

"I thought you two were going at it like a couple of teenagers, so what went wrong?"

David had a quick look around to be sure that Kate was not in the bar before explaining in subdued tones.

"At first, I could not believe my luck and even though I had quite a few way-out sessions with girlfriends, Kate made them all seem like amateurs. We made love in my car, in her kitchen, in a barn as you know and really anytime and anywhere. I am ashamed to admit it, but it began to be too much for me and I actually heard myself complaining that I had a headache and was just not up to it. Can you believe that? Me refusing to make love. I found my, you know, was getting quite sore with so much use. I swear that Kate must be trying to make up for years of neglect by that husband of hers and I am now making all sorts of excuses to avoid her advances, but I do love the woman. She thinks the world of you and I was hoping you would have a quiet word and persuade her that we can spend our time together without having sex all the time."

Hearing this, I was stunned.

"Surely you must have tried explaining your feelings about overdoing the lovemaking?"

"Of course I have, but with my reputation she is convinced that I am losing interest and it makes her even more active. I know you can explain it to her gently and much better than I can. Perhaps then we can settle down to a more normal relationship together, since I don't want to lose her. She will be coming in tonight and looking for me, so do you think you can spend just a few minutes to have a chat with her."

We had been friends for a long time and I could hardly begrudge him a few minutes of my evening to speak to Kate.

"Alright David. If she comes in tonight within the next half hour, I will try to explain the situation, but I will be away with my family for the next three days and then it would have to wait. Are you going to be staying here?"

To my surprise David was already on his feet and obviously anxious to get away as quickly as possible. After pausing briefly to thank me for agreeing to help, he hurried off before Kate arrived. The half hour was almost up when I saw Kate standing at the bar and nervously looking around for her lover. Her face registered first surprise and then concern when she saw me walking towards her and offering to buy her a drink. I explained that that I had just been speaking to David Kane and I needed to have a word with her, which made her even more apprehensive. I lead her to my usual table carrying both our drinks with a visibly worried Kate following behind. We sat down and I explained that David had to attend a meeting, but asked me to apologise for him. As I began to raise David's problem, I could see her becoming a little less tense.

"I am really glad that you and David are getting on so well after meeting at my barbecue."

"We are and he is the most wonderful man I have ever met."

"He told me that he loves you, but there is just one problem."

Kate's head jerked up as she waited to hear what I had to say next.

"Yours is a very physical and loving relationship, but there is more to enjoying each other's company than constant lovemaking. David loves you and is quite happy just to be with you, without spending so much of the time making love. Why not hold back and let him take the initiative occasionally since you have nothing to prove and you already have his love."

Kate gave a big sigh and relaxed in her chair.

"Oh Tom. I have been so worried and thought David wanted nothing more to do with me. I have always been unlucky with my men and I was convinced that I was losing him, which made me try even harder to keep him loving me. I don't want to be making love so often, but when we first met, he told me he was starved of love and I was his dream woman. I am happy just to be with him too and will let him make the moves and decisions in future, just so long as we can stay together."

I told her that was all that David wanted and he would be in touch. Kate threw her arms around me and gave me a big hug and I noticed there were tears on her cheeks. I said goodnight and left, but noticed Rod standing behind his bar and wagging his finger at me. I guessed he was probably thinking that I was being a little too friendly with Kate, but I was happy to have helped my friend and knew it had been the right thing to do. I had nothing on my conscience and would tell Helen exactly what had happened over breakfast in the morning.

When I called at her house next morning Helen was dressed and ready to go to the local hospital. She told me that she was feeling much better, but still not ready for the long car journey to Aberdovey and warned me to take care driving over the tortuous Welsh country roads. I mentioned having to help David Kane and his problem with Kate and Helen thought he was lucky to have me sort out his love life for him.

"You men never stop complaining when women are too tired, or unwell to fulfil your sex fantasies, but when Kate did everything she could to please him, he just was not able to keep up and had to turn to you for help."

Hearing these critical comments, I kept my silence, as you do.

Chapter 11
Sand Sea and Ice Cream

I was last to arrive at the hotel in Aberdovey and found my family already enjoying drinks as they were waiting for me in the lounge and were clearly anxious to have their dinner. The small hotel was solidly built in local weathered stone to withstand the winter gales which often roared in from Cardigan Bay and I guessed that it was Victorian. Possibly because it was his first stay away from his usual crawling ground, grandson Martin was not in happy mood and when I bent down to give him a kiss, he gave me a clip on the ear. We booked a corner table for six in the restaurant and Martin immediately started banging the tray of his highchair with his rattle until Karen began feeding him. Still not happy in a strange location, he moved his head from side to side as she tried to put spoons full of food into his mouth, before knocking the spoon from her hand. Suddenly I felt really glad that as a grandparent, my patience would not be tested in the same way. Thinking that perhaps he was not hungry, Karen stopped feeding him and he immediately began crying again and his high-pitched wails turned every single head in the restaurant. Poor Karen had no choice other than to leave her own meal and take him up to their room after telling us that he was probably overtired. When my son in law finished his meal, he followed Karen to allow her to return and finish her own meal as he took her place looking after Martin.

Meantime the conversation at our table was lively and I was asked to describe some of the highlights of my eventful overseas holidays. My experience with the belly dancer on the Nile steamer and escape from the pole dancers in Pattaya was well received, although my daughters thought I was a typical innocent abroad after assuming that they had been told the whole story. Abby's new boyfriend Craig worked in marketing, which gave us common interests to discuss and avoided those uncomfortable silences which often arise at a parent's first meeting with his daughter's new boyfriend. I liked him and was relieved that Abby had made a good choice, although I knew that my opinion would not influence her in any way.

I had a single room on the top floor of the hotel and could reach into the bathroom as I sat on my bed. The room may have been small, but this was certainly not reflected in the amount I had been charged. Had Helen been able to join me we would have had a double room with more space at a reasonable price as well as our usual lively conversations when we were in bed. I was beginning to feel lonely and missed our advantages as a couple already. The hotel was just across the road from a small sandy beach and there was a large public car park for our cars nearby. This made it much easier to transport baby equipment and beach furniture down to the water's edge. It was a sunny day and there were sailboards for hire. Since my juniors all wanted to try their luck at standing upright on a sailboard as they skidded over the water, I volunteered to look after Martin in my grandfather's role. Having previously tried and failed to remain standing for more than a minute on one of these slippery fibreglass boards, I was quite happy to do my duty and remain on firm ground with Martin.

My daughters were doing quite well and were able to maintain their standing positions on the boards, but their men were spending more time climbing back on the boards than sailing them. Fortunately, my daughters had gained valuable training and experience when on holiday with me as teenagers and were confident surfers, much to the embarrassment of their male partners. Martin was sitting quietly beside me until I built a really magnificent sandcastle and then enjoyed himself smashing it up so that I had to build another one. After demolishing six of my magnificent masterpieces, he began losing interest, much to my relief. Scooping up damp sand and carefully smoothing it into shape for turrets and battlements was tiring work and I thought it was time for a walk and an ice cream, which would be good for both of us. After carrying Martin and his pushchair up from the sand and onto the promenade we made our way along it to the shops. I bought him a tub of ice cream after deciding he could do a lot more damage with a cornet. We sat together on a bench and I fed him with the wooden spoon and was relieved to find there was no head turning and he was ready for each of my deliveries. It was very pleasant to be sitting in the warm sunshine with my first grandson and I remembered all the times I had looked after my own children until they eventually grew into troublesome teenagers. Thinking about my nights of disturbed sleep and the temper tantrums of noisy infants, I decided that I was quite happy in my new role as grandad and part time carer. However, when my triumphant daughters and subdued partners finally abandoned their sailboards, I was still relieved to hand Martin back to his mother. After lunch we took a ride on the Talyllyn Railway up into the mountains and Karen explained to Martin that it was a puffa train. At some point she would have to correct puffa trains and moocows, but babies are better at recognising noises than words.

On Saturday night over dinner, I explained that I would return home in the morning. I was concerned that Helen was not well and I was so far away if she needed my help. Everyone thought it was the right decision and asked me to give Helen their best wishes for a quick recovery. It was a long drive with frequent holdups as I was trapped first behind cars towing boats and then caravan convoys on the narrow roads. There were also frustrated drivers deciding to risk their lives and mine by overtaking on blind bends and hilltops. With one stop for a toilet break, petrol and snacks, I reached home by midday to find that Helen was not in and guessed she was still working at the hospital and covering for a colleague. Just to be sure I telephoned Helen and she was surprised that I had cut short my stay with the family and told me not to make such a fuss over her. Since she deserved a relaxing break after working all day, I persuaded her to have dinner at an Italian restaurant and she said it was nice to have me back. There was a candle on our table as we enjoyed our food and when I told her I had missed her Helen reached across and kissed me and I felt like a teenager again.

The Tea Caddy investment club met on Monday and after their top-secret discussions, Helen joined me in the bar of The Yorkshireman, but refused to give any hints as to their stock selection. All she would tell me was that their choice would never be considered by men, which had me puzzling over the possibilities. The Yorkmisers were due to meet on Wednesday and I was looking forward to hearing which stocks our three members would recommend before we chose one for our own first purchase. Perhaps by then one of the men would have persuaded his wife, or partner to disclose the mysterious Tea Caddy choice. I could not believe that women would be able to outdo the men in their first stock purchase, but thinking about Helen's subtle comment I was beginning to have concerns that our reputation could be at risk.

On Tuesday evening we both helped Albert to carry his orchids to the pub for his presentation and to arrange them behind the screen where he could easily reach them. I was surprised to see more than thirty residents take their seats and watched their faces as Albert displayed and described each orchid. He had brought ten of his favourite plants and in the bright lights of the meeting room their colours and the delicate formation of the blooms were spectacular. He explained that each plant was grown from cuttings because he had found that to be a more reliable method than starting with seeds. Cuttings proved to be more consistent and predictable than using seeds and gave faster results. There were lots of questions and as I watched I could see the same interest and enthusiasm on faces in the audience which we had ourselves when Albert spoke to us in his bedroom filled with orchids. Quite a few asked if they could buy some of the orchids and although Albert was quite happy to give away his plants, I suggested that since he had to buy the pots and grow the orchids from cuttings, he should be paid something towards his costs. We settled on a price for an orchid in a pot and Albert was given orders for twenty plants by enthusiastic residents. Helen and I insisted on buying Albert a drink and Rod did the same and we eventually drove him home after he told us that it was his best night in years and he was thrilled to be paid for doing work he loved.

As we drove back to my home, we both felt delighted that Albert's talk had been so popular and that he would now have more contact with other residents to liven up his lonely life. I made coffee and we relaxed in the lounge as I told Helen about my stay in Aberdovey and how happy I was to be back and sharing the evening with her. Taking hold of my hand she surprised me with a request.

"I think it is now time for us to begin looking for a suitable house on the estate, then have a quiet wedding and make it our home."

I looked at her in amazement. She no longer needed me to prove my ability to resist designing women and was also ready to move to a new bigger home. Once again, my imagination began giving me unpleasant thoughts about possible reasons for her decision. Seeing the surprise on my face Helen explained.

"You have already shown how much you love me and I know you do your best to keep ladies from involving you. I feel sure I can trust you and want to marry you, particularly now that I have a special reason."

My phone rang just as I put my arms around her and I had to struggle to hold her and the phone as I took the call.

"Oh Tom. Is that you?"

It was Trudy and by the sound of her voice, she was very distressed and I asked her if there was a problem.

"After our lunch Dickie went to sleep in his chair and I got on with some cleaning. When I got finished, I took him a cup of tea and he looked up at me and wasn't speaking properly. I didn't know what he was saying and his face was sort of twisted. I knew there was something wrong with him and rang for the paramedics straight away. They were here within minutes and took him to York hospital. It was all so sudden and I have been at the hospital for hours ever since, waiting to hear what was happening, but they have him in intensive care and I am so frightened. I knew you would want to be told."

"Oh Trudy, I am sorry. We will be with you within an hour and will meet you at the hospital."

Trudy thanked me and put down her phone, since she was obviously too emotional to say more. Helen had been trying to make sense of my comments to Trudy, but realised that something was seriously wrong. When I explained to her what had happened, she was shocked and agreed that we should drive to York and help Trudy as much as possible. Hopefully Dickie would pull through, but unless he had changed his will, I would still be his executor if he died. I had gone through a similar experience when my wife died and would also have to collect his shotgun and add it to my licence before advising the police. Trudy had no shotgun licence and it would be illegal for her to keep a shotgun in the house since only Dickie had a licence. Fortunately, there were no traffic holdups and we were at the hospital in less than an hour. As soon as Trudy saw us, she threw her arms around me and sobbed on my shoulder. Her daughter was with her and we went with them to get hot drinks from the vending machine.

Dickie was overweight, too fond of wine and did very little exercise as well as being five years older than I was. He had given up smoking ten years previously, but the damage to his lungs and arteries could already have been done. I put my arms around Trudy and told her how Dickie had helped me when my wife died and she told me how much he meant to her.

"Since we all met in Cyprus he has made me happier than I have ever been before in my loveless marriage and every day with him is funny and special. I don't know what I would do if I lost him."

As we were drinking our coffee, a nurse spoke to us and assured us that Dickie was over the worst and would now need a good night's sleep. We offered to take Trudy and her daughter home and arranged to collect Trudy the following morning. Next day we were back at the hospital and Trudy, Helen and I went to Dickie's bedside and found him lying pale and motionless with tubes connecting him to a bedside machine which was helping his body to recover. He opened his eyes and smiled at us, but did not speak and instead we briefly described our

Vietnam holiday and how the dog had snatched my neighbour's trousers in the barn, which brought a smile to his face. Helen and I then left to allow her daughter to sit with her mother beside Dickie. As we were leaving, I had a word with one of the doctors and he told me that Dickie had suffered a mini stroke and should be back home within days.

After taking Trudy and her daughter back to her home we drove off to Fairfields and I suddenly remembered Helen saying she had a special reason for getting married, before our conversation was interrupted by Trudy calling about Dickie.

"So, my love, what was the special reason you had for suddenly deciding to marry me, as well as my natural charm and flash shower of course?"

Helen snorted at this, but refused to tell me until we were home, she had prepared a meal and we were sitting down in the lounge enjoying coffee. Her silence was beginning to get me worried again and my imagination was working overtime in picturing all sorts of unusual situations and calamities, but I would just have to wait for her to choose the right moment. On the bright side I was hoping that it was a house she had chosen, or perhaps she wanted a new car to replace her ageing runabout. Eventually, with our meal over we were sitting together and drinking our coffee in the lounge when Helen smiled at me and gave me details of her special reason.

"Well my darling, in my professional opinion I am pregnant."

I could not believe what I was hearing and stared at Helen as I waited for her to tell me that she was just teasing me after hearing about my experiences with Martin at Aberdovey. Although her eyes remained fixed on my face, she said nothing more and I suddenly realised that she was actually serious and I really was going to become a father again. I put my arms around her and kissed her before responding.

"If you are sure darling, then it's fantastic news and I already have a lot of experience as a dad and know that you will make a wonderful mother."

Helen's eyes filled with tears and she wrapped her arms around me and put her head on my shoulder. She told me how she had made repeated tests because she could not believe that at fifty-two years of age, she was to become a mother for the first time.

"You do realise Tom that our lives are going to be totally changed and you have already brought up a family. Are you sure you are willing to start again now that you are retired? It is certainly not going to be easy for us to bring up a child."

"Helen, we have been blessed with an incredible gift even if it has come as a complete surprise to both of us. Young couples having their first baby have to cope with their jobs as well as setting up a home with no experience of children and often very little money to manage on. We are retired, we have homes and enough money and can give all our attention to our baby. First, we must get married, quietly as you have always suggested and I hope quickly. Next we must find a new home for us as a family of three and work to make it ready for when our little one is born. We will then give him, or her the best childhood we possibly can. You know what I think so tell me how you feel about becoming a mother?"

Helen sat up and took hold of my hand as she told me about her feelings.

"When we visited Karen and she let me hold your grandson, I felt his small warm body in my arms and realised what I had missed in my life and what I thought I could never have. Then I had two periods after thinking I had finished menstruating. I thought no more about it until I began to notice gradual changes in my body and realized they had to be signs that I was pregnant."

"Was that the reason for the tummy problems?"

"Yes, but we women have to put up with our body changes as we face the menopause and I didn't want to get you involved."

We spoke for hours about what we should do as parents and it suddenly occurred to me that our baby would be either an uncle, or aunt to my grandson Martin. Imagining the reaction of my family, friends and acquaintances at The Yorkshireman, we thought it wise to wait until Helen began to show signs of pregnancy before releasing the news, or with my reputation they would be sure I was simply kidding them. That night we both had difficulty getting off to sleep as one or other of us would have another thought on how to prepare for the new arrival to pass on to the other. Fortunately, with her experience as a midwife Helen did not need any advice on how to prepare before the birth in seven months' time, but did suggest that there were classes for expectant fathers as well. Having brought up three very active but very normal children, I assured her that my hands on experience was better than taking classes. Helen was not convinced.

"Science has also improved baby equipment and handling in the last thirty years my love and you might be surprised what you could learn."

"If it helps to avoid spearing my thumbs with safety pins when changing nappies, I might be interested."

"There you are you see. Terry towelling nappies are not used now so you don't need safety pins anymore with disposable nappies, which makes my point."

"OK. As I said, if it helps, I will take the courses, but you must say nothing about this to my daughters."

As I thought about all the things we would have to do, it struck me that as in business we were now working to a deadline and would have to plan ahead to be sure that we had everything ready for our new arrival.

Chapter 12
New Home and Honeymoon

We were wide awake at 5 am the next morning and decided that we had too much on our minds and too much to get done to stay in bed any longer. After our very early breakfast, we sat in my lounge to plan our baby campaign and make sure we were available for Trudy until Dickie was out of danger. When I made coffee for us in the middle of the morning, we had a list of things to do and a time plan. I wanted to put my house on the market first, but to my delight Helen insisted that it should be hers because of my fabulous shower. After the sale Helen would move in with me until we found a larger house and then I would sell my house. We would have our honeymoon in Hawaii as soon as Dickie was out of hospital, but if there was no time to marry first it could wait until our return, since we did not want to risk travelling whilst Helen was too pregnant. If Dickie had a relapse, or another stroke Trudy would need our help and we would postpone both our marriage and honeymoon.

I rang Trudy to ask about Dickie and she was more relaxed after learning that he had a good night and was sitting up in bed. She was going to visit him in the afternoon, but told us to stay at home and see him later in the week when he should be stronger. My next call was to a local estate agent to value both houses and provide details of suitable larger properties on sale in the area. An agent would meet each of us in the afternoon and bring details of suitable houses we might like to visit. With Dickie on the mend, we could now set dates for the honeymoon, followed by our wedding.

Helen was waiting in her house after a frantic session of cleaning and tidying every room, plus the mandatory bunch of fresh flowers in her lounge and room fresheners to cancel out any hot dog aromas from Billy. Her estate agent Raymond arrived promptly and began his tour with his notebook in hand to record room sizes and key selling points. He was overweight and middle aged and Helen assumed he had been nominated to relate to a single pensioner selling her house. She was tempted to tell him that she was not going into a home, but getting married and having a baby, but stayed silent as she followed him from room to room. At the end of his tour he told Helen that there was a strong demand for compact homes like hers and she should have no problems selling it quickly. He quoted a price range which was higher than either of us expected and told her that his colleague Janet, who was at my house had details of properties for sale. Helen wondered if Janet was also middle aged and overweight like Raymond, but with my reputation she suspected that Janet would very likely be young and attractive.

Meanwhile at my house I was greeted by Janet, who was probably in her mid-twenties, slim and blond. She told me that she would do her best to sell my house after she had found the larger house we were looking for. It was a popular area and she had lots of customers looking for properties just like mine. In her short skirt and high heels Janet seemed dressed more for cocktails than house surveys, but I assumed that she wanted to use her power dressing to reassure me that she was a capable, as well as an attractive estate agent. Janet was particularly impressed by my shower and showed so much interest in the range of controls that for a moment I was tempted to offer her a trial, but fortunately wisdom prevailed. Since my house was an end property with a side entrance and paved front garden requiring little maintenance, she assured me it would be ideal for older customers wishing to downsize. The price she forecast would show me a healthy increase since I purchased it when I was also downsizing. She wondered why I was moving.

"It is a well-maintained property Mr Hartley. Are you moving out of the area?"

I could not resist shattering her image of pensioners selling their homes.

"No, I am getting married and starting a family, which is why I need a larger property in the area."

Her face registered her disbelief, but after a long pause she assured me that she was sure she would be able to find the right property for me and asked what sort of price range I had in mind. Doubling my house price, I gave her an approximate figure and she promised to bring me a list of houses in my price range to look at. As she was leaving, I could not resist further boosting the reputation of seniors.

"I play a lot of tennis and have little time for television, which is why I prefer big families instead."

There was another long pause before she said goodbye and assured me that she would have a list of suitable properties for me to consider by the end of the day and would bring it to my house.

Ten minutes later Helen arrived and asked how I had got on with my estate agent. I told her that my attractive young lady estate agent had admired the shower and seemed ready to try it, but I explained that it was reserved and she was very surprised when I told her I was moving to have a baby. Glaring at me for my joke about the shower, Helen quickly corrected me.

"You are not having a baby my love. You have already made your vital contribution and now it's up to me to cope with the pain and discomfort to make you a proud father. Why was it I wonder that you had a young lady and I was sent an overweight old man to view my house. I'm sure you have some sort of homing device to attract women."

Ignoring her comments, instead I raised the question of Billy.

"We are going to be very involved both in the day and the night and I wonder if we will also have time to take Billy for walks and clean up droppings in our new garden."

Helen frowned and told me it was too early to decide about Billy and once again I said no more to let things take their course. After adding the likely value of both houses and part of our bank balances we had a maximum cash figure to use for our house purchase, but would also need money for redecorating and emergencies. Fortunately, we both had pensions from our employers and as we were retired, we hoped to do any redecorating ourselves. Now we would have to find a house to match our requirements and cash available. At our age we were unlikely to be given a mortgage and preferred to avoid increasing our outgoings with a child to bring up.

Trudy rang to tell us Dickie was back at home and ready for visitors and we arranged to see him in the afternoon. When we arrived, he was sitting in the lounge and seemed his old self, but was helped to his feet by Trudy when he visited the bathroom. The doctor had warned him to change his diet and avoid, or drastically reduce his alcohol intake since after a mini stroke he was now more likely to have a full stroke with dire consequences. Trudy showed us his diet sheet and assured us that she would make sure he followed it. We told them our news about our baby.

When they heard that Helen was pregnant there was a stunned silence as they overcame their shock before hugging us both and telling us it was wonderful news. It made me appreciate the likely response I would face in moving from being a grandad to becoming a dad again. They were surprised to learn we were about to book our honeymoon and would marry on our return. They insisted that once again we should allow them to take care of Billy, since dog walking would be beneficial for both of them. Hearing this made me think that our return from honeymoon would be a good time to suggest leaving Billy with them permanently. Dickie was surprised that we were not getting married before our honeymoon, but Trudy agreed that we should now be giving the baby our priorities since there were travel restrictions on pregnant women.

Back home at Fairfields estate we picked six houses from the list Janet had delivered and drove to each to park and study them from the outside, as well as checking the neighbouring homes. Some houses were flanked by others with badly overgrown gardens, or camper vans, cars, or pickup trucks parked on the garden, or kerbsides, which might make it too busy, or noisy for a young baby. Only one house appealed to us, but the paint was peeling on the woodwork and although the garden was well established, it was also very badly neglected. The house had been built pre-war and was at the end of a quiet cul-de-sac. It was a large semi-detached house and had space on the drive for two or more cars, plus a garage with a door which appeared not to have been opened for some time. The houses on either side were well maintained with attractive gardens. We contacted the agents to arrange a viewing during the following morning.

We arrived at 10 am to meet the owner Mrs Hedges and found a smiling grey-haired little lady greeting us in the doorway. After inviting us in and offering us tea she explained that after bringing up her family they moved away and then her husband died and she looked after the garden, the house and herself for the last ten years. Unfortunately, at eighty-nine she had to accept that she could no longer manage on her own and was selling the house to pay for her accommodation in a retirement home. She relied on a cane to walk and asked us to look around on our own because she could not climb the stairs.

We had to walk though barriers of cobwebs before finding three good sized bedrooms with built-in wardrobes and a large bay window in the main bedroom. The bathroom upstairs had its original cast iron bath and a large separate toilet next door. I had never seen so many, or such large spiders and we had to brush them off each other as we broke through their networks, built during years of house neglect. Downstairs the kitchen was small, with a doorway into a medium sized dining room with French windows opening on to a big garden. The lounge had a large bay window and high ceilings, but the fireplace was original and dated, whilst the entrance hall floor was laid out with attractively patterned ceramic tiles. There was also a large cloakroom alongside the hall which was fitted with a shower and toilet. Helen really liked the house, but was worried about the amount of work needed to clean, modernise and restore it. With our inspection finished we were invited to take more tea and Agnes asked us why we were moving and was amazed to learn the reason. She struggled to her feet to kiss Helen and congratulate her on her wonderful news and told us how her own children had made her life so happy as she watched them grow to be adults. One was in Canada and the other lived in Ireland, but they both visited her with her grandchildren once, or twice every year. As we were leaving, she said she hoped we would have her house so that she knew it would be in good hands after spending most of her life within its walls.

Over lunch Helen told me that she thought she would be happy living in the house Agnes wanted us to have, if I thought we could carry out the work and afford the repairs needed as well as tackling the overgrown and long neglected gardens.

"Well love, I completely decorated my own big house and sorted out the garden in three months before selling it and that was working on my own. With your help and encouragement, I am sure I can do it again and the house price is well below our maximum budget level."

Helen hugged me and showed how much she wanted the house with her next suggestion.

"We don't really need to take a honeymoon, either before or after marrying Tom, since we already had holidays on The Broads and in Vietnam. Why not spend the money and the time on the house instead, move in quickly and be on hand to use as much time as possible to make it ready for our baby? We could work together all day on decorating and in the garden and settle in the house at the same time. If we can manage to live in the house, surely we can get most of the work done in the next seven months."

I thought this was a great idea, but before we finally decided to buy, I wanted a survey made to be sure that there were no major hidden problems. Pre-war houses were usually well built by craftsmen, but the house was some eighty years old. I rang the estate agency to tell them to push on with the sale of both our houses and agreed to buy Agnes's house subject to survey. The price already allowed for the neglected condition and we would not want to haggle with Agnes, provided that no major faults were found in the survey. Dickie was surprised to hear our honeymoon was cancelled and how instead we were hoping to spend the time working on the pre-war house we both liked. Trudy heard part of the telephone conversation and cut in.

"That's good news Tom, you will now have time to get married and have the same surname on the baby's birth certificate."

"Thank you Trudy. That makes sense and it will be well worth making time to launch Mrs Helen Hartley into the Fairfields estate. She will be in touch after we choose the date."

Dickie was a retired surveyor and advised me to check the wiring and roof timbers in view of the age of the house. He also warned me that the bathroom and kitchen would certainly need updating. When he also offered to come with me to make a more detailed inspection and calculate how much it was likely to cost, I was glad to accept. Since he was not yet allowed to drive after the stroke, I arranged to collect him from Haxby. When I mentioned Trudy's suggestion to Helen about getting married before the birth, I was told to get on with it, since she was having one of her bouts of nausea and was hurrying to the bathroom. Having been given the go ahead I began making the necessary arrangements at the Leeds Registry office where Trudy and Dickie were married.

The Wednesday night meeting of the Yorkmisers investment club went very well and our three-man team had done their work and suggested three good companies for us to consider as investments. Our choice was an insurance company which paid good dividends and was doing well in the market. In spite of our efforts to discover the ladies Tea Caddy choice, so far, we had learned nothing, other than the fact that all the women members were sworn to secrecy. The ladies hoped that their choice would be more successful than the all-male club selection. Hearing this our investment trio was urged to consider companies which could appeal to ladies in case they had somehow obtained insider knowledge.

By the end of the week the survey on Agnes's house at 28 Chestnut Grove had been completed and a full report was given to us. We would need to fit a new combi gas boiler, roof insulation, double glazed windows, a full set of roof guttering and a garage door. The kitchen, bathroom and cloakroom needed updated fittings and tiling and all the woodwork and interior walls needed complete redecoration. The survey also recommended the removal of ivy from the walls, which had penetrated the roof space and the house would benefit by having the brickwork repointed. Ivy can make houses look rural and attractive, but its' branches attach themselves to walls and can penetrate and expand gaps in cement pointing and force their way under the roof eaves to invade the loft, or even bedroom area.

Ivy branches can grow to become as thick as a man's arm and they very firmly attach themselves to walls. It would be difficult and very time consuming to remove and I might need help if I ever found the time and energy to tackle it. We wanted to carry out as much of the work as possible ourselves before our baby arrived, but knowing that we would be replacing much of the kitchen and bathroom, the work would have to be carried out before I could redecorate them. Our work would have to begin by concentrating on stripping and painting the walls and ceilings of all the other rooms. Most rooms had been papered with layers added over many years and if, as we expected, it proved difficult to remove and the walls were damaged in the process, we might need to have damaged areas skimmed by a plasterer.

We studied the surveyor's report and Helen became quite depressed as she thought about the cost and work involved, which would stretch our budget to the utmost limit. The house had been on the market for some time and I guessed that would-be buyers had been put off by the extensive and expensive repairs needed. As we were trying to decide whether we should proceed and what we could afford to have done first we received a telephone call from Agnes. She had spoken to the surveyor to ask how much work was needed and the approximate cost. She told us that she wanted us to have her house now that she was leaving and she already had enough money to pay for her care for the limited time she expected to need it. She would be happy to deduct half the repair cost from the purchase price, which would give us £10,000 towards repairs. She also told us that she wanted nothing else from us except that we live in her house and bring up the new baby. We were delighted to accept her generous offer and Agnes invited us to her house for tea, but instead Helen insisted that we bring her to our home where we would provide her with dinner that evening.

I called the Estate Agency to buy the house at the lower figure and over dinner we thanked Agnes for her generous gesture and toasted her with champagne. We assured her that whenever she wanted to visit us, we would collect her from the retirement home for an afternoon in 28 Chestnut Grove to see our progress and meet the new baby. She told us that after her husband died her family wanted her to move in with them, or at least move to an apartment to make her life easier. She had been living in her house for over sixty years and after bringing up a family, she could not bear the thought of leaving the home which held so many happy memories for her. Accepting that her refusal to move had resulted in the poor condition of the house and garden, the price reduction would clear her conscience. We all enjoyed the evening and exchanged stories of our work and families. She asked if Helen was expecting a baby boy, or a girl and agreed when Helen told her that she had deliberately not checked at this stage. I mentioned that deliveries were arranged, but not exchanges and had my shin kicked by Helen, while Agnes looked a little confused. After my attempt at humour had fallen flat, I kept silent, as you do. As we left Agnes at her front door, she told us how she envied the wonderful times we had ahead of us, but also warned that there was nothing easy about bringing up a new baby. Thinking about Martin and his tray banging and screaming, I gritted my teeth as I visualised the problems ahead of us, but said nothing to Helen to avoid dampening her euphoria over the coming birth.

I called in to see daughter Karen who admitted that when she heard about Helen's tummy upsets, she did briefly think it might be due to pregnancy, but soon dismissed the thought in view of Helen's age. She gave me a big hug, but could not help laughing as she visualised me coping with nappies and prams again after so many years. She telephoned her sister Abby, who was equally startled to hear that her father was himself becoming a father again and after she too had stopped laughing she wanted a word with me.

"You never cease to amaze me, Dad, but the last thing I expected was to hear that you were becoming a father again at your age. I just can't wait to watch you pushing a pram and my congratulations to you both."

Both girls urged me to telephone son Michael in Australia and I promised to contact him later in the day to save waking him up in the middle of the night. I telephoned him at eight next morning, which was early evening in Australia to give him the news about the house and he was pleased to hear I was settling down and giving up my globe-trotting. When he learned that Helen was having a baby, there was a silence before he too began to laugh and tell me that nothing I did surprised him anymore. He also had news for me about a local girl he was hoping to marry. We agreed it would be best for him and possibly his girlfriend to visit us once we had settled in the new house.

Following Helen's order, I quickly arranged our wedding at the local Registry Office with Trudy and Dickie as witnesses and registrar Monica to do the honours, who also wished us luck and told us she was sure her friend Magda would be pleased for us. Helen was wearing the sapphire necklace given to her and Monica admired it and was quite emotional when she learned about the background behind the gift. Since Helen was still suffering with bouts of nausea, we opted for a quiet wedding dinner at The Yorkshireman pub, so what could be more local and laid back than that? We invited my daughters and partners and Karen was able to persuade a friend to look after Martin for two hours so that she could join in. Unfortunately, news of our wedding had somehow leaked and we were greeted with streamers and applause from our many friends and FGC members who had gathered in the bar and were waiting for us to arrive. We were then treated to a champagne toast led by The Yorkshireman host, our local councillor Rod. It was not exactly the quiet evening we had planned, but it was a wonderful evening amongst our family and friends, who promised us all the help we needed with the new house and garden.

Fortunately, as yet no one suspected our big secret about our baby, but Helen was beginning to gain weight and it would soon become obvious that it was not due to middle age expansion. Within a month, or two we would have no difficulty convincing our friends that Helen really was pregnant.

Chapter 13
Chestnut Grove

We were surprised to receive an offer for my house at the full asking price from a cash buyer who had just returned from working abroad and wanted a low maintenance modern home in our neighbourhood. At the time we were still negotiating with two couples interested in buying Helens' house, but both prospective buyers were locked in a chain involving the sale of their own properties. Although it was not what we had planned, it was too good an offer to miss and I would now have to move into Helen's house and put my furniture in store. Fortunately, Agnes was quite happy for me to start clearing the giant weeds in her garden and insisted on having me in for frequent tea breaks and light snacks at regular intervals. Living on her own she was glad of my company and obviously enjoyed feeding me and listening as I told her about our plans. We needed to sell both our houses to pay for the Chestnut Grove house, but if there was an extended delay, I was prepared to sell off my investments to complete the purchase and avoid losing the house. Hearing about our difficulties, Agnes told us not to worry, since the delay would give her longer to stay in her own home. She also enjoyed having company with me working in the garden and helping her in the house with items she could not reach, or were too heavy for her to lift. Helen then began the formidable task of cleaning the upstairs rooms in preparation for our decorating and joined in our tea breaks after I had picked off the cobwebs attached to her hair and clothes. We all got on really well and Agnes was delighted with our presence and told us she hoped it would be a long delay.

I put off tennis, golf and shooting to concentrate on the garden and was surprised to find some of the local residents joining me in the evenings as I battled the foot-high weeds. The community spirit I wanted to develop on the estate was now benefitting me as well and Agnes and Helen kept my helpers well supplied with tea and biscuits. Billy loved roaming around the large garden and was startled to find frogs and hedgehogs in the long grass and began chasing them. Unfortunately, he got over excited one day and bit a frog and then began snuffling and sneezing because of the awful taste. He very quickly learned that prodding hedgehogs with a paw, or trying to bite them could be painful and he changed to following and barking at them as they scuttled through the grass in his new domain. He was very excited to find that he now had two large trees. I watched as he circled and sniffed around both and was obviously puzzled to find no trace of previous dog contacts, before baptising both to claim ownership. With a regular flow of helpers to work on the garden, I set up my barbecue over the weekends. Helen served hamburgers and hotdogs to our volunteer workers, but warned them about the furry predator who was always prowling around and hoping to snatch any unguarded food. Amongst the volunteer workers was David Kane and Kate, who suddenly appeared with David who came equipped with his own garden fork.

"Hi Tom. We heard you could do with some help and you have certainly done all you can to help us, so here we are."

No mention was made of the change of pace in their love life, but Kate was wearing the tightest and smallest shorts I had ever seen and the two seemed relaxed and happy as they worked together in the garden. I noticed that whenever Kate bent over to reach a weed, the men around her suddenly found a reason to pause in their work. It made me wonder what would happen if Marigold joined our work team in one of her customary very revealing outfits. Eventually I wanted to lay a small paved terrace outside the French windows to make room for a pram and two doting parents and I also needed to lay a lawn, but neither of these were priorities at this stage.

At last, the sale of Helen's house was completed and we were able to finalise the purchase of the Chestnut Grove property. Agnes was quite sad to move to the retirement home and told us she had really enjoyed spending time with us, which helped to make her final weeks at her family home so enjoyable after years of being on her own. Helen and I were checking on the state of our drive surface when we met our new neighbours, Joyce and Roger Green, who told us that they had been living in Chestnut Grove for over twenty years. I had noticed a lady with a white cap walking in the garden next door and mentioned it to Helen. When we were standing face to face, I realised that Joyce had a mop of white hair and wondered if I should get bi-focal glasses. After being invited into their home for tea, they told us that their son was living in London and Roger had retired three years previously after selling his small engineering business, while Joyce was a retired schoolteacher. Their house was immaculate and made us conscious of the enormous task ahead of us in bringing our cluttered new home up to anything like a similar standard. Roger was a model railway enthusiast and showed us the extensive layout he had built in his back garden, with bridges and tunnels and a wooden hut where he could sit and control the network. Noticing a Guinness beer truck amongst his rolling stock, I joked that he could always build a branch line through the hedge into our garden and send me supplies on hot days. Taking my suggestion as an invitation, he told me it would be no problem to arrange and would be an interesting project. I received a dig in the ribs from Helen for misleading him. Roger told us he was always willing to help if we had any electrical, or mechanical problems and offered me the use of his extending ladders when I wanted to work on the guttering, or finally do battle with the sea of ivy enveloping the house walls.

After we left to return to our own untidy and dusty house, Helen told me how pleased she was that we had friendly and helpful neighbours, who, like us were retired. She was also very relieved after previously having Kate as my neighbour.

"I was sure we would have an attractive widow living next door with your talent for meeting friendly ladies and it was a pleasant surprise to meet Joyce and Roger, but we still have to meet the neighbours on our other side."

I had already noticed two very attractive women getting into a car on the drive of our other neighbours' house, but decided to say nothing, as you do. They were probably just visiting and if not, it would be safer for me to spend my time watching the model trains moving around Roger's garden. Dickie spent a full morning checking over the house before we moved in and helped us to decide how we should spend our limited funds to modernise it. Afterwards we were having a quiet drink in The Yorkshireman before taking Dickie back to York, when Rod joined us to ask how our house move was progressing. He gave Helen a big hug and noticed that she was putting on weight and joked about it.

"Marriage must agree with you Helen. You seem to have put a bit of weight on, unless you are pregnant of course."

"As a matter-of-fact Rod, I actually am pregnant."

Rob started to laugh and then began to sense that she was not joking and a surprised look slowly spread across his face before he hugged her again and congratulated us both on the news.

He called his wife over and within minutes the news had spread to other customers who were shaking my hand and kissing Helen. In no time at all, our quiet drink had turned into yet another celebration party. After many good wishes and lots of advice and free drinks, we managed to escape and drive Dickie home. Out secret was out and we were now not just newlyweds, but also an expecting couple.

Amongst the members of the FGC, we had a joiner and a plumber, who both offered to help by installing our new kitchen and bathroom. We were then able to shop around and buy the units and fittings we chose at wholesale prices for them to install. They quoted very reasonable rates for the work and the overall savings helped us with the cost of the house rewiring and skimming walls, where plaster was damaged. The kitchen was very small, with both a serving hatch and door entry to the dining room and Dickie suggested that before fitting new units, we should think about extending it and removing the hatch. We took measurements and asked Helen what she wanted before deciding to extend the kitchen by ten feet and fit sliding glass doors to replace the sagging French windows in the dining room. With the time and cost savings on the kitchen and bathroom, we hoped to have most of the work done before baby arrived, if only we could keep up our furious pace of cleaning and decorating.

The builders began work on our kitchen extension by laying the concrete base before breaking off for their lunch. The weather was good and the two builders sat on our garden bench to relax and eat their sandwiches. They were served tea by Helen, who walked past the freshly laid cement and noticed the trail of doggy footprints from side to side. Knowing the culprit, she pointed out the markings and the builders picked up their floats and carefully restored the surface. When they returned to the bench to drink their tea and eat their sandwiches, they were startled to find that someone else had already eaten them. Once again Helen knew who was responsible and told the builders she would make them some fresh sandwiches. I was working in one of the bedrooms and when I looked through the window and saw Billy sitting behind the builders, I thought he was trying to make friends instead of waiting to steal their food. In the evening Helen told me about Billy and the cement and sandwiches and I again mentioned my concerns.

"We just don't have time for Billy at the moment and he is not getting his daily walks and is probably bored. When baby arrives, there will still be lots of work needed on the house and we may still not have enough free time to give him the attention and exercise he needs. He filled a gap in your life, but soon you will have a child to fill your time. Perhaps Billy would be happier with Dickie and Tracey, who love taking him for walks and it would be good for Dickie."

Helen nodded her head, but did not respond to my suggestion and I said no more, since Billy was her dog and it would have to be her decision.

When I first married, I left the choice of colours, curtains and carpets to my wife, but as a widower I was forced to make these selections for my town house and quite enjoyed the experience. I was now keen to be involved in our choices at Chestnut Grove, but unfortunately my tastes were almost the direct opposite of Helen's, since I favoured bold colours and she liked pale pastel shades. We had no time to waste and since the house had six rooms, we agreed that we would each choose the colour mix in three and Helen would pick her rooms first. She selected the fittings and tile colours for the kitchen, but gave me some options and I chose the lounge and did the same for her. We accepted that we were no longer living on our own and now we both had to compromise to meet two views, which I thought was a good way to begin our marriage.

Having sold both our houses, our Chestnut Grove house was filled with furniture and appliances as well as bedding and linen and we needed to decide what to keep and what to get rid of. We had duplicates of everything, including washing machines, cookers, microwaves, steam irons, ironing boards and many other household items and furniture, which all had to be moved from room to room as we were decorating. After clearing cobwebs in the same corner of the dining room ceiling three times, the determined spider replaced them to maintain his fly traps every night. Since it never showed itself, the only option was to use an anti-spider spray to keep it away and it did the trick. As the builders worked on the kitchen extension, we relied on a microwave and electric kettle in the dining room for our meals and hot drinks as we began decorating our lounge. At the end of each afternoon, we changed from our dusty, paint spotted clothes to eat and relax at The Yorkshireman before returning home, changing again and carrying on with cleaning and painting for an hour or so. We found this took less time than preparing a meal at home with our limited facilities. It also gave us a break and something to look forward to near the end of each day after months of cleaning and decorating. It was difficult to remove all the paint splashes on us and fellow diners were quick to tell us they liked the colours we had chosen. In the house we had nowhere yet to sit down and relax even if we could find the time and our only options were decorating, or bed.

After Agnes found she had difficulty climbing the stairs to her bathroom, she had her downstairs cloakroom extended to contain a shower. This was now a great help for us when builders began refitting our bathroom and installing our new multi-jet shower, which we both agreed was an essential addition. Day after day we battled with the dust and cobwebs as I washed down the ceilings, while Helen cleaned the walls to get them ready for painting. After years of neglect, the spiders and other crawlies had infested skirting boards and festooned every nook and cranny and we popped them into a plastic bag and put a paint pot on top to prevent them escaping. Our days were long and we were exhausted by the time we finally fell into bed each night. We were getting frustrated by the clutter in the house and thought about the car boot sale due to take place on Sunday morning in the car park of The Yorkshireman pub. We might be able to use it to dispose of unwanted items, which had to be moved from room to room whilst decorating, free up space and hopefully add some cash to our fast-diminishing funds.

We spent the night before the sale gathering together all surplus items in our hall and then chose the selling prices and put price stickers on each item. We hired two folding tables and were busy setting up our display in the car park at 6.30 am, after unloading goods from my car to be ready for the 8am opening. I took photographs of larger items, such as wardrobes and a washing machine to show on our stand and offered to deliver to buyers' addresses. Most customers were from our estate and knew us after joining in our FGC activities. Many also knew we were now married and sympathised with us about the work involved in repairing and redecorating an older house. We took flasks of coffee and sandwiches to keep us going and by midday we had sold most of our stock, including a wardrobe and washing machine. Since Rod needed his car park for his lunchtime customers, we had to return all unsold items to my car before relaxing and joining other car boot retailers for lunch at The Yorkshireman. Helen was now having to find larger clothes to cope with her expanding waist size and I was teased about nappy duties and sleepless nights ahead of me, which I still remembered from when my older children were born.

The Post Office had our new address and in the mail I received a letter from my ex-work colleague Peter about a reunion lunch at Harrogate. I told Helen that I was too busy to attend, but she insisted that I join my old colleagues and tell her what happened between Peter and Jan and her family living in his house. She also insisted that it would give me a break from my leading role in tackling cobwebs and spiders, particularly since she could not stand having spiders on her. After working in old clothes for months, it felt strange to be wearing a suit again as I joined the group of retired workers in the bar of the hotel where the lunch was held. I noticed that the numbers had reduced since the last reunion and I was told that two of the group had died and others now needed walking sticks, or were unsteady on their feet and could not make it to the reunion. Peter arrived and I saw immediately that he had lost weight, as well as hair since our last meeting and looked ill and tired. As we circulated together to meet and chat with as many as possible of our old work colleagues, he told me that the past year had been the most awful he had ever known. We were called to the dining area for lunch and were unable to sit near each other, but agreed to speak again when we had finished our meal. At the previous reunion Peter had told me about his growing problems with his much younger partner Jan and her demand to be given half ownership in his home. I warned him that his problems would increase if he agreed to her request and left him to decide whether to give in and accept or end the relationship. As we sat down together in the lounge, he told me about the trauma and disgust which he endured in expelling Jan, her son and her mother from his house and his life.

"I could not stand the thought of having to live alone again after the joy of sharing my life with a vivacious and attractive woman like Jan, but told her that I would not give her half my house. I also insisted that her mother must immediately go back to her own house. Jan was furious and I was again attacked by her 16-year-old son Rodney for upsetting his mother. The police had to be called and he was taken into custody for assault and Jan and her mother left my house, before collecting him on his release and returning to the mother's house. I was not prepared to risk more violence from Rodney and accepted that I would have to exclude all of them from my home, but still hoped to persuade Jan to move back on her own. I called in a locksmith to change my door locks and prevent them from gaining access after Rodney tried to kick my door down and threw a brick through my window. I had to get a court order to prevent them from returning and had a security door fitted as well as bars on my front windows.

A month later Jan telephoned me to tell me she was sorry and wanted to move back in on her own, but by then I was aware of a medical problem and information about her that made me decide to have nothing more to do with her. During the telephone conversation I reminded Jan about her lifestyle before we met and she slammed the phone down on me. Previously, I seemed to have no energy and put it down to stress and my age, but the area around my groin was swollen and I had a small sore, which then cleared. I was also losing weight and called to see my doctor who had known me for years. After examining me and running some tests, he called me back and told me that I had syphilis and gave me penicillin injections to clear the infection. I knew that there could be only one source and asked him if my guess was correct, but he told me it was not for him to say, since his patients' records were confidential. I pleaded with him to tell me more and he eventually suggested that I speak to a man we both knew, who told me that in her teens Jan had taken drugs and paid for them by having sex with wealthy older men willing to pay her. She was attractive and built up a list of affluent clients. Eventually, one of her older regular customers paid for her to take a rehabilitation course and break her drug habit, but while she was away on the course, he died. On her return she had expected to marry him, but met me and certainly chose me as his successor and lied about her background. Rodney's father was one of her clients and his violent mood changes may be due to her carrying the syphilis germ. I am now cured and know that I am just a stupid old man and that I have had a lucky escape to get my health and my life back. You told me what I had already suspected, but did not want to accept. I know it will be difficult, but I have to get used to being on my own again. I miss Jan very much, but no longer have to put up with Rodney, or her unpleasant mother. I thank you for that and hope to see you again next year at the reunion."

After urging him to get out of the house and become involved in all sorts of social contact activities, we shook hands and parted. I returned home after a good lunch and dodged stepladders and paint pots to find my busy co-worker. Immaculate in my suit and smart tie, I was greeted by a paint splattered Helen, waving her paint brush at me from the top of her stepladder.

"Hi love. You can get that fancy clobber off and get back in your decorating clothes. But first how about making me coffee and then you can tell me all about your friend and his attractive young partner."

After a quick change of clothes, I was soon up my own ladder with my roller and spreading a bright white cover over the faded grey of the ceiling. Working alongside me Helen listened with her paint brush poised as the sad story unfolded and she really felt sorry for Peter as I told her how he had finally managed to extricate himself from living with his unscrupulous partner and her family. She was relieved that he had made the right decision, particularly after hearing about the syphilis infection and Jan's early life as a prostitute.

"The poor man and what an awful, scheming woman. Those people would have made his life an absolute misery if he had given them half ownership of his house."

I was glad Helen had persuaded me to meet Peter and it was a relief to know that my ex-colleague was now free to look for new activities and friends to fill the gap in his life.

New plastic double glazed windows had been fitted in our house and after our decorating was finished in the lounge, we moved in carpets and furniture so that at last we had one comfortable room where we could relax, if we could find the time. With work continuing in the bathroom and kitchen, there was still dust and clutter in most of the house and as well as the inconvenience, Helen was also having to cope with nausea and vomiting. She began having unexpected cravings for food she would not normally even consider eating. Having never smoked and given up alcohol as soon as she knew she was pregnant, she snacked on fruit and ice cream instead of chocolate and pastries to avoid putting on too much weight.

There was a problem in fitting the multi jet shower in our new bathroom because of limited space, but by removing the adjoining wall and including the previously separate toilet, we had ample room. When our bathroom was finished at last, we celebrated with a glass of wine before using the multi-jet shower at the end of another hard day of cleaning and decorating. Refreshed, but still very tired, we fell into bed and were asleep within seconds. With three months remaining before our baby was expected, builders were making good progress on our kitchen extension, but for cooking we still used our microwave and electric kettle in the dining room. We moved our washing machine and tumble drier into the cloakroom and after months of living with dust and bare floors, we were sure that our house would be ready for the arrival of our baby.

Chapter 14
Motherhood

Work on our kitchen and bathroom was finished and we were alone at last in our house after the workmen had left, but we still had to carry on with the decorating. Yet to be done was my work building a terrace outside our dining room with the new sliding glass doors also to be installed. With only weeks to go, I would not let Helen do anything which might jeopardise our baby and insisted that she did not lift, climb, or even use the paint roller, since I was sure that I could complete the work on my own in time. When we were using our new multi jet shower after another busy day working on our house, I teased Helen.

"I have to use more soap on you now love since I have to cover both of you."

Helen groaned as she smoothed her extended stomach and told me that she did not expect to be carrying her baby for very much longer. Apart from the garden, only the cloakroom and one bedroom were still to be done and if Helen was right in her calculations, I had three weeks left before the birth of our baby boy. We now knew the gender, because Helen had finally watched her own scans at the hospital where she had spent most of her nursing career. As the baby grew inside her, we were fortunate in having maternity clothes given to us by daughter Karen.

After finishing off the work on the last of the bedrooms, we had just cleaned up and were relaxing with coffees in our new kitchen when we received a visit from David Kane and Kate. They were impressed by the changes in the house since their last visit and in her short skirt, Kate wandered around our kitchen as she stroked the unit tops and fittings and complimented us on our colour choice. They told us they were getting married and David wanted to know if I would be his best man. He had never married and was hoping that with my experience of two marriages, I could give him some advice. I congratulated them and told him I would be delighted to help as his best man. Kate was beaming with excitement as she stood beside me and put her arm on my shoulder before also seeking my advice.

"You two have made such a great start to your marriage and achieved a miracle by having a baby in your retirement. David has always wanted children of his own and I would love to know your secret because David and I would do anything to have a baby too."

Helen carefully edged closer to me and I guessed she was concerned that the woman might be hinting that I could take a positive role in helping her to achieve her ambition. Watching our visitors and thinking about Kate's provocative approach with men, I wanted to steer the conversation to less controversial topics.

"Exercise is really important Kate and you two have been quite active in taking all the monthly walks with the FGC, but have you thought about getting a dog?"

Kate immediately looked horrified and told us that she had never been an animal lover. David looked interested, but only until he saw the look on her face, no doubt remembering our dog Billy and the barn. Returning to her ambition, Kate told us that at forty-six, having taken early retirement, she expected to be within child bearing age, but she had no time to waste if she was to give David a child. Helen offered to help in any way she could with her experience as a midwife. Kate told us she had already made an appointment with a doctor for advice on preparing her body and she and David were now concentrating their lovemaking on the times in her menstrual cycle when she was most likely to conceive. David shrugged his shoulders and looked embarrassed, but assured us that he would do everything he could to help Kate to conceive. After the couple had left, Helen wearily put her arms across her tummy on top of junior and gave me her view on the visit.

"I hope she wasn't testing our reaction to having you perform to give her a baby. She is a very determined lady and already has Dave, or David as she insists on calling him, under control to let her do it."

I put my arms around her and tried to calm her down.

"No chance of that my love, I am already fully booked for the next ten years."

This made her laugh, but she then asked if she could also reserve the following ten years and of course I agreed and went off to measure the cloakroom walls for tiling. An updated shower, toilet and wash basin had been installed and it was now up to me to get the walls and floor finished. As an expectant father, I was determined to get this done before baby arrived, unless of course he arrived early. He did.

Two nights later, in the middle of one of my incredible dreams, Helen shook me awake to tell me it was time to get dressed and take her to the hospital. Fifteen minutes later we were on our way with me keeping one eye on the road and the other on Helen, in case the birth began during our journey. Images of me helping Helen to have her baby at the roadside, with her screaming out instructions began to pass through my mind and only stopped when we arrived outside the hospital entrance and I helped Helen to make her way to reception. The problem with an overactive imagination is that it brings worrying thoughts as well as good ideas. Sitting in the waiting room surrounded by other expectant fathers, with many wearing tattered jeans and trainers, I looked across at one who must surely still have been a student. Most were in their twenties, or early thirties and my grey hair and smart chino trousers and polished leather shoes made me conspicuous and brought some very odd looks from the rest of the soon to be fathers. I was sitting next to a young man with shoulder length hair, a moustache and beard and heavily tattooed arms. He was very restless and kept getting up to pace around and then return to his hard chair. It was identical to mine, which was making me sit sideways at intervals to ease my discomfort and was certainly not designed for long term stays. Finally, he must have noticed me and spoke.

"You here for your daughter mac?"

At first, I wasn't sure if he really was speaking to me, because with his head down, his voice came from inside a screen of long ginger hair. I smiled at him and shook my head.

"No. My wife is having her first baby and I am just hoping everything will go well for them both."

"Ain't you a bit old to be having a baby mac? You still working?"

"No. I retired a few years ago and it was quite a surprise to find my wife was expecting, especially since we only just got married."

"Wow tiger. Still got lead in your pencil then and you ain't wasting any time, are yuh? I'm impressed. Can't be many pensioners like you having a baby."

I was tempted to explain that it was actually my wife who was having a baby, but sensed that it was wiser to say nothing. Some of the other fathers in waiting had heard our conversation and there were smiles and startled looks all round before one comedian asked me what I put in my cocoa before going to bed at night. Fortunately, one of the youngest men was then called to go and meet twin daughters. Looking shocked as he heard the news, the young man staggered off following the nurse and the subject changed to having twins, or triplets and the cost. Someone mentioned expensive special prams and wheelchairs and another the cost of two sets of clothes. As new parents with little money to spare, there were worried looks around the room. Over the next two hours, men were called to meet new arrivals and others replaced them, including my long-haired friend, who left me suffering on my hard chair in spite of regular walks to the coffee machine and toilet. After falling asleep on the chair, which shows how tiredness can overcome discomfort, I felt someone shaking my shoulder. Then I heard my name called before coming awake to face a smiling nurse, who invited me to come and meet my new son.

Entering the maternity ward with the beds all taken by mothers sitting up beside their partners, with both gazing down in awe at their new babies, I spotted Helen in the far corner. After waving to her I walked over and gave her a kiss before listening as she explained the problems which delayed the arrival of our son. She was wearing her new nightgown, which I had been sent back to collect during our panic minutes before driving off to the hospital. Her hair was nicely done and her face seemed to have a remarkable glow and special look after achieving her main ambition. A nurse arrived with a small bundle wrapped in a blanket and I saw my son for the first time, with his little pink face and tiny wrinkled fingers. Thankfully, Helen did not ask if there was any family likeness, since with such small features, I had never been able to find any with my older children as babies, nor now with our new arrival. After hearing about our baby's reluctance to emerge, I suggested to Helen that like me, when he was in a comfortable position he naturally wanted to stay. This predictably brought a comment about our first night together.

"Unlike his dad I hope he does not attack women who mistakenly get into bed with him, but no doubt he will inherit your inclinations and make friends with all the girls in the area."

Since Helen would always blame me for reacting quite normally when I found her warm body pressed against me, I did not mention that as a consequence, we now had a baby son. I remembered reading the book *Men Are from Mars and Women from Venus* which explained the gap between male and female logic.

The early delivery had taken us both by surprise, which left me to complete our preparations. I was given a list of items to buy and left my wife and son at the hospital to drive home, sleep and try to finish my tiling in the next few days. Alone in the house, I kept working with short breaks for snacks and finished the cloakroom tiling the next day. After visiting Helen at the hospital and spending time watching and hearing my new son, on the way home I called at The Yorkshireman. My friends all asked about Helen and the baby and Rod insisted on drinking a toast both to the baby and to me for my achievement, which brought some chuckles and comments from customers. I definitely heard the word stud mentioned, but just smiled and said nothing. Then Dave Kane grabbed me and insisted on shaking my hand and congratulating me, which made me feel embarrassed, since it was Helen who had carried the baby for nine months before giving birth to our son and I only played a minor, but essential role.

Dave invited me to sit down in a corner and I wondered if he had more problems to discuss on his relationship with Kate. I listened as he described Kate's fixation with getting pregnant and her demands that they make love whenever she found she was ovulating. She made regular checks on her temperature and her insistence that he perform had begun to turn him off, so that he sometimes failed to get an erection. Kate then worried that he was losing interest in her, which made his failure even worse and left them both depressed. She had bought a pregnancy testing kit and each time she used it in the bathroom, he could tell by her face if the results remained negative, which made him feel inadequate.

I patted his arm and tried to convince him to be more enthusiastic and support Kate's efforts.

"Most men complain that when they are feeling amorous, the wife is too tired, or not interested, so you are one of the lucky ones. Kate loves you and wants to have your baby while she still can, which means you must take advantage of every opportunity and accept that it could take time. Remember, even when Kate does conceive, she will still be carrying your child for nine months before giving birth, which is a much bigger contribution than she wants you to make. You are really fortunate that Kate is willing to do all she can to have your child. Believe me, having a child of your own is so satisfying and special that even if it takes months, it will still be worth it, so stop complaining and give her more help."

His frown cleared and his face lit up as he shook my hand again and was about to rush off when I offered him more advice.

"If you are on one of the Walking Club outings, for heaven's sake don't let Kate take her thermometer in case she finds she is ovulating and you have to find the nearest haystack, or hedge to perform."

His worried look returned, but he saw my smile and realised I was just having him on after the barn incident. He shook his head and got to his feet.

"There is no way that is happening again in a barn, or any other public place. She always has that damned thermometer with her and I think she has made a special pocket for it on her knickers. But you are quite right. Kate is doing this for us both and I should be doing all I can to help her. I still have a lot to learn and with you as a friend and my best man, I am really lucky."

The wedding would take place in two weeks and I thought how delighted they would be if by then Kate had actually conceived. Knowing how determined she was, I thought they had a very good chance. He went off to wait for his next call to perform and I went home to sleep after another busy day. In the morning I made my final check around the house and cleared away any dust, or clutter I found, so that everything was ready before collecting Helen and the baby. Having worked in the garden manhandling concrete flagstones for our terrace, when Helen passed me our little bundle as she got out of the car, he seemed so small and light that I felt nervous about holding him too tightly. I lowered him gently into his cot and was anxious not to disturb his sleep. No doubt he would soon be disturbing mine, but we fathers know how to put up with these sacrifices. Helen intended to breast feed the baby, which meant there was no need for me to get up to boil water for night feeds, but help could still be needed to get rid of air breathed in during the breast feed. Perhaps we would be taking turns in back patting and air letting, since no new baby technology is involved as far as I know and I do have previous experience.

Once we knew that Helen was carrying a baby boy, we discussed the name and when Helen suggested Christopher, her father's name, I was happy to agree. It would probably be shortened in use to Chris, but this was fine and since the middle name is rarely used, we did not give him one. We had forty-two days to register his birth, which was probably intended to give parents time to decide, or change their minds before visiting the local registrar for a birth certificate bearing the name. Billy was very interested in the new arrival at Chestnut Grove and we had difficulty keeping him out of the lounge whenever baby cried, almost as though he too had a father's instinct. Unfortunately, he kept getting underfoot and twice Helen nearly tripped over as he strayed too close to her feet. Noticing me watching, but saying nothing, the second time this happened Helen finally made her decision.

"Perhaps it would be better for the dog and make it easier for us if we offered Billy to Dickie, since he really needs an incentive to take regular walks."

Nodding my head, but glad that Helen had finally made a decision, it was agreed that Dickie would be asked if he wanted to give the dog a new home and when I telephoned him, he was delighted. Next day we were at Haxby to show the couple the new baby and deliver Billy to his new home. Trudy took Christopher in her arms and Dickie took Billy out to the garden after his car ride, since he was well aware of the dog's fast leg lifting ability. I followed and we left the ladies to discuss the technical details of the baby's delivery. Being a natural coward, I had not accepted the offer to be present at the birth, which was fortunate, since it would have been a three-hour vigil. Responding to the shouted call to tea, Trudy assured me that my son had my nose and instinctively I touched my face and hoped she was not going on to compare other parts after her long chat with Helen. Billy settled down very quickly, helped by us having brought his basket. When we drove away, he took no notice because he was too busy eating food we had also brought to maintain his routine. I explained to Dickie that the dog's favourite meal was builders' sandwiches, but he would also settle for anglers' biscuits, or egg and bacon breakfasts. He thought I was just kidding him, but I knew that he would soon find out about the dog's food snatching talents.

Helen was sitting in the back of the car with Christopher and looking at her in my rear-view mirror, I could see that she was upset at having to leave Billy behind.

"I know you will miss him love, but think of the wonderful new baby in your arms who must now be our main concern. We still have teething, walking and talking ahead of us, followed by potty training, school time and worst of all, teenage time. Our lives are going to be very full and we have already made an incredible start to our marriage with a new home and new baby. Billy will be here whenever we come over to see Trudy and Dickie, who will be taking him for regular walks and giving him all their attention."

Hearing Helen sniffing, I thought she was being critical of my advice, or missing Billy until I saw in the mirror that it was the baby she was checking and found he had filled his nappy. Thankfully, we were half-way home and instead of changing him in the car she told me she would do it as soon as we got there.

At the hospital Helen had given me a list for shopping, including a large pack of disposable nappies. I was surprised to find how simple it was to fit them on the baby, instead of juggling him on a knee and wrapping him in white towelling, before securing it with a safety pin without piercing a thumb, or the baby. Common sense and good design have made this chore so much easier and quicker for mums and dads these days. As Helen headed for the bathroom, I changed and went into the garden to finish off laying the flags for our terrace.

Just as I finished my work, neighbours Joyce and Roger came visiting and as Roger stopped so that we could stand together to admire my recently completed terrace, Joyce went inside the kitchen where Christopher was being fed. Roger was waiting for a garden shed to be delivered and needed my help in laying the base. I asked if he knew our other side neighbours. He told me that the mother Doris Johnson-Thompson was a pensioner and after marriages to two affluent, but heavy drinking husbands now deceased, she lived with her two unmarried daughters. Chloe, the eldest was a wild driver feared by all the motorists in the area and Ramona was a nature lover and nudist, who took advantage of sunny days by wandering around the back garden with no clothes on. His news got me quite worried after having carefully checked nearby drives and gardens before buying our house, but not anticipating an adjoining back garden with a wandering nudist. I explained my concern.

"Helen will not be surprised, since I had an over friendly lady living next door previously, but assuming that Ramona keeps her clothes on in her front garden and I can always raise the fence height and plant some quick growing conifers."

"Good for you mate. Most men hereabouts have bought binoculars, since Ramona is well worth watching. You might have a treat in store."

Our two wives came out to join us and Joyce was holding Christopher. I told her the new terrace was intended for the pram and sunbathing, since it was so popular in the area. Roger began to laugh and gave details of our nudist neighbour to Helen, who slapped me on the shoulder before complaining.

"I knew it. You told me you had checked the neighbours and now you will be spending time in our garden and ogling a naked woman across the fence."

Hoping to help me by changing the subject, Roger asked where our dog Billy was today and with watery eyes, Helen told him the dog was now with friends in York, because the man needed regular walks after a stroke. Joyce took the female view and complained that the bedroom curtains were never drawn and

Ramona often undressed near the window. Before Helen could return to my naked neighbour, Christopher promptly brought up his last feed all over the back of Joyce's dress. Both women hurried into the kitchen to clean off the milky mess and relief showed on both our faces, because as we all know, men are less likely to be left holding the baby. After allowing time for the clean-up, we walked into the kitchen to offer to help, but having got our timing right, fortunately we were not needed.

Helen had made a good job of cleaning the dress, but Joyce now needed to go home to change since her dress was damp and smelly. Having been a mother, Joyce was accustomed to baby spills in various forms and told Helen not to worry and that her dress only needed to go in the wash. After our neighbours left, Helen still needed consoling and I put my arm around her and offered to make coffee.

"Never mind love, we will just have to be prepared for the odd embarrassment as baby works through his feeding and nappy phase. I remember being more worried when mine were out of sight at school and university, or with the boyfriend, or girlfriend they brought home. Karen arrived home once with a boy in torn jeans with shoulder length hair, earrings and tattoos. My son Michael brought a girl whose skirt was so short I had to keep studying the ceiling to avoid seeing her thong."

Helen laughed and relaxed before getting ready to go off to the second meeting of the Tea Caddy investment club, while I stayed home to look after Christopher. After giving him a feed before she left, we both hoped he would sleep for the hour, or so before she returned, since I was not equipped to take her place. Fortunately, the baby stayed asleep as I crept around the house, desperately anxious to avoid doing anything to wake him up. When Helen returned, I was able to relax and since the baby was still sleeping, I wanted to know the result of the first Tea Caddy investment. The actual investment was still being kept secret, but I was told that it had increased by an incredible 25% during the month. However, as a generous gesture to help the men, we would be given details of the chosen company after three months. This would give the ladies a commanding lead before the men would be able to add the stock, unless the men's first investment had also done well. The Yorkmisers club was due to meet on Wednesday and Helen would stay at home to look after Christopher as I attended.

There were now twenty-two members and they were all waiting to hear if money had been made, or lost on our first investment. The outgoing trio of members who selected the share had smug looks on their faces as they announced that our investment had covered the broker cost and stamp duty to show us an 8% profit. Members were not impressed, until they were told that this represented a worthwhile gain on our first modest outlay and at this rate of return, we could have almost £2000 by the end of our first year. Another member, whose wife was in the Tea Caddy club then brought gloom to the meeting by mentioning the 25% increase on the ladies first investment, which was still being kept secret. I said nothing, since Helen was the Tea Caddy chairperson and my wife. We hoped that our second choice of investment would be more successful to spare our embarrassment. When I returned home, Helen asked how the Yorkmisers investment had fared and smiled, but said nothing when she heard our return was much smaller than the very successful Tea Caddy choice.

Obviously, we could cope with one of us going out, but wondered how we would manage if we wanted to go out together, but were unable to take our baby. My mother lived nearby when my children were babies and looked after them when my first wife and I attended company functions. When the children were older and we had moved a hundred miles away, we were fortunate in being able to find babysitters we could trust in our home. Our new baby would certainly restrict our outings together and we accepted that tennis, golf and shooting clays would have to be suspended until Christopher was out of nappies at least. Next weekend we would be at Kate and David Kane's wedding, which could be a problem for us. I always called him Dave, but Kate insisted on using his full name, even though she was happy to have her name Catherine shortened to Kate. I put it down to more female logic.

One of the FGC projects still outstanding was our production of a video showing the initial garden project, help for local residents and the formation of the Walkers Club, as well as the Yorkmisers and Car Boot Sales. We could sell our finished video to other groups wanting to copy our schemes instead of having to go and speak with interested parties in different areas of the country. Since videos are easily copied and hiring involves administration costs, a one-off sale would be easier. Fortunately, I had taken photographs of most of our work and the still shots could be included with the movie and narrative to show some of the before and after situations. My spare time was limited, but whenever I could I began jotting down ideas.

Chapter 15
The Yorkshireman Baby Club

The following day I was raking over the rough ground in the back garden in preparation before laying the lawn, when I sensed I was being watched and turned to see an attractive young woman with a mop of frizzy dark hair watching me from my boundary fence. As we faced each other she waved me over, gave me a big smile and spoke.

"Hi. You the new neighbour, or the gardener?"

I dropped my rake to walk over and shook hands before giving my answer.

"My wife and I bought the house about six months ago and we have worked every day to get rid of cobwebs, spiders and clutter to modernise it before our baby son arrived."

"Gee, so you are a new dad as well and I can't believe you have done all this while I have been in America. I knew Agnes wanted to move to a home, but to go away and come back and see the house and garden so different is quite a shock for me. It will be great to have a real family living next door, although I will miss Agnes who is a lovely lady. My name is Ramona by the way."

"I'm Tom Hartley and my wife is Helen and our baby is Christopher. Did you enjoy yourself in the US?"

"I loved it and worked as an au pair in Miami until the husband started asking me for other services. After that I got jobs in bars and hotels to keep myself during my six-month visa. I love sunshine and it was always easy to find a quiet spot where I could lie on the warm sand and let the sun cover my entire body. See, I have an all over tan."

Ramona opened her blouse and with no bra, she showed me her deep tan and glimpse of most of her well-formed chest. It was such a natural gesture that I wasn't embarrassed and it was certainly not a provocative action. After closing her blouse, she asked if she could come around to meet Helen and our baby and

I went indoors to warn Helen we were receiving a visit from our neighbour. As she walked in, Ramona looked at the newly decorated walls and new carpets and said it was so different from the hall she remembered, that she could not believe it was the same house. We went into the kitchen, where Helen had just finished another nappy change, which was currently needed every two hours. Ramona gave Helen a kiss and a hug and told her she was delighted to have us as neighbours and hoped we could be good friends as well. We spoke about her holiday in America and found that like me, her favourite state was Florida and she too was taken with the Gulf Coast and incredibly had also enjoyed the boardwalk and fish restaurants at John's Pass at Madeira Beach. She told us she worked as a waitress there for three weeks before she got tired of the owner's groping. After that she moved north to Tarpon Springs, where she spent her last six weeks in Florida as a barmaid.

I offered to make coffee as Ramona told us that she had taken a degree course in Early Childhood Education and Care at Brighton before spending time abroad. She was now hoping to train as a nurse and specialise in looking after children. Unfortunately, because she was a naturist, kept herself fit and had a good figure, she constantly had to fend off gropers and men propositioning her as a female object, instead of an educated woman. Helen told her about her own career in nursing and the two women found common interest and I wondered if we had found a new friend and who knows, a reliable baby-sitter. After an hour chatting with us Ramona left and Helen and I sat gazing at each other in amazement. Helen spoke first.

"Ramona said something about hoping she didn't embarrass you in the garden, which I could not quite understand."

Trying hard to look casual, I told her that Ramona told me she liked full body sunbathing and when she was standing at the fence, she showed me how brown her chest was."

"You mean part of it, or all of it?"

"Sort of, well most of it, since she doesn't wear a bra."

"So, while I thought my husband was safe working in our garden, you were in fact ogling that young woman's breasts."

"Oh come on love. I know it sounds shocking, but for her it was such a natural gesture that neither of us saw it as provocative, or deliberate. I like talking to her because she is such an open, friendly person and certainly not a sex object."

Helen smiled and said she was only teasing and that she agreed with me that Ramona loved the sun and had every right to strip off in her own garden and sunbathe whenever she wanted, without being accused of being a temptress. It was the men watching her and complaining about her who were the real guilty ones. If it had been a man opening his shirt to expose his tan, or hairy chest, nothing would be said. Instead of pointing out that men had slightly different shaped chests, wisdom prevailed and instead I suggested having Ramona look after Christopher for us both to attend Kate's wedding on Saturday. Helen thought it was possible, but she would like to see how Christopher reacted to being held and perhaps changed by Ramona first. We would have to limit our time at the wedding and reception, which would spare us from hearing too much about Kate and her on going pregnancy attempts.

Next day my work on laying a lawn continued and when I saw Ramona walking towards the fence, before I could speak to her, Helen appeared and invited her to our house for coffee. Startled by the sudden interception, I was unsure whether Helen was protecting me from Ramona's chest, or was anxious to see if our neighbour and Christopher could bond with each other. I went back to my gardening until I was summoned for coffee break. Christopher was quite happy to be held by Ramona, who had just done a nappy change and impressed Helen, I learned later. The Saturday wedding and reception had already been discussed and we would leave our son with Ramona for two, or three hours, since Helen would provide her milk for Ramona to use if Christopher woke and needed feeding. The way the two ladies solved the baby-sitting problem really impressed me, but after all, there are very few men with the necessary experience, or equipment to do so. Christopher was handed over to Ramona for safe keeping on the morning of the wedding and Helen and I were waiting at the Registry Office for Kate and Dave to arrive. The 11 o'clock deadline came, but with no sign of the couple and Helen and I wondered if there had been a rift, car breakdown, or even an ideal moment for conception. Since I had helped Monica the Registrar by filling in for her at a concert, I went to apologise and ask if she could allow us some extra time. Fortunately, she agreed to wait for half an hour before going for her lunch.

Sadly, Kate had no close friends she wanted to attend her wedding, while most of Dave's were his ex-girlfriends, who would certainly have been barred by Kate. Ten minutes later the couple arrived and we hurried inside to have Monica perform the wedding. After signing the forms and thanking Monica for her patience, we left and became aware of the strained silence between the newlyweds. Somehow, I was sure that Kate's thermometer was responsible and when we arrived at The Yorkshireman for the wedding lunch, I mentioned it to Dave, who frowned before nodding his head. As soon as we had eaten our meal, I apologised for having to rush off so quickly, but our young son would be waiting for his feed. We were given hugs by Kate and Dave and thanked for helping with their wedding. When we reached home, we found Ramona reading some of Helen's medical books and a recently fed baby asleep in his cot. We could have stayed longer at the pub, but we both thought we were better off away from the tense atmosphere to allow Mr and Mrs Kane to come to terms with Kate's determination to conceive.

Ramona seemed to feel quite at home in our house and made coffee while we both changed. She told us that she was born in her mum's second marriage to Archie Thompson, who owned a string of betting shops and had his own horse. He was out riding when his horse shied at a low fence and he was thrown off against the fence and killed when she was six years old. Her older sister Chloe was born when her mother was married to her first husband George Johnson, who ran a bus and taxi service. He spent much of his time working to fill gaps when employees failed to turn up for early, or late bookings. George was a workaholic and died when Chloe was ten and her mother had already begun seeing Archie and married him a year later. Her sister never took to Archie because she knew her mother had been unfaithful to her father by having the affair.

It was not a happy home and the three women lived very separate lives, which was why Ramona was so pleased about finding us as neighbours. She knew that she was spied on by neighbours with binoculars when sunbathing because she had noticed the sun reflecting off the glass, but although she removed her bra, she told us she always wore a bikini bottom, or thong in her garden. There were not so many warm sunny days which were suitable for sun bathing and she was determined to take advantage whenever she could.

After her experience in Florida, Ramona had decided that she wanted to be a full-time nurse looking after children and those with special needs. She already had the necessary qualifications and would be starting a full degree course at Leeds Becket University in five months' time. Helen was hoping to find her work at our local hospital until she began her studies and it was surprising how quickly the two had become good friends. After Ramona left, I made a show of checking and polishing the lenses on my binoculars and as I expected, it brought a quick response from Helen.

"Don't you dare use those in our garden. I'm sure you will get a good enough view over the fence anyway, so try to concentrate your energy on building our lawn."

Our phone rang and it was Rod our councillor with some very sad news. Albert, our orchid expert had been found dead on his kitchen floor when the window cleaner was at his bungalow. His daughter Dorothy was now making the necessary arrangements, but Rod thought I might want to offer my help since we had been such good friends. We had heard nothing from the newlyweds after leaving them at the pub, so I hoped it would be safe to leave Helen looking after our son as I went off to ask if I could do anything to help Dorothy.

When she saw me at the door, she gave me a hug as tears ran down her cheeks and told me how much her father had appreciated being introduced to fellow residents and growing orchids to meet the flood of orders. She was sure that his last six months had been so much happier as a result. He must have known his end was near, because he had left instructions that his entire orchid collection should be put on display at The Yorkshireman for local residents to choose and take home. However, one striking crimson orchid was put aside for Helen, after Albert had cross-pollinated a hardy and a strong flowering species to create a new variety, which he named Helen. I offered my help in arranging to have unwanted items collected by a local dealer and left with Helen's orchid after offering to e-mail FGC members with the funeral details. I was sure that Rod would be quite happy to display a notice in The Yorkshireman with details of the funeral arrangements. We expected that many members and residents would want to show their affection for Albert by attending his funeral.

Helen was delighted with the beautiful flower and her eyes filled with tears as she learned that Arthur had named it after her. Our sad moment was shattered by our doorbell ringing and I found myself looking at a shamefaced Dave Kane. As he sat down in our kitchen where Helen had just changed our son, he apologised for the late arrival at the Registry Office and the tension between him and Kate at the wedding lunch.

"We were dressed and ready to leave this morning for the Registry when Kate made another of her damned temperature checks and found she was ovulating. She was convinced that it was a special sign on our wedding day that she would conceive and insisted that we strip off and make love. She is always enthusiastic, but this morning it was almost as though she was possessed and would not let me go. Finally, we broke off and rushed to shower and get dressed, with me annoyed that she had made us late for our own wedding. Thanks to you and your friend Monica we were saved, but Kate kept me on edge all morning after days of wondering when I would be told to make love."

Helen and I locked glances and her eyebrows rose as Dave sat wringing his hands before telling us he knew how determined Kate was to conceive and he was doing his utmost to help after our talk. Incredibly she was convinced that this morning their intercourse would make her pregnant. He wanted to believe she was right, if only to finally escape from her unpredictable demands. After the wedding Kate was so convinced that she had now conceived that she had gone to bed to rest and give the embryo time to form. Left on his own on his wedding day, he had come to apologise and explain the reason for their late arrival. I opened a bottle of my best red wine and wished them both luck and success in their efforts to have a child. Helen was happy to leave us alone to finish off the bottle and by the time he left, Dave was in a much happier mood. The news about Albert's death came as a shock to him and he wondered about writing an article for his paper under the title *The Orchid Man of Fairfields Estate.* He would certainly be attending the funeral, provided of course that Kate would release him from his baby making duties.

Ramona became a regular visitor to our house around morning coffee time and insisted that she would be happy to look after Chris whenever we wanted to go off for a break on our own. She began borrowing Helen's medical books and said it was easier to read them in our home, because of the loud music and arguments between her mother and sister Chloe. Although many residents spoke about having Chloe try to drive into the boot of their car, or pull out in front of them, so far she had not threatened me. We decided to take advantage of Ramona's offer and went off one morning for a game of tennis. As we were walking to the tennis courts, we met Arnold and Marie, our affluent strip-off enthusiasts and stopped to chat as Marie greeted us.

"Hi you two. Long-time no-see. We thought you two must have moved away from the area since we never see you on court these days."

Helen smiled at her and explained our absence from the courts.

"We now have a baby son of three months and have moved to a bigger house, which has kept us far too busy for tennis."

Marie was genuinely pleased for us and embraced Helen and kissed me on the cheek as she congratulated us, but with a look of sadness, or perhaps envy showing on her face.

"Congratulations and how wonderful for you both and have you got married yet?"

Helen put a protective arm around my shoulders and told her that after finding we were expecting a baby, we decided to get married and moved to a bigger house and our son now took priority over sport, but today we have a baby sitter. Arnold said nothing and continued to look bored as he gazed around the sport ground instead of becoming involved with a couple who had walked away from his seedy manipulations. We said goodbye to Marie and received a curt nod from Arnold before he hurried off without waiting for his wife to follow.

When we got back to our car, Helen said she liked Marie and felt sorry for her because she was forced to give up having children and a normal marriage in exchange for security and luxury in her life with her rude and arrogant husband Arnold. Since Marie had made her choice, I could not agree with Helen. Returning home, we found our son sleeping peacefully and Helen said that either Ramona was lucky in being with Christopher when he was sleepy, or she had a special way with babies. Whatever the reason, she was our perfect baby-sitter who could help us to recover at least some of the leisure activities we enjoyed before Christopher took over our lives. Ramona had lunch with us and since the sun was shining, as she left she mentioned spending the afternoon topping up her tan in the garden. I immediately said I had more work I must do on my lawn and Helen gave me a big smile and said she would bring Christopher out on the terrace to benefit from the fresh air and then she could keep an eye on both of us.

Fortunately, most of my work would keep me near the fence and having spread the grass seed, I was stamping down the topsoil to make it level when Ramona strode past and waved to me. I heard a shout from Helen to tell me I was wanted on the phone and tore my eyes away from our neighbour. The caller was my son Michael wanting to know if we would be at home for the next week, or so, since he was thinking of coming to visit us with girl-friend Catia. They were planning to arrive at the weekend for two weeks and wanted to know if we had a spare room. My son only wanted one bedroom and I remembered staying with my first wife's parents when we were engaged and were still put in separate bedrooms. Fortunately, there were no squeaky floorboards and her parents were heavy sleepers, which allowed me to quietly slip into Mary's room at night.

Times have changed and subterfuge is no longer needed when couples want to be together.

Helen was quite excited about the visit and I contacted both daughters to tell them that Michael and his girl-friend were coming. Karen wanted to get together to plan for their arrival and I arranged a family meeting over coffee at Chestnut Grove in the afternoon. Uncle Christopher and nephew Martin could then gurgle at each other as we discussed the arrangements for the visit. Michael knew the area well after taking his degree at Leeds University and would probably make his own choices of where to take Catia sightseeing. Not wanting to take up too much of his visiting time, we settled on a family dinner to be prepared by Cordon Bleu chef Helen and weather permitting, a barbecue using my new terrace. Michael could be added to my car insurance during his visit to allow the couple to use it to go touring, while I worked in the garden and tried really hard not to glance at any sunbathing neighbours.

Albert was cremated and the small chapel was filled to capacity, with more people waiting outside because anyone who had ever met Albert remembered him as a very special person and wanted to pay their respects. At the end of the service as his coffin glided away through the curtains, I felt a stab of sorrow as I remembered my first wife's funeral, but she will always be in my memory and life goes on after a loved one is taken from us. With so many attending the funeral, Dorothy had arranged a light buffet at The Yorkshireman. Ramona and I helped to move the fifty, or so orchids from Albert's bedroom to the function room and placed a notice inviting residents to take one. Although Ramona had never been inside The Yorkshireman before, she had worked as a barmaid in bars throughout the USA and immediately noticed the welcoming atmosphere and got on well with Rod. Someone suggested putting contributions in a box as a memorial to Albert and with the money collected, we were later able to buy a wooden bench and plaque bearing his name. The bench would be sited alongside the flower beds in our estate garden, where it could be enjoyed by other retirees. Dorothy was really touched by the gesture and burst into tears.

Helen had just accepted a small glass of red wine and was chatting with Ramona when a jubilant Kate charged up to us waving a slip of paper, followed by her very relieved and equally exultant husband.

"We did it. We did it and now I am pregnant. The test result is positive, see."

Kate waved a slip of paper in front of Helen, who took it and read the figures showing that the test really was positive and Kate was right about conceiving on the very morning of her wedding. We listened politely as Kate said she had a premonition that her perfect time to conceive had come and the wedding just had to wait. She was sorry to have arrived late, but she had been right and they would now have the child they both wanted so much. Rod was listening and said two more of his older customers had also told him they were pregnant and it seemed to have become an ongoing feature of the estate. One lady was aged forty-nine and the other forty-six and he wondered if it was the beer, or his shepherds' pie at The Yorkshireman which was responsible for the middle-aged baby surge. Seeing me looking sceptically at him, he winked. Kate sniffed and said in her case it was very early middle age. Dave Kane nudged me and said it could make an interesting article for his column in the paper and asked if I had any comments, which I did. Leaving the three ladies, we edged away to have a quiet chat and I warned him.

"Just make sure you don't make the heading 'Wrinklies Baby Boom', or our friendship will be severely strained. When we retire, we expect to relax after our working life, but bringing up a child is a fulltime job. Believe me, in spite of the sleepless nights and disruption of a cosy lifestyle, it will still be the most rewarding experience ever for the lucky couple."

Dave assured me there would be no reference to wrinklies and made a note. He told me how relieved he was that he would no longer have to perform when Kate found she was ovulating. Unfortunately, she had already decided to give up wine as well as sex to be sure that no possible harm could come to her baby. Kate was already bombarding Helen with all sorts of questions on birth and motherhood as Ramona stood beside her holding Christopher and listening patiently. I took Dave to one side to reassure him about the abrupt termination of his sex life and looking at his gloomy face, I tried my best to cheer him up.

"Look Dave. All your efforts were worth it and you are going to be a dad. Only a couple of weeks ago you were complaining about being forced to have too much sex and now you are worried about having none. Perhaps you will just have to play more tennis to burn off the energy for the next nine months."

"Ha ha. You know yourself that when you can't have sex, you want it even more and Kate is a very physical woman. I just can't imagine not having sex for nine months with my sex drive."

He seemed genuinely worried about coping with no sex and thinking about the attractive women I had seen him with over the last three years, I thought he might be driven back into the arms of one or two.

138

"If you get desperate Dave, perhaps Helen can speak to Kate about giving you a monthly allowance, which shouldn't harm the baby."

For a moment he thought about my offer and then began to smile and wagged a finger at me.

"You are having me on again you rotten sod. You always look so serious when you are giving me advice, but when I think it over later, I can tell you were wrapping it up in that quirky humour of yours. Kate is a very determined woman who wanted to give me a child and made sure she got pregnant. I don't think Helen, or anyone else is going to change her mind about giving up sex, but I'm happy to have her try and thank you for your offer."

Seeing Kate standing near the pub door, Dave waved to Helen and then he and Kate left. Although Ramona had been standing alongside Helen during the entire discussion on babies, Kate completely ignored her after being introduced by Helen. She now wanted me to tell her what our intense conversation had been about. I told her how Kate was now planning to make Dave celibate during the length of her pregnancy and she started to laugh before giving me her views.

"You men. You are never satisfied. First, he complains about too much sex and now he is moaning because he's been banned. We women can never please you."

"I'm sure you can my darling, but Ramona is looking puzzled and perhaps you should tell her about the background."

Helen explained about Kate and David wanting a baby and how she insisted on making love whenever she was ovulating and was now delighted to find she was pregnant. Now she wanted to avoid any possible harm to the baby by insisting that they give up sex while she was carrying her baby. Ramona felt sorry for Dave for first being required to perform and now facing an abrupt ban. Helen was looking at me and smiling as she told Ramona that there was no risk to the baby during intercourse, but Kate had yet to come to terms with her pregnancy after trying so hard to conceive. She would certainly be given assurance by her doctor and would also want to avoid stress in her marriage. Helen was sure Kate would eventually change her mind when she realised the possibility of forcing her man into another woman's arms. We walked back to our respective houses so that Christopher could have his feed and I wanted to do more work on the FGC video project.

Once Christopher was asleep in his cot, Helen came and sat beside me to read my notes, which were scattered across the settee beside me. Putting my arms around her, I warned her that with my son and girlfriend arriving, there would be few times when we would be alone and able to enjoy impromptu passionate embraces. Helen kissed me and explained that unfortunately there was a problem.

"I have to clean the oven you burned yesterday cooking that pizza and I will probably be far too tired afterwards."

Naturally I immediately volunteered to clean the oven, but only because it was accidentally burned when I was using it. It was good of Helen to remind me about this unfortunate mishap, which of course I would be very happy to correct to help my busy wife.

With my son and his girlfriend arriving at the weekend, we had prepared our newly decorated spare bedroom for our visitors and checked that there was not a cobweb, or speck of dust anywhere in the house. Helen had already decided on her menu for the family dinner while I was looking after Christopher. Ramona had looked after him while we were at Arthur's funeral service and she wanted to know more about my family and son Michael in Australia. She thought the name Catia was very unusual and wondered if it could be of eastern European origin, which had not occurred to me. Within days we would be meeting Catia and would then have an answer.

There were still a few orchids left after many of the residents had taken up Arthur's generous offer to give them away to anyone who wanted one. Rod took one and I took another, but since Helen already had two, I wondered if Ramona would like one.

After being given the flower, she held it in her hand and admired the delicate peach-coloured petals before saying that it was so lovely and quite exquisite, but she would have no idea about feeding and watering the plant. Hearing our conversation, Helen joined in and showed Ramona her own plants and explained how little attention they needed during their long lives. Ramona said she would love to have it and would look after it. We had gained a new orchid convert.

Chapter 16
Good on Yuh, Mate

Ramona was quite happy to look after our baby as we went to the airport and waited nervously at the Arrivals barrier for my son and his girlfriend to come through. Just as we were thinking they had missed their flight, we saw a familiar figure walking towards us with a slim dark haired and very attractive young woman, with both towing large suitcases. Michael put his arms around me and gave me a hug as he welcomed me in his best Australian.

"Good on yuh mate."

After disentangling myself from my bearded and suntanned son, I was then embraced by Catia, who kissed me on both cheeks before telling me that she had heard all about me from Mikey and had been looking forward to meeting me for months. Catia had big brown eyes and long jet-black hair swept back in a ponytail. Her smile lit up her entire face, but I could not help noticing that she was also showing early signs of pregnancy. I introduced Helen, who also received hugs and kisses from them both and we walked outside to my car. First Karen, then Helen, then Kate and now my son's girlfriend were all recent, or mothers-to-be with a wide age gap between the oldest and youngest. Somehow my quiet and comfortable life-style seemed to have completely changed since that afternoon in Aberdovey when my grandson Martin was enjoying himself smashing up my magnificent sandcastles on the beach. Until then, my only contact with babies was as a grandfather and occasional carer, whereas now my life seemed to have become permanently involved with nappies, ovulation and pregnancies.

Since the couple had been given breakfast before landing, we drove straight to Chestnut Grove and exchanged information on activities in Australia and Yorkshire during the car journey over The Pennines. Catia's father had worked in the wine trade before leaving Portugal to settle near Toowoomba in

Queensland. After working for local winegrowers, he eventually bought his own vineyard and it was now very successful, but with two brothers working in the business, Catia had chosen to train as an engineer and subsequently met my son Michael. They became engaged as Helen and I were selling our houses, which was why I had asked him to postpone his planned visit until we had moved in, redecorated and settled in Chestnut Grove. When Catia found she was pregnant, they decided to get married, but said nothing because they knew we were struggling to cope with a new house and Helen's pregnancy. Instead, they had now come to Yorkshire to celebrate our marriage, their marriage, our new baby and the coming birth of a second grandchild for me. Michael had also just accepted a new job, which was mainly office based in Brisbane and the Australian Mr and Mrs Hartley were hoping to move to their own apartment in six weeks' time.

The young couple were obviously very much in love and although my son would now be remaining in Australia, I understood his reasons, although he would be far away from me and his sisters. Still, we could always fly to Australia to see their new house and baby as they were doing with ours, with a stop-over at Singapore on the outbound and inbound flights. We did not think we could cope with spending a full day in an aeroplane with a direct flight from the UK to Australia. Catia was really excited to meet Christopher and Michael was amused to watch her hugging the baby.

"Just remember Catia that you have your arms around my brother and our baby will be his nephew."

His wife gave Christopher a kiss and told Michael what she thought about his brother.

"Well, at least he is nowhere near as hairy as his big brother and he smells so much nicer."

Helen laughed and said that he did not smell quite so nice after he had filled his nappy. Helen and Catia stayed chatting in the kitchen and were quickly engrossed in discussing babies and deliveries as I took Michael out to show him my new terrace, after first having a quick check that my neighbour was not sunbathing to distract him. Once Michael had finished admiring my terrace and partly laid lawn, he explained his marriage and career change.

"I was really glad about you getting married, Dad, and Helen is a really lovely person and you are just right for each other. I thought you were fooling me when you said Helen was pregnant, but watching you two with my little brother, I can see how happy you both are about having a child together. With Catia, I was smitten the moment we met and could not believe my luck when she invited me to move in with her. She has a big family and our wedding in Portuguese style was incredible. We would have liked to have you both there, but knew you were in the middle of your house move and your rush to get ready for the baby. The Santos family house has ample room for you to visit us and meet Catia's family and we will be coming here again when our baby is old enough to travel."

As we were chatting, a tall woman with shoulder length dark hair and bright red lips appeared at our fence and waved in our direction.

We moved closer to hear what she wanted and were greeted by another of our neighbours.

"Hello. Is one of you Mr Hartley?"

I smiled at her and spoke as I put my arm on Michael's shoulders.

"We are both Hartley's, but I am your neighbour and this is my son who is visiting from Australia."

"Oh, sort of two for the price of one today then. I'm Chloe and I believe you have already met my sister Ramona, who loves looking after your baby boy. I work in the entertainment industry and spend most of my time in London, but during my home visits I have seen workers in your garden and Ramona has told me about all the changes you have made in Agnes's house."

We shook hands and I invited her to come and have coffee and meet us all. We sat around in our lounge and chatted as we got to know each other. I guessed that Chloe was in her late forties and learned that her mother had been a dancer before marrying, which may have encouraged Chloe to choose the entertainment sector. I recognised her as one of the glamorous ladies I had previously seen on our neighbours' drive. She worked mainly as a choreographer and was very much in demand. Chloe was very interested in the FGC after hearing about the orchid lecture and help for elderly residents from Ramona. When she told us about her experience in musicals and dancing, I wondered if she would like to be involved in the FGC.

"We already have walking and investment clubs here, but if you had the time, I know that Line Dancing would be popular and would involve all ages and both sexes."

"Sorry Tom. My work takes up most of my time and I often have to turn work away, but Ramona is a terrific dancer and knows most of the routines. I would be quite happy to pass on any new dances that are introduced and she can teach your members, at least until she begins her full training as a nurse. I doubt that I could be available for every meeting, but might like to join the ladies investment club."

As she finished speaking my daughter Karen arrived with baby Martin and Michael hugged his sister and then introduced Catia. While our ladies were all chatting and comparing baby progress, I thought it was a good time to take Michael with me to visit my neighbours' train layout. Chloe had soon made her exit since she was unlikely to have been enthralled by non-stop baby talk. As we walked to Roger's house, I told Michael about Ramona's fondness for sunbathing topless in her garden.

"No big deal for me, Dad. The beaches in Australia are filled most days with topless ladies and some are quite happy to take everything off to get an all over tan."

After greeting us, Roger took us to see his extended layout which had taken him more than three years to build. We sat in his control tower, or wooden hut and watched as he moved trains through tunnels and over bridges, before generously allowing each of us to operate the controls. Time flies when you are enjoying yourself playing with toys and we were startled to see Joyce waving at us and pointing towards my garden. Three ladies with one holding a baby were standing at the fence and making it clear that our playtime was over. After thanking Roger for letting us play with his giant train set, we hurried back to the family, who had eventually noticed that we two were missing. The weather forecast was good and the ladies had decided in our absence, although I suspect our presence would not have changed the outcome, that our barbecue should be held on Saturday. Fortunately, I had stored all my equipment, but we might need to buy more chairs to cope with the expected numbers joining us.

Our family numbered six adults and two babies, plus Trudy and Dickie with Billy, both neighbours and Kate and Dave Kane. Rod and his wife could not leave their jobs at The Yorkshireman because Saturday was a busy day for them. I teased Rod that with his growing income from the bar and restaurant takings, plus his retainer as our councillor, it was time he thought about installing a manager. His response was swift and predictable.

"As usual Tom, you are quite right and since you have nothing to do all day, I think it would be the ideal position to keep you out of mischief."

I should have known that it was almost impossible to score over Rod, who spent most of his time dealing with difficult, or drunken customers who had to be put down diplomatically so that they remained as customers.

On the day of our barbecue Chloe and Ramona arrived without their mother, who had a heavy cold and wisely abstained in the interests of the other guests. I could tell that Roger recognised Ramona, even with her clothes on when she gave him a hug. He told me he had only glimpsed Chloe's face in his car mirror when she raced up behind him and he was trying to avoid a collision. Fortunately, he did not mention her driving as they were introduced. When Kate in a plain trouser suit and a glum looking Dave arrived, Helen and I exchanged glances and guessed that she was still denying him his conjugal rights. Helen had lost most of the weight gained with the baby and was now able to wear more glamourous clothes. With Catia, Ramona and Chloe, plus my daughters turned out in their party dresses, the men in plain chino trousers and sports shirts were very much overshadowed.

Our dog Billy raced into the garden to check that his two trees were still bearing only his own signature liquid and after a quick sniff check, he marked his return by baptising both and took up his position near the barbecue jointly operated by me and my son. As usual I was in charge of cooking on the barbecue, while Helen was serving salads she had prepared with help from Catia. Baby Martin was now walking and once or twice when Karen was distracted, we heard the sound of breaking china as he grabbed, or swiped crockery within his reach. Fortunately, our own baby still spent most of his time feeding, sleeping and filling his nappy, but gave everyone who approached him a beautiful smile. I assured everyone that this showed he had inherited his father's friendly manner, which Helen insisted would certainly lead him into trouble, just like his father. Roger was telling my son in law about his extensive train layout and Joyce was helping Helen and collecting empty plates. Everyone was busy chatting and eating and with the help of the sunshine, our barbecue was proving to be very popular.

Dave came and stood beside me, since he was not in the mood for socialising during his enforced period of purdah. My son was now wielding the cocktail shaker with practised skill I thought and serving the drinks. Kate was speaking with Helen and probably seeking even more information on pregnancy. Anxious to avoid mentioning his enforced celibacy, I was telling Dave about my ideas for making the FGC video, which led him to my possible interview by BBC Leeds in their Round & About programme. His contact had mentioned to him that our FGC activities could interest viewers and Dave assured me that if I could get my video done, he would show it to his contact to encourage a visit.

We were joined by Ramona with Chloe and Dave asked them if they would be interested in getting involved with the FGC video. Chloe seemed to be in a very friendly mood, probably after sinking one or two of my son's lethal cocktails and offered to help as she explained.

"I have worked on a number of film screenings and Ramona enjoys mingling with the public, even when she has to keep her clothes on."

Ignoring her sister's comments, Ramona told me that she liked The Yorkshireman and would be happy to fill in behind the bar and help with FGC schemes. Imagining Ramona's striking bust as she served drinkers behind the bar and Marigold's exposed thighs in front of the bar, I was convinced that Rod's bar takings would be bound to soar. It also gave me another idea on involving local residents by enticing them into the pub. Dave's mood had definitely improved since the girls joined in our conversation and after having enjoyed a few cocktails to cheer himself up. Hearing Chloe's jibe at her sister he laughed and there was a noisy dialogue as different ideas for scenes on FGC activities were discussed. The laughs and noise must have caught Kate's attention and seeing Dave enjoying himself with two friendly and very attractive ladies, she stormed over and confronted her husband.

"You are making a fool of yourself. I want you to take me home now."

Having issued her request, she was already making her way towards the drive and Dave shrugged his shoulders and explained to the startled girls that his wife was pregnant and currently at the emotional stage. As he was walking after Kate, he had given me some good advice, most of which I followed.

"Time to get that video done Tom and it will be more interesting with these glamorous ladies on screen instead of an old pensioner like you."

He told me later that after not saying a word to him during the drive home, when they arrived, Kate removed all his clothes slowly and they spent the rest of the day in bed. Jealousy can work wonders and change attitudes.

Ramona and Chloe decided to leave and waved goodbye to my family and friends and I collected the few remaining burgers, onions and rolls and took them over to the group surrounding Michael at the bar. Knowing about my preferences, he greeted me with a Singapore cocktail, while Helen accused me of provoking Kate.

146

"You lot were making so much noise over there and suddenly Kate noticed you and Dave laughing with our attractive neighbours and rushed across to rescue her husband. I knew you were safe because I was keeping an eye on you. What was all the chat about?"

I explained that Dave was urging me to make the FGC video, which could help him to persuade BBC Leeds to feature our group on their Round & About broadcast. I added that he had been enjoying too many cocktails and was also keen to have Ramona and Chloe included to add a touch of glamour. Hearing this, Helen gave me one of her hard looks, but I avoided falling into the trap.

"Not that it will be without glamour of course, with you and Kate taking part after all your keen involvement and we could also include Billy to appeal to animal lover viewers."

My daughters put their arms around Michael and suggested that he should take Catia to York and he asked if Helen and I would like to go along. Since it was pretty level ground, Helen thought we could take the baby in his foldup pram to visit the Minster and castle walls. Abby suggested staying the night and looking at the city streets and Viking and Railway Museums. Dickie then warned us that it was race week and it would be difficult to find accommodation with the city full of punters and unfortunately their bungalow only had two bedrooms. It was time to settle the details and I made my own suggestion.

"It is only a short drive to York and there is no need to stay overnight. We could spend one day visiting city attractions and another at The Knavesmire for the races, or take a trip up the river Ouse for tea and biscuits at the Bishop's Palace."

Michael thought this was sensible and after choosing the days for both trips said he also wanted to take Catia to visit Whitby and drive across the North Yorkshire Moors. Their visitor programme was filling up nicely.

Billy was sitting nearby licking his lips and salivating as his keen nose tortured him with the aroma of cooked burgers stored just out of his reach. Thanks to our warnings about his snack snatching talents, everyone had held their food in their hands, or kept it beyond his reach. After being denied unwatched snacks, the dog was suffering with hunger pangs and first removing the bread, I fed him two well-cooked burgers which he wolfed down in giant gulps. As dusk fell, my coloured lights added to the festive atmosphere and when my daughters and partners left, Michael, Catia, Dickie and Trudy went indoors for coffee. Roger and Joyce thanked us for an enjoyable day and said they were tired and ready for bed and I put away my cooking equipment. Although it was not a long drive to York, Helen tried to persuade Trudy and Dickie to stay the night and return home in the morning, but Dickie insisted on driving. She had watched him drinking too much during the evening in spite of his doctor's warning and did not want him to drive, but he wanted to get home. We agreed to meet them in York for lunch, since they were already very familiar with the city and its tourist attractions and Dickie wanted to avoid walking on the busy streets after his stroke.

When we had finished our breakfast next morning, we drove to York and left our car in the large park-and-ride area on the outskirts before using the included bus service to take us to the city centre. We made The Minster our first stop and with Helen pushing Christopher in his pram, we began walking around the magnificent Gothic cathedral built in 1472 with stone quarried from nearby Tadcaster. The enormous Great East window is the largest stained-glass window in Europe and with light streaming through the coloured glass, the effect was magical. Michael wanted to take Catia to the Central Tower and climb 275 steps to the viewing point so that they could take advantage of the panoramic views over the city. With Christopher in his pram we would not be able to join him and wanted to stay together. Instead we walked down the choir aisle and were enthralled by the magnificence of the arched roof and the exquisite stone columns, which must surely rival those of the Alhambra in Spain. Our enjoyment was suddenly shattered as Christopher began to cry and in the enclosed space his high-pitched yells were magnified and echoed. Startled visitors suddenly all turned to see what we were doing to our baby to cause him to scream so loudly. Fortunately, there were signs directing visitors to toilets where we could seek refuge. Helen rushed Christopher off, with me trailing behind and trying not to trip over my feet as my eyes kept turning to admire the incredible stained-glass windows, military colours and battle honours. There were baby changing rooms alongside the toilets and Helen soon found that our baby needed a nappy change. When we returned to the main body of the Minster, Christopher began to cry again, but fortunately a few octaves lower. I wondered if he was a baby atheist, or did the building atmosphere somehow make him frightened? Whatever the reason, we had to take him outside to spare our embarrassment and the eardrums of the other Minster visitors.

Once Helen was nicely settled in a nearby café, I went back to wait at the bottom of the Central Tower, in case Michael was one of the few people in the

Minster who did not hear our baby's screams. A sympathetic guide, who must have appreciated the removal of my noisy son, smiled and told me that during the sixth century when Christian missionaries were wandering the country, they used churches as centres and priests also lived there. This resulted in them being called monasteriums, which in Old English are known as mynsters, which is how York became entitled to be called a Minster.

When he and Catia returned and we explained the cause of our rapid retreat, my son agreed to meet us in the café when they had visited the Undercroft, which has Roman, Viking and Norman stonework laid as the building was destroyed and rebuilt over the centuries. Since it was a fine day, our next visit was to the nearby stone steps taking us up to the top of the massive stone walls which circle much of York city centre. The walls, or bars, were built on the original Roman fort of Eboricum and extended during Viking occupation and later during the medieval period. The massive stone walls stretch for two miles, are 13 feet high and 6 feet wide. As we walked around them, we were able to look down into the city and at the traffic which passed below us. The term Bar was used when barriers were first used to restrict movement through the city gates and were again used when tolls were collected for entry. Occasionally I could not prevent myself from turning around whenever I heard someone shout "Dad". When Karen gave birth to Martin, it came as a shock to become a grandfather, as well as being dad to my children. Now my titles had increased again and I had to accept being dad and grandad, as well as daddy to baby Christopher.

Once out in the fresh air, our baby was a model of quiet contentment and beamed at us whenever we checked on him. We completed our wall walk in good time to meet our friends at one of the many Italian restaurants in the city and when we had finished eating, it was time to return home before the late afternoon traffic build up. We planned to return in the morning for a river cruise to the Archbishop's Palace at Bishopthorpe.

The next day the sun was again shining on us and Yorkshire was making a good first impression on Catia, who had been advised to bring warm clothes for her first visit to England and the UK. We had arranged to meet Trudy and Dickie in Museum Gardens before our cruise and with Helen pushing our pram, I was walking behind and admiring the riverside buildings and passing river traffic. Having just taken a photograph on my phone, I hurried after Helen and noticed a smartly dressed woman standing near a very large crouching dog dropping a large pile of poo on the riverside path. Without stopping to collect his mess, she then jerked the lead to begin walking away and disgusted by her behaviour, I shouted after her.

"Are you going to leave your dog mess for others to find madam?"

The lady turned to glare at me, before continuing to walk away and I shouted at her again.

"You are on camera madam and I am sure your neighbours and York Council will be very interested to see you on Facebook tonight and no doubt contact you about fouling their riverside path."

Hearing this, the woman stopped and with a very red face returned and scooped her dog's mess into a plastic bag, before holding it up and insisting that I take another photograph. Pointing my phone towards her, I thanked her for her public-spirited act and assured her that she would not now feature on Facebook. Hearing my shouts, Helen had stopped to watch, before asking me how I planned to put my films on Facebook and I explained.

"Actually, there are no films love. I just wanted to shame her into clearing her dog mess."

Shaking her head at me, I was criticised and praised by my wife.

"You really are a devious person Tom Hartley, but your motives are mostly good."

We then saw our friends coming towards us and walked with them to the Lendal Bridge boarding jetty, while Helen told them about my encounter with the dogpoo lady. They were glad I had stopped at least one dog owner from fouling their beautiful city, walking away and possibly allowing others to get involved in the mess.

We boarded a river boat for our tour south to the Archbishop's Palace and a friendly attendant helped us to take Christopher on board in his pram. Helen and I had to sit alongside him on the lower deck while my son and Catia sat on the open top deck to enjoy unrestricted views as we moved downriver. We were quite happy to have our movements restricted until Christopher began walking as part of our parental responsibilities, but nevertheless hoped he would be an early walker. As we glided slowly along the Ouse, we listened to a commentary from the boat captain on the points of interest on the riverbank and the history of York. Two rivers, the Ouse and the Fosse meet in the city centre and first the Romans and then the Vikings used the Ouse to make their way to the city from the sea. Unfortunately, with two rivers flowing through the city centre, it is frequently flooded. The level of the river Ouse can rise from its' usual 5' level to

15′ or more with heavy rain and a high tide driving water inland. I remember having to walk from a city centre hotel across wooden planks when staying overnight for a business meeting and saw Clifford's Tower cut off by flood water. Although we were able to see the Archbishop's Palace at the riverside, there was no opportunity for landing and I complained to Helen about not being able to take tea with the archbishop. Helen assured me that he had probably been warned about my presence and gone walkabout. The boat simply turned around to take us back to Lendal Bridge jetty. Back in the city Michael and Catia went off to the Jorvik Viking Centre, which had low ceilings and funny smells. We dared not allow innocent visitors in an enclosed space to be deafened by screams from our son. Instead, we arranged to meet at the National Railway Museum with me pushing the pram and hoping that with so much open space and large exhibits, our son would behave himself.

Walking alongside, or even beneath the giant locomotives never ceases to thrill me and even Christopher seemed to enjoy himself inside the enormous building with gleaming engines and luxurious carriages built for wealthy passengers. With so much to see, time flew and Helen and Trudy had to shout to drag Dickie and me from admiring the record-breaking Mallard steam engine, as Michael and Catia joined us. As the ladies took tea, we men had another chance to study the exhibits with Michael, who was only twelve years old when he was last at the Railway Museum. As Trudy and Dickie went home, we took the shuttle bus back to our car after a busy and enjoyable day together.

There was an FGC meeting the following evening and Michael wanted to take Catia to the North York Moors and visit Whitby. The couple drove off after breakfast in my car and I worked in the garden and prepared for the meeting with my new proposals. Helen stayed at home to look after Christopher and be available when our visitors returned from Whitby. Ramona was quite keen to organise Line Dancing classes and I wanted to couple it with my next project, mingles. There were many elderly residents on our estate, both couples and singles, who had no transport and relied on the limited local bus service, which resulted in many spending most of their time at home. My idea was to introduce a once a week mingles night when FGC members would offer to collect and take-home residents who wanted to meet up in The Yorkshireman to enjoy a meal, a drink, or just to mingle with others for one night a week. It might also help those who had partners suffering from dementia who needed relief from their 24 hours care if only for an evening.

Helen suggested inviting a local hairdresser to offer simple cut and trim services. If this facility proved to be popular, we hoped that Rod would agree to close off one of the toilets for the evening for wash basins to be used for more demanding treatments. The FGC members were in favour of adding line dancing classes, mingles evenings, the hairdressing and using funds to subsidise, or pay for Xmas lunch for needy elderly residents. They also approved having a video made about FGC to sell to other communities interested in following our lead. Income from video sales, car boot meetings, advertising on our estate garden hoardings, plus FGC bulletins should grow and be supplemented by occasional contributions from Rotary and pub quiz nights.

Kate and Dave Kane attended so that Kate could give details of her next planned walk to club members and the couple now seemed to be very relaxed and happy together. I noticed that Kate had now accepted everyone calling her husband Dave instead of the full David. As Kate was busy speaking to members about her walk, I had a drink with Dave and learned that his sex ban had been lifted after Kate rushed him away from his lively conversation with Ramona and Chloe at my barbecue. I guessed that Kate had realised that she was likely to drive Dave to seek favours elsewhere and decided it would be wiser to keep him happy. Rod joined us and said he would have to take on extra staff to cope with the extra business our FGC activities were bringing him. I had a suggestion.

"Why not offer Marigold an evening job as a barmaid. Her plunging necklines should increase sales and you could increase beer prices for customers in pole positions at the bar and stop them blocking the view of other customers."

Rod tilted his head and thought for a moment before responding.

"We never did find out what happened when you found her sunbathing topless in her garden and she always makes a fuss of you when you arrive. Now you are trying to persuade me to put her behind my bar so that you can admire her cleavage whenever you order a drink."

"She was not topless, just almost bottomless and I was braving wild dogs and killer letterboxes at the time just to get your damned leaflets delivered."

"Quite right. It was a brave effort and thank you Tom. But you must admit even dangerous work can sometimes have its rewards."

Dave suggested Rod might consider offering evening work to Ramona, who was also popular and well known to locals, especially those with binoculars after her regular sunbathing sessions in her garden. I mentioned that many locals with binoculars would not recognise her after probably never seeing her face. She would also be busy running the Line Dancing classes one night a week. Turning to Dave, Rod said he had heard that he had been a big hit with Ramona and Chloe at my barbecue and now we were both trying to choose our friends for his extra staff work. Dave knew Rod was only teasing him, but admitted that he had been impressed by the sisters, who just happened to be my adjoining neighbours.

"That Chloe could be like a smouldering volcano. She is a good looker and has a wicked gleam in her eye, as well as a strong sense of humour. I am very happy with Kate and looking forward to our baby, so I won't be the one to light Chloe's fire, but I think she fancies Tom here."

Before I could respond, we were joined by Ramona who had been listening to the FGC meeting comments and had spoken with members interested in joining her dance class. She told us that most interest came from the ladies, but she hoped to have a more mixed class and wondered if I could ask for male volunteers. Rod immediately suggested that Dave and I were light on our feet, but we claimed family commitments kept us too busy. I said it was time I got back to my family and Ramona said she would walk back with me. Dave winked at me, but suddenly lost his smile as he saw a frowning Kate heading his way. As we headed back to Chestnut Grove, I asked Ramona if she planned to join the FGC and get involved aside from running dance classes. She was sure she would join the Walkers Group and possibly the ladies Tea Caddy investment club, since she wanted to learn more about stocks and shares. To my surprise she took my arm and told me how pleased she was to have us as neighbours.

"Mum is not very interested in our community and prefers to stay indoors because of her arthritis. Chloe is away in London most of the time and although Agnes was a lovely lady, she was mainly housebound as well. You and Helen have been so kind to me and I enjoy looking after Christopher and can't wait to help out with the dances and your other schemes."

As we reached my house, I saw Roger painting his front door and as he turned to wave, Ramona gave me a quick peck on my cheek and hurried off. Roger stood with paint brush poised and a surprised look on his face after seeing Ramona kiss me. Not wanting him to jump to conclusions, I explained that she was an emotional young girl and appreciated my help with the FGC and Helen's efforts to find her a place at the local hospital. He nodded and said I had seen much more of her than most of the neighbours.

"Do you mean with, or without binoculars Roger and by the way, your paint brush is dripping on your shoe."

"Touché Tom. Very few of us have ever seen the mother and Chloe always seems to be stalking us in her car, or away in London. Of course, you live next door to them and Ramona is the friendliest and is good with your baby. She must be delighted to have a lively couple as neighbours after being away in America for so long."

"We like her Roger and at the meeting tonight we agreed to start Line Dancing one night a week. We will also be having a mingles night when FGC members take elderly, or incapacitated older residents to The Yorkshireman to meet up with other residents. When they want to leave, they will then be given lifts home. It should help people like Ramona's mum get out and meet other residents, so why don't you and Joyce come along."

Roger put his paint brush back in the pot and told me he would talk it over with his wife, then went back indoors. Helen was in the kitchen and our baby had been fed and changed and hopefully would sleep for the next few hours. Radio Leeds had telephoned to ask when we would be available to take part in their Round & About live programme and I told Helen that I had permission to make a video about the FGC. I also mentioned being kissed by Ramona and watched by Roger. Helen shrugged her shoulders and gave her view.

"I know you can't help being friendly with everyone and a peck on the cheek in the street is nothing to worry about. I know I can trust you and so do people who know you, especially now you have a new son to keep you busy."

As we were enjoying coffee together, our overseas visitors returned and Michael assured me that the garage would soon be able to repair the dents and scratches on my car after he had driven it across the moors. Seeing the horror on my face, he admitted that he was only kidding. He has a wicked sense of humour and I have no idea where he got it. Nevertheless, when I took my car out of the garage in the morning, I could not resist checking and fortunately it was unmarked. The couple went off on their own most days so that Catia could see other Yorkshire attractions and Michael drove to Chester, as well as Howarth and Holmfirth. The time since they arrived seemed to have flown and their UK holiday was almost over. Helen cooked a superb dinner for the family on their last night before their long flight back to Australia the following morning. With my two daughters and son with their partners and babies Martin and Christopher, Helen and I felt that we were so fortunate to be part of a real family. As we men were showing our appreciation by washing the dishes, pots and pans afterwards, Michael thanked me for making Catia so welcome. He also told me how happy he was that I had married Helen and how amazing it was for me to become a father again in retirement. Receiving an invitation to make the long journey out to see their new baby and house, I promised to talk it over with Helen. With a stopover in Singapore on both flights, I thought we would be able to cope. Christopher should soon be walking and talking, but if we could find the money, it would be easier to fly Club Class and being retired, we could choose the days and times with cheaper flights.

During our usual bedtime chat, I asked Helen about visiting Michael in Australia and she thought it would be a wonderful opportunity to meet Catia's baby and her family. She had always wanted to visit Australia and agreed to a stop at Singapore with perhaps a visit to the grave of Patrick Mulcahy. She also suggested that with the cost of refurbishing the house and the arrival of our baby, we could always sell the necklace Patrick had given her. She had not worn it since her wedding day and our social activity was usually low key, which would make wearing her necklace appear ostentatious. It was a magnanimous offer, but I knew I must do my best to avoid having to sell Patrick's generous gift. As we kissed goodnight Helen told me how wonderful it felt to be with my daughters, son and partners and be a part of a real family after being on her own for most of her life. In return I told her how wonderful it felt to be married to her after finding myself alone. The following morning, I made an early start for the drive across The Pennines to Manchester Airport, but Christopher had a cold and Helen stayed at home to look after him. As usual traffic was heavy, but we were in good time for the flight for their first stage to Dubai and after hugs and a kiss from Catia, the couple walked through to the Departure Lounge and I drove home. As we were having our evening coffee, we were sad that the couple had gone back, but glad to have the house to ourselves again and be able to have a playful tumble on our settee once the baby was asleep.

Chapter 17
Stars of the Small Screen

I was looking after Christopher as Helen went to have her hair done and if there was any free time, I wanted to work on the FGC video. Helen kept her car in our single garage, while mine was on the drive because we used it more often. Unfortunately, that morning her car would not start and she had to take mine as I called the garage to come and sort her car problem. The mechanic told me that he had fitted a new battery because the car was not being used frequently enough to keep it charged. When Helen returned and heard about the repair, she had a suggestion.

"We can save money on tax, insurance and running costs by getting rid of my old banger and it will be a start to our Australia fund. It will also save you from scraping ice from your windscreen on frosty mornings if your car is kept inside the garage instead of mine."

This was a very sensible suggestion and showed me that Helen had now fully accepted being part of a sharing couple. The next day the camera crew arrived to record aspects of our FGC activities for Yorkshire TV.

We were all prepared and I was interviewed first as the instigator of the scheme to involve local residents and improve facilities on our estate. Fortunately, I had a photograph of the abandoned garden area before we cultivated it and this was featured, followed by views of the finished garden with its low retaining wall, benches and lawned area. Helen spoke about the group of residents who had completed the work and ignoring her hard stare, I mentioned that we had to shower off the dirt afterwards. Kate explained her role in leading our organised walks and was a polished, if lengthy speaker. To end the session on a humorous note they then included a couple of photographs of walkers under attack by Canada Geese. Two residents spoke of help with their gardens and customers at The Yorkshireman were interviewed at the bar, with Marigold standing behind to add glamour and holding a beer pump handle in each hand. Rod pointed to the FGC emblem at the pub entrance and mentioned the number of retired ladies who had given birth on the estate. Asked if he knew the reason, he suggested that it could be their active lifestyles, or perhaps it was his special shepherds pies. The two investment clubs were described and a female member of the Tea Caddy Club explained how they were doing far better than the men in the Yorkmisers Club. The interviewer discussed having separate clubs for the sexes and how it created interest, as well as competition. The film was to close with a group of line dancers moving towards the camera, but there was an unfortunate absence of males. Ramona persuaded Dave and me to join the line-up and as the line moved forward, I moved back and Dave was also lost on which way to move to keep up with the ladies. We were assured by the female programmer that our mistakes would be excluded by showing a still view. When we later saw ourselves stumbling about on television the next day, our mistakes were included and we put it down to a feminist attack on men. Helen agreed with us that it was unfair, but also mentioned that it showed the film was live, since men never follow properly.

With the television programme aired, we received a steady stream of requests from other areas for information on setting up similar activities and suggested that forward orders for our video should be placed. The pressure was on and we included much of the television programme in our video, interspersed with details of each of the activities. After calculating packing and postage, we should make a modest profit on each video sold to help in building our funds. Rod generously agreed that the pub darts team should be renamed the Fairfields Garden Club and wear t-shirts carrying our banner to advertise our community services during their away games.

As we were getting back to normal after the departure of our visitors, Helen found my prize-winning watercolour of Crathes Castle, created outdoors during an eventful painting course to Scotland before we became a loving couple. After giving her an edited account of my experiences, I had promised that one day I would like to take her to see the castle and its wonderful gardens and make a new painting. This would include a group of Japanese schoolgirls who had stopped and made complimentary comments about my work. At least I felt sure they were complimentary, but they were bowing and speaking in Japanese, although I also received some really big smiles. I was surprised that Helen had remembered that

I wanted to visit the castle and repaint my watercolour and even more surprised by her comments.

"Look Tom, we cancelled our honeymoon to save money and work on the house, so why not take a short break to see this wonderful place and then you can create a new painting with those ideas you mentioned to me?"

Naturally I was happy to agree and left Helen to make the hotel bookings, since I was working on another service by our FGC. Our first mingles evening was held at The Yorkshireman and twenty-two residents attended, six of whom were collected by FGC volunteers in their cars. Rod had generously laid on free snacks and the drinks were served by our very own television stars Marigold and Ramona, who brightened the lives of the elderly residents, but mainly the males. David, accompanied by expectant wife Kate had picked up a couple with husband Peter suffering dementia and his wife Gloria his all-day carer. Kate was normally very slim and there were now early signs of the baby growing inside her and Dave had begun talking about becoming a father instead of complaining about too much, or too little sex with his wife. During the evening Peter watched someone add tomato sauce to his food and promptly added some to his coffee. Nothing was said by understanding onlookers and a volunteer collected another coffee for Peter. The guests seemed to enjoy the relaxed and friendly atmosphere and the other customers were glad to have the opportunity to help. At the end of the evening the mingles residents were all taken home after thanking Rod for providing them with refreshments and a relaxing evening in good company. Asked if they would like to have regular weekly, or monthly mingles gatherings, the results were inconclusive and the FGC committee settled for monthly until demand justified more frequent meetings.

While I was working on the FGC video and mingles meeting, Helen had been busy planning a five-night trip to Crathes Castle at Banchory near Aberdeen and the weather forecast for the area was warm and dry. We would not return until just after a Yorkmisers Investment Club meeting, but Helen assured me that the FGC could spare me for a few days outing with our family. We drove north up the A1 and stopped for coffee and a toilet break at Washington before continuing on to North Berwick to stay the night, instead of finding accommodation in the busy and more expensive Edinburgh hotels. It is a very attractive town with a golf course between the town and the sea and good views of nearby Bass Rock Island with its large protected gannet colony. Unfortunately, there was a steady rain downpour and it was not the weather for a couple to walk around while pushing a pram. Next morning, we followed the motorway across The Firth of Forth and after a stop for lunch halfway, we finally reached our hotel outside Aberdeen in late afternoon sunshine and relaxed in the garden before dinner. Taking our time over breakfast we later drove to Banchory and Crathes Castle.

After parking our car we walked around the castle to the large lawned area at the rear, where I set up my canvas stool and foldup easel to give me the same angled view of the castle I had painted on my last visit as a painting student. Fortunately, it was a warm sunny day and Helen left me to my painting to go walkabout with Christopher. I set about working on my creation for almost an hour while waiting for the arrival of Japanese schoolgirls, or any other enthusiastic admirers of amateur painters. I began my painting by placing schoolgirls in the foreground and since only their backs would be visible, I decided to turn two heads to show the girls had Japanese features. My back would also be showing, but perhaps my figure in a floppy sunhat would make me appear more like an accomplished painter. I had visions of matching David Hockney's style in having a picture within a picture. On the previous visit I had trouble mixing paints to find the correct colour to match the weathered stone and mossy face of the castle walls. Fortunately, I had made a note of the colour mix on my last visit, which saved time in putting paint to paper. When Helen returned an hour, or so later with a cold drink for me, my painting was already taking good shape and she went off again to walk near the lake and look at the herons and kingfishers. The curved shape of the towers and angled castle view took time and patience to reproduce and there were also visits by interested tourists, who suddenly appeared behind me and commented on the painting. One pointed out that I had missed a small wooden building built against the castle wall. I explained that amateur painters are allowed to remove difficult or ugly structures which might spoil the view. He nodded his head and went away happy to have learned something about watercolour artists. It was lunchtime when Helen returned and I packed up my instruments and equipment to take my family for lunch in the castle tearoom.

We spent the rest of the day in the walled garden with its herbaceous borders and magnificent Irish Yew trees trimmed into incredible shapes, including a giant yew archway. There were a number of nature trails and as we explored the extensive grounds, we saw buzzards circling above in the sky and red squirrels leaping amongst the branches of the trees. Helen really enjoyed the visit and Christopher was well behaved and never stopped smiling at us. My painting was not finished, but with the essential outline and shapes already added it should not be difficult to paint in the final details at home. Once we had eaten dinner in our hotel, we were glad to go to bed after a full day outside in the bracing Scottish air. In the morning when we were having our breakfast, we could see the rain lashing the windows outside and knew that spending time exploring the local rural landscape was out of the question. We decided instead to return to North Berwick and hope that we would leave the rain behind us, but as we arrived in time for lunch, the driving rain was still bouncing off our car roof. My previous visits had always been in sunshine and now with dark skies and puddled roads it showed a depressing view of the resort. We found a restaurant with space in the car park and rushed inside with Christopher wrapped up to protect him from the rain. Over lunch we agreed to skip spending the night in North Berwick and drive on to Alnwick after Helen telephoned ahead to book a two-night stay at an hotel.

A friend had told us about the attractions of Alnwick and although it was late afternoon when we booked in, the rain had stopped at last and after hours of driving we were glad to walk around the attractive town centre before having dinner in the hotel, which was pram friendly. The following morning, we visited Alnwick Castle which featured in the Harry Potter films. In the extensive grounds we found an enclosed Poison Garden, which displayed a range of deadly plants with a guide providing a narrative and booklets for sale, in case any of the visitors required details for future use. Many of the growing plants would be included in ordinary gardens and would therefore be readily available, if needed. Most visitors were female and apparently poison is the favourite murder method for ladies. Perhaps men would be more interested in growing vegetables, or using less subtle murder methods.

The waterfall feature was really spectacular and we stood nearby to watch the water cascading down the stepped series of waterfalls with 120 water jets. Suddenly we were startled when the central water "bomb" exploded and shot fifty feet into the air. After walking amongst the free-standing sculptures and more water features, we had snacks and drinks inside the modern Pavilion Restaurant with its glass wall allowing diners to admire the gardens. The magnificent castle itself was crowded with visitors, but with a pram to push we chose to forego an inside tour until Christopher was walking and we were more likely to justify the expensive entrance fees. As we were leaving by the entrance to the grounds, we were fascinated to see the large Tree House Restaurant, built within the branches of a number of trees and linked by wooden walkways. With steps to gain access, it was not pram friendly and we would certainly have to come back again in a couple of years' time to enjoy the experience and food. The Alnwick Tree House is the world's largest.

Our next stop was at Barters Bookshop in the old railway station, which had an enormous range of used books at bargain prices. An extensive model railway track had trains constantly circling around the bookshop on top of the bookcases so that children and some men could watch them whizzing around. Naturally there was also a station buffet and a children's room filled with toys to keep them amused, while their parents were browsing amongst the books. We really liked Alnwick and would definitely return when Christopher was old enough to appreciate all its attractions.

Before leaving Northumberland, Helen suggested a visit to Holy Island and we drove over the narrow causeway to visit the small community, which is completely isolated each time the tide comes in. Anxious to avoid being marooned by the returning tide, we had a light snack and a leisurely walk around the small community island before driving back along the causeway. Choosing the scenic coast road took us past the massive bulk of Bamburgh Castle. We parked to admire the building and location, but it began to rain yet again and we postponed a visit for a later date and after making our way home we arrived in early evening. In spite of the rain, we had a pleasant time at Crathes Castle when the weather was kind to us and my painting was now ready to be finished as soon as I could find the time.

During a busy working life with many very long days, the dream of one day being able to relax with lots of free time and leisure had always been in my mind. Having retired and found so many interests to pursue, my leisure days were now never long enough and the myth was shattered.

Helen suggested that I hurry down to The Yorkshireman to catch the end of the Yorkmisers Investment club meeting, while she put Christopher to bed and unpacked. By the time I arrived at The Yorkshireman the meeting was over and everyone was heading for home, or the bar. I was easily persuaded to join the remainers to hear about the meeting outcome, while they asked about my holiday break in Scotland. One of the trio considering investments had received a hot tip from an unnamed, but very reliable source and the meeting had sold its existing shares, which were making modest increases to use all its funds to buy the hot tip company. It sold a range of clothing on-line and had already doubled sales since start up a year ago and was expected to be taken over by a larger competitor at twice its current share value. It sounded too good to be true and when I mentioned this, I was called a Jeremiah and told I needed another drink to cheer me up. As I was about to leave, I was asked to arrange the share purchase and was given details on a slip of paper torn from a diary as I left. In the morning I went on-line to buy the shares before spending a leisurely day working in the garden and cleaning the car. Helen and our son enjoyed the mild weather sitting on our magnificent terrace and she would be attending the Line Dancing class in the evening while I looked after Christopher. A week later while reading the paper, it came as a shock to learn that the company I had bought for the Yorkmisers club had found a rich seam of rare metal on its prospecting area in Greenland. I had been told I was buying an on-line clothing company and certainly not a mining company. Could I have bought the wrong company by mistake? I would need to find the slip of paper and it should be in my waste basket where I thought I would have tossed it after making the purchase.

Before I could check the basket contents, Ramona arrived to join Helen on a shopping trip and I was to baby sit until they returned after lunch. Christopher was now teething and needed a lot of my attention to console him during the long hours without his mother. I was thrilled to spend time with my baby son, but nevertheless was relieved to hear the sound of my car returning to the drive. Two ladies with heavy shopping bags hurried into the kitchen and as Ramona made the coffee, Helen took Christopher from me and his mood changed immediately as he felt his mother's arms around him. As we drank our coffee I was told about the crowded shops during the sales and the fantastic bargains both ladies had snatched away from other bargain seekers. When Ramona left, I was treated to a fashion show as Helen tried on the clothes she had bought and naturally, when asked, I assured her that the style and colours were just right for her. Watching Helen strip down to her undies to try on skirts and dresses made me realise how much more a woman in undies appeals to a man than when in the nude. My spirit rose and I took hold of her and gave her a long kiss, only to be told that the baby needed changing and that if I cleared up, we could always shower together later. I promised to clear up and returned to my search of the basket.

There was no sign of the missing slip of paper after I tipped the entire contents onto the floor, but still failed to find it. Without it I could not prove I had bought the company chosen by club members, but perhaps the rare metal find would boost the mining company share price and compensate for missing out on the clothing company profit. It would be the last time I took instructions after drinking with tipsy club members who were unlikely to remember if the details were wrong.

My face must have reflected my worries and over dinner Helen asked if there was something wrong with the food and I told her what had happened. She reminded me that I had just driven for hours and still rushed off to attend the meeting, before drinking on an empty stomach. Perhaps the mistake was predictable, but with the company name written down I was sure it was not my fault, but it would be impossible to prove without the missing piece of paper. I would just have to wait for telephone complaints from members, or embarrassing questions at the next meeting and hope that the gap between the two share prices would not become too large. To my surprise and relief, no one seemed to have seen the newspaper article about the Peter Low Group Mining Company and there was no mention in the papers about the takeover of the clothing company Piccolo.

Helen checked on Tea Caddy performance and was delighted to learn that the ladies were still showing far better growth on their investments than the men, which made me even more embarrassed about my possible error. Whatever I did over the following days, my first action every morning was to check the share prices of the two companies to find how much my error had cost our investment club. Suddenly my gloom vanished as fortune smiled on me and I read that the company I had bought in error was doing very well.

Chapter 18
Rare Metal Triumph

Our second mingles night was held and three extra residents over the previous meeting attended for the evening. Thanks to the steady growth in his turnover, Rod decided to try adding cabaret and hired two entertainers to keep his customers happy and staying to spend more on drinks and food. The woman had a clear and pleasant voice and was accompanied by her partner on keyboard as they sang a selection of popular hits. With Marigold and Ramona helping him to supply the many customers, I could tell by the satisfied look on Rod's face that takings were covering the cost of hiring the entertainers. Perhaps a weekly cabaret night would be added to the many Yorkshireman activity evenings.

Helen and I were sitting with some of the minglers and they told us that after being nervous at the first gathering, they spoke with friends and agreed that it provided a pleasant break from their lonely existence. Their only concern was that it was in the evening and while some were accustomed to going to bed early, others did not like being out at night with quiet streets, or darkness. This made me wonder about suggesting afternoon mingles gatherings, which would be extra business for Rod and more popular with elderly residents, although neither Marigold nor Ramona would be available because of their day jobs. Of course, amongst the younger and more active retired residents there might be some who were willing to look after the minglers. We might also invite a hairdresser to be present to widen the appeal of the afternoon gatherings. The evening ended with prolonged clapping for the entertainers and for our beaming landlord and local councillor Rod.

At home and after Christopher had been put to bed, Helen and I had our usual bedtime chat and I outlined my ideas about amending our mingles project and she was sure it would be a success because everybody gained. Although pleased that she agreed with the change of timing, my mind kept returning to my error in buying the wrong company and the next meeting of the Yorkmisers was due the following night. Helen attended her Tea Caddy session on Monday and told me they had chosen another share for their portfolio, which was also showing gains and this news just added to my worries. We all like to hope we have a guardian angel to protect us when we are in trouble and mine was with me the next morning. As usual I read the paper after breakfast and my eyes were immediately drawn to an item headed Piccolo, which stated that the company had gone into liquidation after failing to pay its' suppliers. The competitor rumoured to be negotiating its takeover had found that the accounts had been doctored to hide heavy losses and immediately cancelled negotiations. Hearing me shout "Yippee", Helen was startled and asked if I had won the pools. When I explained she was disappointed that she would not be having a new car, but delighted that I would not be walking around the house in a miserable mood any longer. Next, I checked the price of Peter Low shares and had another pleasant surprise when I saw that they were 50% up and expected to show further increases when they began extracting rare metal ore. Now I was looking forward to attending the Yorkmisers next meeting after saving the club funds, but would have to admit that it had been done by accident. My double stroke of luck was almost too much for Helen, who raised her hands in amazement.

"Honestly Tom, I think you must be Teflon coated since you always seem to get away with it even after flying by the seat of your pants, or in your case boxers. Now you will be praised as the club saviour after buying the wrong shares."

I tried to justify my error and incredible share purchase.

"I know I had a few drinks the night of the meeting, but I was quite sober when I bought the company written on that missing bit of paper the following morning. The trouble is, without that little slip of paper I can't prove it was not my mistake. Fortunately, I can tell them that for the club, it was a very lucky mistake. I am going to suggest that in future the buy note will have to be signed by all three in the group and raised at the meeting with no more bar instructions."

Ramona appeared at our door and Helen told her about my idea to move mingles meetings to the afternoon. Hearing this, she looked a little doubtful and wondered if we could cope.

"There are lots of people to help out in the evenings, but not so many during the day. Perhaps they could meet and just chat amongst themselves."

Finding enough helpers in the afternoon could be a problem, but we might be able to hire a minibus if our local Rotary club, or sponsors agreed to cover the cost and Rod agreed to the time change.

At the meeting the Yorkmisers members were surprised that their chosen shares had not been bought. When a member then held up a newspaper article about the bankruptcy, there were groans and muttering as they thought about their lost funds. Their attitude changed immediately as I told them that instead the club held shares in a very successful mining company. I accepted the blame, but the member who gave me the paper admitted that he might have confused the similar sounding names and we agreed to share the blame and the glory. After the meeting we naturally went to the bar to celebrate and I felt someone put their arms around me and turned to find a smiling Chloe standing alongside. Ramona had told her about the company share mix up and she already knew that I was the man of the hour as I stood amongst friends at the bar.

After congratulating me on my accidental triumph she told me that her London apartment was being decorated and she and her girl friend were having a break together in the north. I was invited to join Connie at their table for a drink and recognised the woman I had once seen with Chloe on her drive. They worked together in the entertainments industry and were long-time friends and perhaps a lot more I suspected. She also complimented me on the mingles meetings and hoped that it might be possible to persuade her mother to attend. We were then joined by Rod and Dave who had both been at the Yorkmisers meeting and were delighted that the club money had been saved. Rod now had more free time with the extra bar staff and explained to the girls.

"Your sister and Marigold are doing a great job and now I can spend time with my most important customers and glamorous lady visitors."

The two ladies gave Rod big smiles and Connie blew him a kiss as I introduced them. As Chloe leaned forward to shake hands, her blouse top sagged open under the weight and Dave and I saw that she was not wearing a bra. I assumed it was a family habit, since Ramona also went unsupported. Miraculously her blouse just managed to hold in the contents and spare our embarrassment. Dave had already been fascinated by Chloe at my barbecue and now had difficulty keeping his eyes away from her chest. Sensing that it was an automatic male reaction, I nudged him in the ribs and he turned to smile at Connie instead. After being assured that both ladies knew about mingles, Rod told me he had no objection to allowing an afternoon meeting, but his pub would be quiet and lacking in atmosphere and entertainment at that time. He was happy to have the residents meet and chat amongst themselves, but would they be happy with this? I said I would have to think over a possible change and Rod wished the ladies a pleasant break in Yorkshire and went off to check on his takings, leaving us to enjoy the close attention of the visitors. Connie asked what we did and was interested to learn that Dave was a reporter and asked about his experiences as Chloe told me how much my son was like me and how she had always wanted to visit Australia. The ladies left not long afterwards and Rod returned to give us the benefit of his wisdom and experience.

"I had no worries about you old codgers being eaten alive by those two, since I am pretty sure they are an item and with men it will be tease, not please."

When I returned home and told Helen about the meeting, Chloe, Connie and Rod's comments about their relationship, her reaction took me by surprise.

"You may enjoy flirting with women Tom, but you are still not smart enough to work out when they prefer other women to men. I knew after meeting Chloe at the barbecue and told Kate that she had nothing to be worried about, but she chose not to listen to me."

As the weeks passed, my first act every morning was to check the stock market and unbelievably, the Peter Low shares continued to increase in price. I calculated that Yorkmisers gains now raised our total to well above the Tea Caddy total and we men no longer felt embarrassed by the ladies FGC achievements. Helen claimed a mistaken purchase in no way showed the same skill as the ladies' clever stock selection, but as they say, money talks and our gains continued to run well ahead of theirs.

We had never experienced vandalism on our quiet estate and the Yorkshire television programme had highlighted this as it covered FGC services available to our residents. Naturally I was surprised when I received a phone call to ask if I had seen the damage at the estate garden and since I had not, I rushed over to see for myself. Our shrubs and plants had been completely smashed, or cut down, but the low stone walls and benches survived because they were well secured on concrete bases. Unfortunately, the vandals had thrown white paint over the benches and had obviously come prepared with cutters and paint, but fortunately, no sledgehammers. It had to be a spiteful and planned attack after our estate was featured on Yorkshire television. The gardens of nearby residents had also been stamped on, plants were uprooted and two cars parked on drives were left with flat tyres. Perhaps the car owners were fortunate that all the paint had been poured over our benches, which left none for their cars. The police were promptly informed and we received an incident number, but were told it was unlikely that the vandals would be caught, although they could make a guess about where they lived. There were many angry volunteers who joined in our Saturday working party and some generously brought shrubs and plants from their own gardens, or purchased them to replace those destroyed by vandals. The benches were completely covered in paint, which would take time and lots of hard work to remove. Someone suggested painting over it instead and happened to have a good supply of canary yellow paint, which we used. The change from the original brown to the bright yellow colour was startling, but the general view was that it actually brightened up the area. Speaking to Helen after checking if she was covered in dust and needed a really good shower with a willing helper, I said the garden had actually been improved and she agreed.

"I think it does look better, which of course it would do with your Teflon cover for all disasters and no I am not all that dusty. However, if the oven was cleaned, I might be persuaded."

I suppose this was a mild form of blackmail, but with a house and baby to look after, the daily work load has to be shared and the oven is only a half hour job at most. When Christopher is finally asleep and we relax together in the evening I know we will both enjoy sharing our multijet shower. When we are together in the shower with our bodies as one and the jets of hot water pummelling us all over, our aches and worries seem to be swept away leaving us relaxed and able to enjoy a good night of sleep after yet another very busy day.

Business was very good at The Yorkshireman, but as he was closing up one night, Rod found his wife Rachel fast asleep on a chair in the kitchen. He knew that the long hours were now taking their toll and he would have to make some drastic changes. Extra staff at the bar and kitchen had helped to cope with the increased business, but they were both on the premises 24 hours of every day and most of the time they were kept busy. They were earning more money than ever, but they were left with little leisure time and they had not seen their daughter, or grandchildren for three months. His work as a councillor took up more of Rod's free time, but fortunately he was able to meet residents needing his help at The Yorkshireman. Council meetings were held monthly and his responsibility for Sports and Leisure in the area was not too demanding. He made some coffee and then woke his wife to tell her they must find a way to give them both more free time and a holiday as soon as possible. They decided they would have to appoint a pub manager and chef at The Yorkshireman to give them time to enjoy the benefit of all their hard work in building up the business.

It was Monday and after working together to decorate our small bedroom, Helen and I had just finished lunch and were surprised to receive a visit from Rod. Helen made coffee and we sat together in our kitchen and learned the reason for the visit. Rod was very worried about Rachel's health and overworking and wanted to take her for a holiday. He and Rachel had also decided that the time had come to appoint a pub manager and chef. He wanted to know if I would be willing to help.

"Much of my turnover is in cash and unfortunately this can be a temptation for light fingered staff who serve my customers. I know the signs and have a quiet word when I find them slipping cash into their pockets and if they keep at it, I ask them to leave. Most customers don't check their change when paying for drinks and staff can take a little on each payment and put most cash in my till and some in their pocket. On a busy night this mounts up to a fair bonus on top of their wages, but some of the smarter customers can either query their change amount, or say nothing, but stop coming to my pub. I know it won't be easy to find a manager I can trust, but I need to give Rachel a break pretty soon and wondered if you would help."

I nodded my head and answered.

"You have always been a good friend to me Rod since I moved here and I will certainly help if I can."

Rod nodded his head and told me what he had in mind.

"I know you worked in business, but running a bar and restaurant is quite different. Would you be willing to work with me during the day and evenings to learn the ropes and then take over for a couple of days to allow me and Rachel to take a break. Once you have experience of the pub business you could also sit in when I interview possible managers to help me to get the right person to take over. I know you are saving to go to Australia when your new grandchild is born and will pay you for your time."

Helen was listening carefully and before giving Rod my answer, I wanted to know how she felt about having me run the pub during Rod's short breaks.

She told Rod that if it was only to be a short-term commitment and help Rod and Rachel, then she was sure she could spare me. Also, the money would certainly be welcome for our overseas trip to Australia. For her part, a long-term involvement could restrict our new lifestyle, which had already seen big changes with the arrival of Christopher. Rod assured her that he would certainly want to make it as short as possible. He hoped to move out of The Yorkshireman with Rachel so that they could spend more time with each other and their family. On this basis it was agreed that I would begin spending time at The Yorkshireman to learn the business before taking over for Rod's two-day breaks and he would immediately start looking for extra staff. After Rod left, Helen looked at herself in the mirror, muttered something and suddenly began to tidy her hair and make-up, as if by doing so she would alter her untidy appearance when Rod had already seen her. I smiled to myself because her efforts now made absolutely no difference, except perhaps in Helen's mind.

After telling her there would now be no need to sell her necklace, I contacted Michael to tell him he could expect a visit from us fairly soon after he becomes a father and he was really excited and said Catia's family were looking forward to meeting us. The Yorkshireman opened at 10 am and closed at 10 pm, with time allowed for drinks to be finished and customers encouraged to go home, which would leave Helen and Christopher alone throughout my working days. It was a joint sacrifice to help a friend, but it would also provide us with very welcome extra money for our visit to Australia. Provided that my involvement was short term, it would be well worth the disruption to our lives.

Helen suggested inviting Kate and Dave for dinner, since we had seen very little of them after attending their wedding with me as best man. Knowing how nervous Kate was about her pregnancy, Helen also wanted to help and advise her as much as possible. Almost as soon as they arrived, Kate produced a photo scan as Dave and I exchanged sympathetic glances and waited as our wives discussed the baby image now showing. Kate was obsessed with ensuring that she had a perfect baby and sought assurance from Helen that there were no signs of abnormality. Finally, we sat down for dinner and began with broccoli and stilton soup, which Helen had made for the first time and was enjoyed by our guests, especially Dave.

"That is really great soup Helen. Perhaps you can give Kate the recipe."

I was feeling suppressed after all the baby talk and made a dangerous response.

"That's easily done Dave, I'll see if I can find the can."

All conversation stopped and Kate looked startled, while Helen looked annoyed. Dave had a sympathetic look on his face and waited for me to be punished and I knew I had to save myself.

"Just my little joke folks. Helen was working on that soup all afternoon and let me taste the results and it was superb. From now on it will be one of her many specialties and I know how lucky I am to have a gorgeous wife, who is also a fantastic chef."

I hoped that by promoting Helen from cook to chef, it would do the trick and it did. There were smiles all round and Dave called me an old smoothie. It was a pleasant evening and during our usual bedtime chat, Helen and I agreed that we should have dinner guests more often.

Since Rod was keen to help Rachel, I started my training two days later and was at the pub at 9 am to help with setting up before opening for customers at 10 am. A cleaner was wiping down the tables and chairs and another was working on the carpets. We checked on the cellar and exchanged empty metal kegs for full ones, before taking crates of bottled lager and fruit juices up to the bar. Ten minutes before opening time Dirty Dickie arrived to fill and check the vending machines in the Gents and Ladies toilets. The man's name was Richard, but because he filled the machines with a variety of shaped and flavoured condoms, as well as tampons, Rod always called him Dirty Dickie. I wanted to know which toilet used most condoms and Dickie told me it was usually the Ladies. He thought the men always had high hopes, but the Ladies were the ones to make the final decision and wisely planned ahead.

I unlocked the door and let three customers into the pub, before filling their glasses with Rod guiding me on how to use the pump handles to fill each glass to the brim. A range of bottled spirits was held in a rack behind the bar and by pressing the glass rim against the measure bar, the correct amount was poured into each glass. For those wanting hot drinks, a versatile machine dispensed a range of coffees, tea, or chocolate, but hot food would not be available until noon when the kitchen opened. A range of crisps and snacks were always stocked behind the bar for peckish customers. I soon became confident that I could serve most customers with their orders, but still had to search for different beers and drinks kept under, or behind the bar. Rod also showed me where I could find details of the fancy range of cocktails which some of the ladies favoured.

Ramona arrived for her evening shift and gave me a big hug, before Marigold also stepped forward to hug me and Rod told them that I could be their boss from time to time, which made both move towards me again to congratulate me. Keen to maintain my position as their future leader, I naturally stepped back. Rod left me behind the bar and kept a close watch on me as I responded to customer orders, although it was clear that the regulars preferred being served by the glamorous ladies, even when they had to wait. Accepting my low rating, I stood poised to serve with my friendliest smile showing. Luckily, some of my FGC members favoured me with their orders and quietly asked if I was having problems making ends meet. After stocking up the mixer bottles under the bar I straightened up and found myself facing a lady with bright blond hair, heavy makeup and very red lips. She must have been well over seventy years old, but was dressed more like a 20-year-old and after giving me a beaming smile and stroking my hand, she told me.

"You must be new here and you just popped up like a Jack in a Box. Give me a Manhattan love."

This was one cocktail I had already read about and I asked if she wanted it in a Martini glass, or short tumbler.

"Give us a tumbler love. Don't like those fancy glasses which are too easy to spill."

As I was mixing the bourbon whisky and sweet vermouth with a few drops of Angostura bitters, she told me her name was Mavis and she had been a regular customer for years. After giving her the Manhattan I moved away to serve Bob, who was another FGC member. He was surprised to see me behind the bar after regularly sharing the other side with me. I explained how I was helping Rod and he told me to be careful with Mavis, who was still desperate to find herself a man in spite of her age. He had called to fix a jammed lock at her home and accepted her offer of coffee, only to find her standing very close beside him in a very revealing dressing gown. He gulped down the coffee and insisted that he had another urgent job to do before hurrying to the door. Whenever I was standing and waiting to serve customers, Mavis suddenly appeared in front of me to chat, or order another drink. It was a busy evening, but I kept an eye on her to judge when to suggest that she should stop if she wanted to walk home unaided. I spoke to Rod about her.

"The elderly lady with the bright blond hair has had four Manhattans and I wondered about advising her to stop."

Rod told me that Mavis had been a regular customer for years and could drink up to six cocktails and still walk away with no sign of a wobble. He thought that she must have built up her alcohol tolerance over the years and we agreed that I would restrict her to six Manhattans. The Yorkshireman had its share of heavy drinkers, which was good for Rod's profits, but drunken customers can cause damage to themselves, to property and to other customers and have to be handled carefully. Pubs which regularly have to call in the police to defuse tense situations, or fighting may well have their liquor licence cancelled. At the end of my first full day as a publican, I walked home looking forward to collapsing into bed, but not relishing the thought that I would be back in the bar by 9 am in the morning. I now appreciated how working seven days a week at The Yorkshireman had drained Rod and Rachel and wondered how I would cope when providing them with two-day respite breaks.

In the morning I received a telephone call from the doctor looking after my ex-colleague Peter to tell me he had died and left a letter for me, which he could post to me unless I was attending the funeral in five days' time. After checking with Helen, I telephoned him to say I would be at the funeral. Next morning, I was back in The Yorkshireman and my second day was not quite as demanding since I knew what to do and where to find most of the drinks, snacks and fruit items. Mavis appeared and again failed to recognise me as the local FGC organiser and Yorkshire TV performer, or even the same barman who had served her the night before. With her bright blond hair, ruby red lips and golden complexion she must have spent some time applying her makeup before coming to The Yorkshireman. She was lively and physically fit, but unfortunately was slowly losing her memory.

Standing behind the bar with a clear view of the tables, I was surprised to see a couple I recognised who were not married to each other, but were nevertheless showing quite a lot of affection. The woman had taken one shoe off to press her bare foot into the groin of the man sitting opposite her while he was stroking her leg under the table… I recognised the man as an FGC member and knew he was not with his wife. When I pointed them out to Rod he had a simple answer.

"See all Tom, say nothing and keep the business, say anything and lose the business. Just remember it's their business and none of our business. I want my customers to think of my pub as a comfortable place to meet and relax. It may be that husbands, or wives are tempted to enjoy chatting with other customers, but if they are lonely, or bored, they will find someone somewhere sooner or later."

Left on my own and thinking about the pub being used for new and ongoing liaisons, I could not understand why no one said anything and wondered if it was because they were all at it. As a customer I had only taken note of my immediate area, but standing behind the bar gave me a full view of the bar and customers as well as some surprises. After my second long day ended, my training was finished. Rod told me he was sure his pub would be safe in my hands when he and Rachel went off to Scarborough for a two-day break. He had more confidence in me than I had in myself.

First, I had a funeral to attend. There were very few mourners gathered at the Crematorium and I was saddened to think that Peter had led an active and successful life, yet now there were only a few friends and no family, or none who cared enough to attend his funeral. There was no sign of the glamorous Jan, whose manipulations had surely cost him the will to live. The small group of elderly men included his doctor, those he played golf with, two neighbours and me to make a total of ten people who remembered him. Peter had been ill for some time and assumed it was due to the disease contracted from Jan. When he finally consulted his doctor, the cancer was too advanced for treatment and he put his affairs in order and left a letter to me with his doctor, who agreed to contact me when he died. After the ceremony I drove home and after telling Helen about the funeral, I sat down to read Peter's letter.

To My Friend Tom,

Although we worked in the same company, we were never really friends, but when I sought your help you became the best friend I ever had and gave me your time and advice when I needed it. I watched you on Yorkshire TV and thought the garden club you set up was a wonderful help for lonely people like me. You made a success of your life and recovered from the loss of your first wife. I lost my wife, nearly lost my job and with your help avoided losing my house. Unfortunately, after finding myself alone again the days and nights were long, bleak and unbearable.

My solicitor will contact you to arrange a payment to your residents' garden club so that it can benefit other lonely people. I was delighted to learn that you now have a son in your second marriage and hope you will accept a contribution to the heavy cost of bringing up a child.

Thank you for your help. I wish that having removed a scheming young woman from my life I had the resilience to fill the void left by her absence, but sadly I find that life without her is dull and empty. I also know that living with Jan and her family would have been even more unbearable and wish I had never met her.

Good luck with your new life and family.

Peter Dreycot.

Giving Helen the letter to read, I told her we would have to wait to learn how much Peter had given to FGC and us, but both amounts would be welcome and it was an unexpected, but generous gesture from Peter. Since his daughter was not at his funeral, we wondered if there had been a rift and Peter preferred to give some of his money to us. Helen told me that although she had never met Peter, she felt that life had been particularly cruel to him as each disaster was followed by another.

Rod asked if I would sit in at the interview with a pub manager applicant and next afternoon we met Darran Halstead, who currently ran a pub for a large company. He was an ex-soldier who had a pension for long service and he and his wife Hazel would like to work for Rod, because they preferred a close personal relationship with the pub owner. I liked Darran, who had an open friendly manner and three years' experience of the pub trade since leaving the Army. Previous applicants had no pub experience, or knowledge of the long hours and hard work involved, which might come as a shock. Rod was offering a salary and a monthly bonus based on pub profits to reflect the effort put into the business by Darran and his wife in developing bar and catering income. Since he was the only really suitable applicant, he was offered the job and agreed to start in one month. By coincidence, the chef who had already been recruited, lived on the estate and was also ex forces, having served in the Royal Navy before leaving to work at a Leeds restaurant. He was looking forward to changing from his busy city centre work to the more relaxed atmosphere in his neighbourhood pub and had the right attitude to fit in to the small operation at The Yorkshireman.

The first of my two days in charge began the following Sunday evening when the owners drove off to Scarborough and left me to look after The Yorkshireman and Mavis, who still asked me if I was a new barman each time I served her. It was a fairly quiet evening and I had no problems closing up and making my way home for coffee and sympathy with Helen. Having once been responsible for a company operation employing hundreds of staff, it seemed incredible that I was now fully extended running a pub with only six staff. The difference was that when working within a corporation, there were many subordinates responsible for carrying out my instructions. In the pub I had to carry out much of the work myself from an 8 am start to an average midnight finish.

Letting myself into the pub at 8 am I was joined by the two cleaners and by working flat out in the cellar and bar area I was ready to open up to my first customers at 10 am. During the day a steady flow of customers kept me busy at the bar, but there were no customers for the restaurant and the new chef was able to begin preparing for evening diners. I made a note to speak to Rod to suggest not opening the restaurant until 5 pm if staff costs produced a loss on lunchtime opening. Instead, peckish drinkers could be served with bar snacks requiring little preparation. As well as the growing evening trade, the pub was also used for weddings and parties, which could now be expanded with a fulltime chef. My two glamorous helpers arrived at 5 pm and after my usual hugs we began serving the evening trade and everything went well. My two days in charge seemed more like a week, but the customers were friendly and my six staff did their job and seemed to enjoy working with me.

Rod and Rachel returned as I was closing the pub on my second night and were delighted to find no police outside, no damage to the premises and takings which were up to standard. My second and final day in charge was marred when a customer refused to finish his drink as we were closing and insisted that he had paid for it and was entitled to take his time. Fortunately, there were some FGC members in the bar and they gathered around and persuaded him to leave voluntarily. Darran and his wife took over The Yorkshireman and Rachel and Rod moved to a house just five minutes' walk from Chestnut Grove, where Rachel could finally relax as a normal housewife, while Rod continued his work as a councillor and laid-back pub owner. He also wanted me to help him in taking up golf, but decided that tennis was too demanding. Darran and his wife Hazel were soon settled in and with their outgoing and lively approach they soon became popular with the locals. We were all relieved that The Yorkshireman would continue to be the centre for our FGC and estate social activities.

Peter left £5000 for our FGC account and the same amount towards the cost of bringing up Christopher, which was a thoughtful and generous gesture from an old colleague. The money given to me by an appreciative Rod for my pub work was added to our Australian travel fund. With our savings we planned to spend four weeks in Australia with my son and wife after yet another Hartley baby had arrived. We calculated that we would have enough money to take the more comfortable Club air fare for the long flight, as well as each way stopover at Singapore. We were looking forward to seeing the new baby and exploring a little of the vast continent of Australia, which Helen insisted would be our proper honeymoon after living in sin, marrying and having our baby long before. Helen and I were already getting ready for our overseas visit and the excitement was building at the thought of the new places and experiences ahead of us. Catia had quickly won our affection and we hoped that we would also become good friends with the other Santos family members. On our return I hoped to work with a very enthusiastic Darran to add FGC services for the estate, which should boost his turnover and bonus earnings, but that is another story.